PRAISE FO[R]

"*Pure Cosmos Club* is an inventi[ve] [...] on spiritual and aesthetic huc[...] knocks them down in this witty, energetic novel. Long live [...]" —Sam Lipsyte, author of *The Ask*

"Binder is our American Murakami. He takes tragic themes and makes them hilarious but also mind-blowing, cosmos erupting. Binder's enormous delight in language and life is irresistible." —Clancy Martin, author of *How to Sell*

"In the world of *Pure Cosmos Club*, art is a vain posture, enlightenment is an elaborate con, and delusion is a way of life. Matthew Binder's ingenious satire captures the absurdities of our fraught moment with a startling mix of laugh-out-loud hilarity and subtle melancholy. It's a novel you won't shake anytime soon." —Jeff Jackson, author of *Destroy All Monsters*

"This absurdist send-up of the haute art world features a struggling iconoclast and the best canine sidekick in literature navigating a Palahniukian landscape of poser blowhards and sky-high art deals. There's not another novel out there like this one." —Courtney Maum, author of *Costalegre*

"Matthew Binder's novelistic dream of our collapsing times is 100% pure!" —Jon Lindsey, author of *Body High*

"*Pure Cosmos Club* is a zany, intelligent romp through the art world that made me laugh out loud just as often as it made me squirm. Playfully skewering the absurd world we live in with energetic, effortless prose, Binder's satire often feels painfully real." —Caitlin Barasch, author of *A Novel Obsession*

"Binder writes with a humorous heart and an uncanny gift to resonate poignantly while you're laughing. It's like Malamud in the 21st century." —Joshua Mohr, author of *All This Life*

"This laugh-out-loud novel is a fresh take on spiritual ascension, told in language so propulsive and gorgeous it announces Binder as a master stylist of prose." —Amanda Stern, author of *Little Panic*

"A novel of high comedy as absurd as our present-day reality. A joy of a ride, gleefully bonkers!" —Paula Bomer, author of *Inside Madeline*

"A dazzling, often surreal, laugh-out-loud portrait of the unheralded artist getting onto the middle years of life." —Julian Tepper, author of *Between the Records*

"Reading Matthew Binder's *Pure Cosmos Club*, one is overwhelmed by the sheer power of his imagination, his capacity to conjure into being not only characters but an entire universe that is as full as ours but in some essential way very different. What's best of all is the way that, ultimately, it's through the eyes of these characters we begin to see ourselves in ways we never had." —Celeste Marcus, *Liberties Journal*

PURE COSMOS CLUB

Copyright © 2023 by Matthew Binder
ISBN: 978-1-7369128-1-2

First paperback edition published by Stalking Horse Press, May 2023

Library of Congress Control Number: 2022942723

Publishing Editor: James Reich
Design by James Reich

Cover image: *Corridors* by Keith Rondinelli, 2020
Used with permission.

keithrondinelli.com

Stalking Horse Press
Santa Fe, New Mexico

www.stalkinghorsepress.com

PURE COSMOS CLUB

MATTHEW BINDER

PURE COSMOS CLUB

STALKING HORSE PRESS
SANTA FE, NEW MEXICO

For D. Foy,
in gratitude.

CHAPTER 1

TODAY, JANIE is picking up the furniture she left when she moved out. Her text last week was our first contact since the incident at the park back in April. It's true I may have been out of sorts, but I don't remember behaving as she claims. I was only there to give her a birthday present, the manhole cover I'd stolen off the street and painted to look like Io, the innermost of the four moons round the planet Jupiter. Years before, on our second date, we'd visited the planetarium. Janie had gazed up teary-eyed at the artificial sky and said Io was the most exquisite object in all the universe. To this day, I can't understand why she called the cops.

She's supposed to be here in twenty minutes, which means I should expect her in ten. She's always said punctuality is one of the five keys to unlocking our true potential. I can't recall the other four, but they must be working for her. She's recently taken a lucrative position at a dermatology clinic in SoHo.

I've been in bed playing my favorite game with Blanche. I lie with my eyes closed and arms folded across my chest, holding my breath, trying to convince her I've passed away. It takes all my self-control to stifle a giggle when she licks my ear.

She entered my life when I took a shortcut through a dark alley on my bike and hit her. The vet said her two hind legs were permanently damaged and recommended euthanasia. Instead, I built a contraption from the wheels of a tricycle. Blanche took to it immediately, of course, and now she scoots through the apartment at top speed.

I don't mean to say our relationship has been without hardship. The day I brought her home, she relieved herself on my favorite jacket. I've recently discovered, moreover, that I'm allergic to her dander and so I am always sleepy from taking antihistamines.

When I can't contain myself any longer and gasp for breath, Blanche goes berserk, bouncing up and down on her front legs, while her bad ones lie behind like overcooked spaghetti. I sweep her into my arms and give her a few pats on the head and a rub behind her ears.

It's not until the buzzer sounds that I realize the apartment's condition has deteriorated in Janie's absence. A black mold has crept across the ceiling, and laundry, dirty dishes, and art supplies are strewn everywhere. More disconcerting, when did this odor first appear? There's a knock on the door. I glance in the mirror. My hair is standing straight up. I lick my palm and try to pat it down, but it's no use.

"Go easy on her, Paul," I think. "It must be hard enough for her already, having so many bad marks in God's account ledger."

Two men are at the door, one black and one white. They have thick necks and smooth, handsome faces. Blanche drags herself over and growls. The white guy bends down to pet her, and she bares her teeth.

"Now, Blanche," I say. "Mind your manners."

"Her name is Blanche?" the black guy says.

"The only name fitting for such a distinguished lady."

"Like from *A Streetcar Named Desire*?" the white guy says.

"Can I help you gentlemen?"

"We're here to pick up Janie's things," the white guy says. "Where is she?"

"Downstairs."

"I'd like to speak with her."

"She'd prefer you didn't," the black guy says.

I bow my head and let them in. They lift the couch, exposing broken paintbrushes, a half-eaten grilled cheese sandwich, the shattered remains of an ant farm, a broken Rolex watch given to me by my grandfather upon completing a scuba diving certification at the local YMCA (the highest level of educational achievement I've attained), and a collection of baby teeth in a Ziplock bag I've held onto since boyhood. The men move with ease and grace. Their voices—much richer and deeper than mine—echo off the walls as they discuss how to navigate the stairs. I gaze out the window. Across the parking lot, Janie opens the back of a U-Haul. In yoga pants and a sweatshirt, she moves effortlessly, like a swan across a lake. I unwrap a package of strawberry Pop-Tarts—one for each of us, Blanche and me. The men return and point to a painting of a horse jumping a fence, one of the first I made for Janie.

"She said we should take the horse painting too," the white guy says.

"I don't have much use," I say, "for old paintings, furniture, lamps, rugs, these kinds of things."

The black guy hoists the bookcase onto his shoulder, while the white guy takes the painting. I close the door and return to the window. The men place my things in the truck. Janie gives the white guy a high-five. Then the black guy takes Janie in his arms for a rather intimate kiss. When Janie catches me watching from the window, she looks away quickly and jumps into the truck.

A stack of books against the wall falls into another, which

falls into another yet. Everything is everywhere. I sit in the middle of it and let Blanche lick my face.

CHAPTER 2

THE SKY is overcast and the air hot and sticky as I make my daily walk to the warehouse where I rent studio space from my friend, Danny. I stay on the shady side of the street, but there's no escaping the heat. Sweat stings my eyes. Already, my face is burned.

A long time ago, I read in an etiquette book that a gentleman never wears shorts unless he's exercising or at the beach. My adherence to this rule is absolute, even as the temperature nears a hundred degrees. When I was a boy, my father told me I have unsightly legs. My knees, he said, were knobbier than a dresser full of drawers. His words left an indelible mark, and now, even while bathing, I make sure to keep my knees covered by a washcloth. A rash has formed where my jeans rub my thighs, so every few steps I have to adjust myself. The farther I walk, the harder it becomes. Poor Blanche is weary of my incessant complaints. Two men pass, dressed in floral shorts and tank tops. I can't help but envy their pragmatic sensibilities.

Back when Danny bought the warehouse from a retired mechanic who used it as a chop-shop for stolen BMWs, the neighborhood was a colorful place, where one constantly found oneself embroiled in all manner of adventure. A stray bullet once shattered the studio's window and put a hole through the canvas I was painting. Another time, I was held up at knifepoint over a box of pork buns. Danny always insisted the building was a prodigious investment, but years later, here we are, and I'm sorry to report he was wrong. Real estate prices have skyrocketed, forcing out the pawn shop where I once got a tremendous deal on a gold chain, and the liquor store that sold loosie cigarettes for a quarter. In their places are a vegan cheese shop and a florist that specializes in lesbian weddings.

For months, I've pleaded with Danny to use his connections to help me get my work seen. But he's always refused, claiming not to want any part in subjecting the public to my "perverted worldview." My work, Danny says, epitomizes everything he hates in art, namely that it takes into account supernatural forces.

"Religion is dead," he once said, "but your provincial superstitions remain."

Nevertheless, he's recently experienced a change of heart.

"At the very least you never bore me," Danny said last week, then told me he's arranged for one of my pieces to be included at a group show organized by his gallerist, Susan.

The thing I admire most about Danny is that he viciously hates anyone who bores him. The man simply can't distinguish between an evil person and an uninteresting one.

I'd been working on a series of paintings of Gwyneth Paltrow. With each piece, she became more satanic and menacing, until finally she sprouted bat wings and horns, holding all of mankind in a saucer of anti-aging cream. Just as I was almost finished, I sliced my finger opening a can of soup, inspiring me to abandon the project.

Instead, I decided to climb a tree. Halfway up the elm I'd picked—it was especially fine, I thought—a branch snapped, and I fell. It was then I had the vision for the work I'm making now, a sculpture of a baby nailed to a cross constructed of cellphones. The difficulty, of course, has been gathering the phones. After exhausting my resources buying used devices on Craigslist and eBay, I was still nowhere near my goal of the five hundred I absolutely require, so I ran a funding campaign on social media, which, somehow, was met with what I can only call apathy, and, at times, even scorn. This left me with no recourse but to rob a Best Buy recycling center, a move that Blanche and I deemed both courageous and bold. Anticipating the major stir my piece would cause in the art world, I penned an open letter to the noted critic Jerry Saltz, of *New York Magazine*. "I think we can agree, sir," I wrote, "that in this sea of idling conformity, even the smallest act of subversion or rebellion cannot but be heralded as a shining triumph."

Public opinion, I've learned, however, is not my friend. The response to my crime has been so unfavorable that Blanche thinks I should move abroad and change my name. I've been so afraid, in fact, that for the last several days I've lain in bed chewing bubble gum and picturing myself dragged from the show in handcuffs.

Danny's parked his Lamborghini in front of the studio, a replacement for the Maserati he drove into a lake last month. Already he's hard at work in his uniform of camouflage shorts and the tie-dye tank-top that shows off the stick-and-poke tattoos he gave himself one night while under the influence of ayahuasca. He's nearly completed his training to become a Sun Dance Chief, studying under a part-Crow, part-Sioux, part-Jew survivalist named Shelley. His final objective is to retrieve the carcasses of four golden eagles.

I don't know how he does these things, but overnight Danny has constructed a ten-foot-long sandbox in the studio in which he's now observing a black and yellow snake. No detail is too minute. Whether the snake slithers, coils, or flicks its tongue, Danny writes a detailed account in his Moleskine notebook.

"I'm glad you're here," he says at last. "I need your help."

Danny leads me to the alley behind the studio, where a pool of blood has collected on the ground. I flinch at the scene, but Danny seems entirely disaffected.

"They should be about dry now," he says, glancing up. "We need to get them inside before the birds pick them clean."

Overhead, a wire has been strung across the alley from which hang what appear to be furry rugs. Something drips onto my face as I squint—a strange phenomenon, indeed, since there's not a cloud in the sky. It's not rain on the back of my hand, however, but blood.

"They're from roadkill," Danny says, and begins to hand me the hides. "Cats."

I'm struck by the juxtaposition: the empty gleam in the eyes of these dead animals belies their lustrous coats.

"How'd things go with Janie this morning?" he says, gesturing me to follow him back inside, where he fills a garbage can with water and a box of salt.

"She sent two men to collect her stuff."

"It's often difficult to imagine what makes one person attracted to another. I never could understand what she saw in you."

I drop the skins into the water, then go to the sink to rinse my arms. But even before I've touched the faucet, I'm stabbed by something, in my leg. I shriek, and when I look down, Danny's snake is retreating to the radiator.

"Your snake just bit me, Danny."

"You should go to the hospital immediately."

"Is it poisonous?"

"It's an Eastern Coral Snake, one of the deadliest in the world, though they're usually very mild-mannered. You must've done something to provoke it."

My leg is really starting to throb. I roll up my pants to find two perfect red puncture wounds.

"Will you drive me to the hospital?"

"Just give me a minute to tie up some loose ends here."

I open Danny's snake handbook for instructions. The author strongly advises against sucking out the venom or even applying a tourniquet. Ice is also discouraged. Without treatment, I learn, I could be dead in hours.

The studio is always hot this time of year, but never have I sweated like this. A tightness has gripped my chest, I can hardly breathe, and a tingling sensation has spread through my face. My vision is blurry. I'm even drooling on my shirt. In no time at all, I'm overcome by a weepy drowsiness and crash to the floor, barely conscious.

Danny says he needs to finish labeling the animal tracks he cast in plaster earlier in the day. If he doesn't do it now, vital data he collected his survivalist retreat will be lost. His reputation is at stake, he says, which I suppose is true. Danny has amassed the largest private collection of paw prints on the Eastern seaboard, and his assemblage of marsupial casts is on loan to the Zoology Department at Harvard.

"You doing okay down there?" he says, as Blanche fans her tail in my face.

I laugh like a hysterical child. "It's just melting away," I mutter, "all the suffering!"

Next to my head, I see a fortune cookie that must've fallen off the table where Danny takes his lunch. I manage to crack the cookie open. "You've been dying," the fortune says, "since your first breath." Waiting for Danny to finish, I think of all the time I've wasted treating myself to life's little pleasures with nothing but regrets to show for it.

When I was in the fifth grade, my best friend Jesse and his family moved to Kansas City. Just before they piled into the station wagon, he gave me a story he'd written documenting an adventure the two of us had shared crossing the city of Denver on our bikes. I spent the afternoon hunched in a closet with a flashlight reading it over and over through tear-filled eyes. Jesse told our story with such poignant tenderness that it was difficult to believe it hadn't been a lost classic by Mark Twain. I sobbed uncontrollably at the thought of losing him. He'd been my only friend since first grade, when he was kind enough to swap lunches with me after my mother had packed me a turkey sandwich, knowing very well I was a vegan.

Shortly after Jesse moved, there was a call for entries in a writing competition at my school. I worked hard on a tale about the time I brought home the class's pet salamander for the weekend only to lose him in the creek, yet nothing I wrote could match the eloquence of Jesse. In despair, I copied Jesse's work and submitted it to the contest.

A month later, the entire student body packed into the gymnasium for the quarterly assembly. First, we were forced to endure the marching band's spirited but uneven performance of the school's fight song. Next, the girls' basketball team was honored for their fifth-place finish in the district tournament. Then the vice-principal announced an upcoming carwash fundraiser. Finally, Mr. Mackey, the chair of the school's English Department, delivered a rambling panegyric about the school's depth of talented writers. I left my seat in the bleachers to fetch a Dr. Pepper from the vending machine. When my dollar bill got jammed, I kicked the machine until the custodian, Mateo, raced down the hall waving his arms and shouting. I had won the writing contest, he said. The whole school was waiting for me to accept the prize.

"What about my Dr. Pepper?" I said.

Mateo rocked the machine back and forth, and sodas of all variety came spitting out. "Take whatever you want," he said.

Upon my return, the crowd rose to its feet and exploded with applause. Mr. Mackey shook my hand and introduced me as the greatest writer from Colorado since John Fante. I chugged my entire Dr. Pepper for strength.

"It's a great honor to stand here before you today," I said. "'Two Bikes, One City' is a tale of friends who don't know how to despair, boys so resolute in their determination to conquer a city that they feel almost humiliated by their own strength of character, boys who were ready to leave behind all they knew, to cut themselves off from the world, like castaways on a desert island, to seek their fortune. I consider myself one of destiny's elect, an adventurer who has triumphed against all odds to write the tale of a generation. Please, when you pass me in these halls, try to think of my accomplishments and be inspired to reach inside yourselves, for it's only there that you'll find the stuff of which you're truly made."

Mr. Mackey started a literary magazine to publish the work. Sales of the story were so strong that the school was able to re-sod the football field. My handwritten copy was placed in a glass vitrine in the administrative offices. Every day I had to walk past it and be reminded of my grift.

Again and again, I promised myself I'd contact Jesse to confess my misdeed, but I always found a reason not to. A year passed before I received news that he had perished in an accident. He had left a note for his mother explaining that he missed his best friend Paul and was riding his bike from Kansas City to Denver to surprise him. Jesse had ridden five hundred and ninety-seven miles of the six-hundred-and-twenty-mile journey when he was struck by a cement truck.

I wake in the hospital with a tube up my nose and a nurse pricking me with a needle. The doctor arrives, and I recognize her immediately as a friend of Janie's. We had met at various social functions Janie had forced me to attend. Her imperious eyes twinkle with misgivings.

"Paul, is that you? What happened?"

"Tttthnaaaake biiiide."

A nurse is sent to retrieve the anti-venom vaccine. It's lucky they have any in stock, Janie's friend explains, as snakebites are uncommon in Brooklyn. When Janie's friend asks how it is I was bitten, I invent a tale about volunteering at the Bronx Zoo, then feign tiredness and close my eyes.

CHAPTER 3

I'VE BEEN in the hospital now for two days. The staff has been kind enough to make an exception to their "no pet" rule. A few raindrops fall outside as Blanche and I flip through a stack of gossip magazines given to us by the nurse. We examine a photo of Nick Lachey and his lovely wife, Vanessa, inspecting produce at a farmers' market. The picture's caption is a quote from Nick, reflecting on his fall from celebrity. "One morning I woke up and realized I have my whole life ahead of me!" This bit of hopefulness triggers Blanche's gag reflex, and she spits up on the magazine. If there's one thing Blanche loathes, it's optimism. God knows, out on the streets, she learned that to foresee the worst helps to prepare against it.

I push the button to beckon a nurse for a dose of morphine, which, as these things often do, sends me into yet another bout of dizzying self-reflection.

Eleven months ago, I walked into a meeting at my job to discuss plans for expanding a digital media campaign to new markets. I'd come armed with a number of talking points scribbled on a napkin from the nearby bodega, where I'd just picked up lunch. I was in a tremendous mood after an event that I'd believed was a fortuitous omen.

For lunch, I'd got a falafel sandwich, a Dr. Pepper, and a bag of pistachios. No sooner had I left the place than I dropped the bag of pistachios into a puddle. There was a hole in the packaging, and my pistachios were ruined. I became enraged, certain this tragedy would mar my day. It was then that I remembered I suffer from a terrible pistachio allergy. The last time I ate them my throat had swelled completely shut. The only reason I'm still here, actually, is the kindness of the stranger who stuck me with his EpiPen. Now, once again, I realized, my life had been spared! I was overcome with joy and stood laughing in the crosswalk while drivers honked and shouted. I couldn't understand why it had been so long since I'd last felt this free.

My father was fifty-four when I was born, the product of an ill-conceived fling. Three years prior, despite having never ridden a motorcycle, he bought one on impulse after watching an old Peter Fonda movie, then taught himself to ride in the backyard. A few days later his wife came out to call him for dinner only to see him lose control of the motorcycle and drive it straight into her. The paramedics rushed her to the hospital for a series of radical procedures, but they all failed, and she died three weeks later.

The only thing that kept my father going was his work as a low-level bureaucrat for the municipal agency that managed the city's telephone lines. That was where he met my mother, a thirty-nine-year-old, multiple divorcée who worked part-time as a receptionist. She once told me that what she first noticed about my father was his "tireless appetite for drudgery."

They went out on a handful of dates before my mother broke it off with him because he chewed his fingernails incessantly. A month later, she learned she was pregnant, the outcome of their one sexual encounter—five minutes, she told me, of passionless sex after too many tequila sodas at a happy-hour function. Out of a sense of duty, they married.

More than fifteen years later, I spent my birthday watching reruns of the classic television show *CHiPs* in which two

California Highway Patrol motorcycle officers cruised the freeways of Los Angeles solving crimes. My father came home from work that night to microwave a frozen Salisbury steak. While he waited, he started a letter to the local paper, rebuking them for advertising women's underwear. But before he could finish, the sound of my high-pitched chortle, which he'd repeatedly complained gave him migraines, interrupted him. Only children and perverts laughed, he shouted, nobody else. Now that I was fifteen, he said, my laughter was forbidden.

After all these years, thanks to my mishap with the pistachios, this gift of laughter had been restored, so that when I stepped into the conference room for my meeting, my spirits were high. But instead of the marketing team, I was met by my somber-faced boss and a lady from HR. My boss repeated that though I was a well-liked member of the team, my performance had never met even the minimum expectations. The nice woman from HR handed me a copy of the termination paperwork and said she hoped the two-month severance package they were offering would soften the blow.

It's true I'd never reached my revenue targets. It's difficult even now to explain where I'd gone wrong. Every day, I donned the business casual attire Janie had so meticulously selected, battled my way through rush-hour commutes, spent countless hours managing my pipeline, and suffered the endless tiresome meetings. No one else worked longer hours, and I'd accrued multiple expense reports full of costly client dinners and bar tabs. In many respects, I was a model account executive. Yet, while my colleagues closed deal after deal, I was subject to an interminable succession of losses.

In today's economy, where hyper-specialization is the key

to success, a man in his mid-thirties has little chance to pursue new skills. I was convinced Janie would leave me when she learned I'd been fired. This was the fourth job I'd lost in as many years. My luck had been no better selling solar panels, commercial real estate, or fancy water machines. While all our friends scaled their respective corporate ladders and bought delightful homes, I had nothing to show for my decade in the city but a scroll of failure.

I didn't tell Janie I'd been fired again. Instead, I got up every morning, read the news with my grapefruit and espresso, donned my work attire, and headed cheerfully off to "work." But really, I was making art in Danny's studio. For years, I'd struggled with the idea I was nothing more than a dilettante. I hadn't jumped through any of the hoops required of a contemporary artist. I considered it undignified to pursue an MFA, and other than my friendship with Danny, I had no relations with anyone in the artistic community. This, too, frustrated Janie to no end.

"If you want to be an artist," she'd say, "you must do the things artists do!"

But her encouragement always rang false. Like all people who make a career of memorizing scientific facts and figures, Janie had little interest in the creative life. Her singular passion was to build a lucrative career that entrenched her as a respected member of the community, and afforded her a wardrobe of designer clothing and an apartment filled with luxury goods. And by her mid-thirties, but for one thing, her dreams had been fulfilled. Now she wanted to build a family.

"Let's make a baby!" she said one night, over our pad thai.
"Now may not be the best time," I said.

Janie couldn't understand. As a couple, she believed, we were doing better than most. She said that lately I'd seemed happier and more steadfast than ever. Somehow, I must have learned to find joy in corporate work, she reasoned. Her misconception, I knew, was due to my having ceased complaining about my job. She was right about my improved attitude. My days in the studio had proven a wonderful panacea. The real problem was, after months of unemployment, my resources were exhausted.

But just as things had turned for the worst, I tagged along with Danny to the racetrack. It took no more than a couple of races to see I had a psychic connection to the action. I needed only study how a horse approached the gate to know if it was a winner. After watching Danny burn through tens of thousands of dollars, I implored him to wager on a gelding named Bruno. The racing form told us Bruno had been running abysmally and was destined for the dog food factory. On this day, however, his stride was as smooth and easy as Denzel on the big screen, so I insisted. When Bruno won by six lengths, Danny gifted me twenty thousand dollars, money, I knew, that would sustain me for months.

This good fortune inspired me to tell Janie I'd quit my job to pursue art full-time. To prove my commitment, I brought her to the studio to view the series of sculptures I'd built out of lawn chairs and PVC piping. Her support evaporated on the spot. I was a derelict, Janie said, with no regard for her wishes or, most importantly, our future family.

Janie is nothing if not decisive, and she left that very night. I was so bereft that I went out drinking alone, telling myself Janie was merely trying to scare me. But the apartment when I got back was empty, as was my faith in the future. I had always sought new adventure, variety, novelty, but now all I wanted was the comfort and security I'd had with Janie.

To win her back, I spent my nights picking flowers that I lovingly placed at the door of her friend's apartment, where Janie was staying. Every day I'd hide behind a bush, waiting for her to leave for work, only to watch in dismay as she passed my offerings without so much as a glance. Finally, undeterred, I resorted to a most underhanded scheme: in a letter, I pleaded to let me give her a baby. I barred not a single hold. I detailed the sacrifices I'd make for our child, including learning the Chinese I'd someday teach him or her, knowing it to be a soft skill that could leverage tremendous advantages. But nothing I said would penetrate. Janie had made up her mind.

I started rifling through her things, letters from past boyfriends, photos from destinations foreign and remote, all these strange and arcane objects that now revealed the complete mystery Janie had been. I placed her underwear over my face, then masturbated on a stack of her cashmere sweaters. The next day, I woke in a pile on the bathroom floor, the underwear thick with vomit. I spent the morning writing a list of requests in my notebook, what I would pray for God to grant me. Why not resort to faith if it could be of some use?

That afternoon, I brought the sweaters to the dry cleaner. Seeing the stains, a little man with crooked teeth laughed so hard he knocked over a pile of folded clothes. A hunched woman whose face revealed decades of toil came out to click her tongue and pick at the stains with a dirty fingernail. Tiny flakes of milk-colored shame drifted to the floor. The sweaters, the man said, would be ready on Friday.

The day Janie came to pack her things, I worked in the

26

studio on a painting of a dead boy in a coffin. At sunset, I shuffled home thinking Janie would be gone, but she hadn't finished. She handed me a check for her share of the rent for the remainder of the lease, and I presented her with a watercolor in which she was nude on a tropical beach, with the vague shape of an angel overhead.

CHAPTER 4

I'M DUE to deliver my latest creation to Susan the gallerist in just a few days, but haven't yet completed it, so at 2 a.m. I sneak out of the hospital in nothing but my gown. The snakebite, the nurse said, had caused my leg to swell so severely that there was no way to get my pants off but to cut them apart.

Blanche and I are about to take our seats in a nearly empty bus when our ears pick up the unmistakable sounds of a kung fu movie fight scene. As we're both connoisseurs of Asian cinema, we race to the back and plop down next to the man watching the movie. It's our all-time favorite Bruce Lee film, *The Big Boss*!

"You don't wear headphones when watching videos on your phone in public?" I say to the man.

"Why should I?" he says. "It's a free country!"

"Turn it up, please, this is the best part!"

The three of us watch, riveted, as Bruce Lee's character single-handedly defeats an entire drug-trafficking enterprise posing as an ice factory business. I karate chop and kick at the seat in front of us. The only other passenger, three rows up, moves to the front. Blanche—exhilarated by the scene's bloody climax—whacks our seatmate in the eye with her tail. The man's concentration is so absolute he doesn't even flinch. When we reach our stop, I thank him for sharing this wonderful experience.

In the studio at last, Blanche curls up on a bed of paint-splattered tarps and makes soft yearning noises as she sleeps. I wonder if in her dreams she still has use of her hind legs.

It's the pleasures that have been stolen from us that are most difficult to forget. Blanche looks so peaceful and content that I decide to join her. Next to her, I can't help but wish I'd had a sister growing up. I chew bubble gum and soon find myself humming softly, tapping my knee with my hand. Thirty minutes later, I'm totally refreshed.

I recite a prayer in honor of Jesse, apologizing for stealing his brilliance and asking him to bless me with the strength to create something as original and meaningful as his story, "Two Bikes, One City." The paper mâché baby I've constructed for my cellphone crucifixion sculpture needs painting. I believe an artist should never put too much intention or meaning into their work, lest it render it stupid or, worse, merely dry. How masterfully I execute the baby's face, nevertheless, is crucial, since its expression will be the principal channel through which the work is interpreted.

My first attempt conveys too much serenity. The eyes are heavy-lidded, almost as if the baby is asleep. Its cheeks are fleshy—too much pink—the embodiment of well-being. The critics will say the work symbolizes humanity's salvation through technology, the cellphone cross the instrument by which the baby is lifted to heaven. They'll accuse me of depicting a spiritual and psychological transformation that ultimately leads to a new identity and way of being. "It is no longer I who live," the painting screams, "but tech that lives in me!"

For my second effort I change the palette, replacing the pink with sallow yellow. The shading under the cheekbones makes the child appear rail thin, its oily skin marked by long abuse. A look of dread permeates the eyes, which practically plead for mercy. A literal interpretation of Christ's death reveals that he was executed by the authorities because of his passion for God, which was itself a critique of the Roman Empire's secular domination. The cross symbolizes what dominant systems do to those who oppose them. Here the cross is an instrument of torture and torment—technology is the all-powerful empire that infiltrates and pollutes our being.

Blanche wakes up and scoots to my side. I take her in my arms and stroke her head. She takes one glance at the baby and emits a panicked bark, as if warding off an invader. It's as obvious to Blanche as to me that I've allowed a passion so violent and absorbing to seep into the work that it's now perverted by its own excess. Surely, this depiction would be lionized by the feeble-minded outrage junkies who champion the loudest and most contemptible artistic statements.

To quit would be to succumb to the pressures of grotesque conformity. If ever there were a time for some hidden talent to reveal itself—a kernel of genius, a morsel of potential toward some grand triumph—it's now.

By 9 a.m., I'm exhausted, yet deeply satisfied. The baby's countenance exudes what any second-rate psychiatrist would diagnose as acute anxiety.

CHAPTER 5

FOR THE last several days, neither Blanche nor I have eaten anything but hospital food. A new French patisserie has opened two blocks from the studio, and Blanche has an unrivalled taste for quiche. Sadly, she went berserk at a bistro last month, and mauled the waitress serving a family of tourists, then devoured all five of the bacon and gruyere quiches the waitress had dropped. Word got out about the attack, so that Blanche and I both have been banned from every bakery in town. It's been impossible to get even a bad piece of quiche, anywhere.

I tie Blanche to a pole a block from the new patisserie and keep my head down when I mumble my order.

"Excusez-moi," she says, "can you please speak up?"

"Two slices of Quiche Lorraine," I say.

The woman leans over the counter to get a better look at me. "Let me see your face," she says. Reluctantly, I look into her eyes. "Just as I suspected," she says, and points to a grainy photo taped to the register, "you are this man, oui?"

In the picture, I'm wrestling with a man wearing a baker's cap, surrounded by overturned chairs and tables while in the background, Blanche is snarling at terrified diners.

"But that was a long time ago," I say. "I've been rehabilitated, as you can see."

"I must ask you to leave, monsieur," the woman says, "before I call the authorities."

In my absence, Blanche got so excited at the prospect of quiche that she fell over in her cart and, apparently, couldn't right herself.

"Don't blame me," I say as she nips at my empty hands. "The woman at the patisserie refused to serve us!"

Back at the studio, a matte black Bentley is parked next to Danny's Lamborghini. The chauffeur is walking up and down the block with a potbelly pig on a leash. When the pig relieves itself, the chauffeur cleans it up, then gives the pig a cheeseburger.

Danny's in his sandbox, his camouflage shorts and underwear around his ankles, whistling as he pees into a cup. A handsome man with silvery hair stands by, cleaning his glasses with a handkerchief.

"What to be and who to be?" he says. "I'm curious what a meaningful and authentic life might look like for someone like you."

"What's the matter, Dad?" Danny says, and hands him the cup. "Are you not happy with how the culmination of all your hopes and ambition has turned out?"

I feign a cough to announce my presence. "I can come back later if you need to talk," I say.

"I was just leaving," the man says. "If the results come back positive," he says to Danny, "I'm giving the Lambo to your sister."

Danny lights a cigarette and pours himself a cup of coffee. "My mother once told me," he says, "that when I was a child my father would often break down into tears because of how bad our relationship was. Can you imagine what it must've been like for him? Here's a man who can easily handle the toughest Wall Street financiers but couldn't manage putting an eight-year-old to bed."

Hearing this, I can't help, once again, but to think about my own father. Our last conversation ended regretfully, so many years ago, shortly after I moved to New York City. He and my mother had insisted I return to Colorado for the holiday season so I could fix some leaks in the roof. I knew my mother would spend the entire visit haranguing me about abandoning them. My father was sick, after all, and we didn't know how much time he had left, something, not incidentally, I'd been told since I was a boy. I can't, in fact, remember a time my father wasn't unwell. When I was twelve, I had to drop out of school for six months to nurse him through a host of auto-immune diseases. Another time, in high school, I was made to give him one of my kidneys. The local news called me a hero.

The last time we spoke my father offered to buy me a bus ticket home, but I refused. In the weeks before Christmas, he left long and rambling messages on my voicemail.

"Every time it rains, the sofa gets drenched. And now your mother refuses to make dinner. How can you leave us like this?"

It was my mother who called on Christmas Eve. I needed to come home immediately, she said. My father had suffered a stroke. I got on the bus that night, but my father was dead before I arrived. That was fifteen years ago.

"A child can break a man's heart," I say to Danny.

Danny ties a blindfold over my eyes. "I need your opinion on something," he says, and leads me across the studio. While on his survivalist retreat, he says, he realized he'd grown weary of painting and sculpting. "What good will another museum artifact do?" From now on, everything he makes must come from nature and have a function. His hands tremble as he removes my blindfold. There's something touching, I've always thought, about a great man's weakness. The dead cats I'd helped him with are hanging on the wall, transformed.

"Backpacks!" Danny says.

It's quite clever, I have to admit as I examine these prototypes, how he's fashioned the animal's legs into straps. Just as impressively, Danny has repurposed the cats' teeth as zippers.

"What do you think?"

"They're wonderful!" I say, and strut about with one of the packs.

Danny yanks it from my shoulders, sets it on its hook, and covers them all with a sheet. "Why do I bother asking you?" he says. "If you knew anything at all about art, you wouldn't need my help getting your work shown!"

This abrupt shift of temperament is rather confusing. It's unclear why, yet by all lights, Danny is somehow grieving. I try to comfort him, but he pushes me away and tells me I'll never understand.

CHAPTER 6

TODAY, I got call from Louis, the son of my mother's sister. Just two months apart in age, we grew up on the same street, but couldn't be more different. For one thing, I was a runt, so much so that while I was held back from my sixth-grade year, Louis thrived. I couldn't even make it through tryouts for the Little League Baseball team, while Louis was the team's star shortstop whose every game my parents forced me to attend. Every home run he hit was like a dagger to my heart. After the games, Louis insisted I sit by his side at the pizza parties while everyone celebrated his greatness. I haven't eaten a slice of pizza since.

Even now, you'd think Louis were older than me by at least ten years. He has a commanding belly, a face lined with wisdom, and a head whose gleaming baldness emanates the character of a battle-hardened general. I, on the other hand, am still burdened with smooth skin, a lean figure, and a headful of curly hair. How much easier life would be blessed with Louis' gifts!

He'd called to say he's bringing the family out to New York City, in celebration of his latest promotion. Never let it be said, he gloated, that perseverance isn't rewarded. His new stature in management entitles him to an extra week of vacation. He'd hoped to use the time to take the kids fishing, but his wife insisted the family visit the Big Apple.

"Too bad for you, Louis!" I said. "The city is noisy, rancid, and crowded!"

Louis can be quite nefarious. Immediately, he changed the

subject by asking if I remembered Madeline. He knows very well that not only do I remember her, but that I'd loved her for as long as I can say. Louis' tawdry fling with her, moreover, was the most hurtful thing my young heart had ever suffered. As it happened, he said, Madeline had died, perished from what the experts call a "death of despair."

"Circus accident?" I said.

"Diabetes," Louis said.

Apparently, after high school, Madeline's weight exploded to the point that for the last two years of her life she was confined to bed. The authorities even had to knock down a wall to remove the body.

Heartbroken, I spend the evening chewing bubble gum and pouring through my high school journal. The anguish I suffered at Louis and Madeline's callousness was unendurable, I remember as I read. The events from an entry dated April 4th, 2001, are especially difficult.

How dare they tarnish the sanctity of the breakfast cereal factory. There's no place more sacred to me in all the world. Its sweet smell of marshmallow and honey is the lifeblood from which I'm nourished. How long has it been since I started going there every day after school? Two years? Three years? It seems I've spent a lifetime on the factory's rooftop, luxuriating in its heavenly odors. I know its every sprinkler head, every piece of hvac equipment, every piece of pipe. It isn't Louis who spent months making an exhaustive log of the roof's landscape. It isn't he who recorded the heights of the different sections of parapet to the fraction of an inch. And certainly it wasn't he who used his stride to measure the distances between the westernmost exhaust fan and easternmost air conditioner—exactly two hundred and twelve steps.

Nor could Louis ever love Madeline the way I do. I'm the one who forgoes lunch at school most days so I can save my money to buy her gifts. I'm the one who teaches himself biology so that I can help her with her studies. And I'm the one who got Madeline out of trouble by telling the police it was Veronica Bensonhaver who drunkenly crashed that Toyota into the post office.

So why didn't my scheme to win her back from Louis work? I had invited them to join me at my cereal factory hideaway. Nothing impresses Madeline more than skateboarding, and Louis masterfully exploited the rooftop's smooth surfaces and myriad obstacles to showcase his skill. After each daring feat, I watched in horror as Madeline would throw her arms around Louis' neck and kiss his face.

When at last the perfect moment revealed itself, I commenced my plan. I mocked Louis' skateboarding skills as mere "child's play" and challenged him to a contest of true courage and daring. Blindfolded side-by-side in the center of the roof, we'd walk toward the edge. Whoever walked farthest without falling off would win. I had walked this stretch of roof countless times. It was exactly one hundred and forty-eight steps from our start to the edge. Louis insisted on only a single rule: No matter what, Madeline was not to interfere.

Madeline counted off our every step. Louis was so confident that he encouraged Madeline to go faster. He wanted to beat me with time enough to work on his flip-tricks before dark. At one hundred steps, I thought his spirit would break, but it seemed actually to harden. He even went so far as to lecture me on a breathing technique he'd learned from a book by Wim Hof. With just a few steps remaining before certain death, Louis giggled. "What's the matter, cousin," I said, "getting scared?" "Not in the slightest," Louis said. "I just remembered a joke, and it made me laugh." Suddenly, I couldn't *remember where I was in my count. Were there six steps left, or only five? After two more steps, Louis said, very casually, "Madeline, please tell my mother to serve hot dogs at my funeral." I began to weep. "Stop it, stop it!" I shouted and ripped my blindfold off just in time to pull Louis from the brink. He would have stepped right off the edge. Madeline raced to Louis' side and stripped off his blindfold as they hugged. "That was a close one," he said, smiling.*

Why does Louis always win in life?

Lying in bed, Blanche snoring on my chest, the question remains the same.

CHAPTER 7

I WAKE up late. The sun is high, and through the windows I can hear the city's endless hum. I roll over so my arm hangs off the bed and roll up my eyes—my *dead* position. Blanche digs her snout into my nose and mouth, searching for signs of life. When she finds none, she presses a paw to my neck, searching for a pulse. But the pads on her paws are too thick to detect the subtle beat. She groans with soulful melancholy. I continue this charade until I can no longer hold my breath, then spring to my feet, and Blanche begins to howl.

The landlord has slid a note under my door. After a short but gracious salutation, the note states that I'm three months behind in rent. It says that I have a week to pay, or I'll be evicted. If that's the way he wants to play it, I think, so be it. The apartment hardly suits my needs any longer, anyway. In fact, I never even liked it. Too much natural light can be a terrible distraction, not to mention, now that the furniture's gone, the high ceilings and wood floors make the acoustics unbearable.

Blanche hates being carried up and down the stairs. Every time we come or go, I have to unstrap her from her wheels so she can commando crawl with just her front legs up and down the stairs, a process that adds forty-five minutes to our commute. Today, however, she must submit to my carrying her. We're meeting Louis and his family. To punish me, Blanche pokes my eye repeatedly, and once we're on the street, she won't budge. Another dog has pooped on the sidewalk. Blanche finds the act of public defecation horrifying. Instead, she always insists on doing her business on the bathroom floor. I try to reason with her, but it's no use. Several wasted minutes have passed when a heavy hand falls on my shoulder. It's the landlord.

"Where's the rent, Paul?"

"I'm not paying you another dime while you're in dereliction of your duties."

"Excuse me?"

"Are you not responsible for the condition of the sidewalk in front of your building?"

"What's wrong with it?"

"Look at that turd!" I say, pointing to the other dog's refuse. "An absolute disgrace!"

"I'm not responsible every time some jerk fails to clean up after his dog."

"Tell it to the New York City Housing Authority judge," I say, and start away with Blanche. Ambling along, my mind enters that aimless state the Surrealists advocated was the most prosperous for unexpected discoveries and new beginnings. An idea for a painting comes: four teenagers along an oceanfront boardwalk, staring at their phones while a magnificent tsunami looms beyond.

My reverie is broken by a man in front of the pharmacy. His cheeks and forehead are marked by a bumpy rash. He can't make sense of his medicine's instructions.

"Can I be of some assistance?" I say.

"The doctor prescribed me two ointments, a yellow and a white. I'm supposed to wear one all day, and the other for just fifteen minutes at a time. I don't know which is which."

I drop my voice an octave to assume authority. "If I were you, I'd get rid of those immediately."

"What do you suggest?"

"Have you heard of Chimayo?"

The man's eyes narrow. "No," he says.

"It's a sacred desert in New Mexico whose dirt cures all ailments. It's very well known. I strongly recommend it, but since you haven't the time, I wonder have you tried ordinary water? There are countless cases of patients healing with it—so long as they believed in its powers. Better yet, get yourself a bar of zinc and carry it in your pocket. I once had a headache for two weeks, but when I used the zinc, I got better in no time."

I toss the man's meds into a trashcan and give him directions to the nearest New Age bookstore. Meantime, Blanche has disappeared. She detests it when I dispense medical advice to strangers, I recall, and must've wandered off. Up and down the street, I holler her name. Passersby confer worried glances. An orange seller inquires.

"Does your dog have any unique features?"

"Floppy ears and a long tail," I say.

"She doesn't happen to have wheels for hind legs, does she?"

"Oh yes," I say, clasping the man's shoulder, "there's that, too!"

He points to a park across the street. Sure enough, Blanche is there, listening to a busking jazz trio. When the song ends, she howls with appreciation. A butterfly flutters past, and Blanche barks. If there's one thing Blanche loathes as much as optimism, it's butterflies.

On the subway, a man in black with a funny hat and long beard is reading his book, his finger moving quickly across the page as he silently mouths each word. A pack of bellowing teenagers get on with their skateboards. One of them tells a joke comparing his friend's mother to a giraffe. At the punch line, I can't help but laugh. His friend, however, doesn't seem to care but merely leans against his pole, munching chips. With his black velvet eyes, wiry frame, and tattoos, he's handsome enough to play the role of the sensitive-but-misunderstood lead in a Larry Clark film.

The man with the funny hat closes his book and sticks it in his bag. A number of coins fall from his pocket. The handsome boy laughs cruelly, inciting the others to join him. They slur the man, who ignores them, but as he moves toward the exit, one of the kids flicks the man's hat.

My heart races, and my hands ball into fists. I struggle to stand up, but am powerless. The man and kids exchange insults. Then the doors open, and the man departs. I'm overcome with emotion, and I vomit. All the passengers, even the obnoxious teens, leave the car, and for the rest of the ride, I'm so shaken I'm unable even to pet Blanche.

At Bryant Park, the buildings are so tall they block the sun. The sidewalks teem with hyper-ambitious workers hustling to important jobs. A woman in high heels and a blazer knocks into me, and then a suited man levels me with his shoulder as he shouts into his phone.

Louis and his family wanted Italian food for their first meal in the big city. Again and again, he raved about a place with the best chicken Alfredo this side of Tuscany, and texted me the address, 2 Times Square. Blanche is so excited I struggle to keep up as she barrels down the sidewalk.

The hostess at the restaurant greets us with a delightful Latina accent. "Welcome to the Olive Garden!"

"It's wonderful to be here!"

The hostess glances down at Blanche. "Is she a service dog?"

"Oh yes, she's tremendously serviceable."

"She's not wearing a vest. Do you have her paperwork?"

"Perhaps a demonstration would be best," I say, and open a menu for Blanche. "Now Blanche, what should I have for lunch?"

In short order, she places a paw under the lasagna classico.

The hostess's mouth drops. "That's my favorite dish, too!" she says, and leads us to our table.

Louis stands to greet us, a stained cloth napkin tucked into his shirt. It's been almost four years since I saw him last, during which he's gained at least twenty-five pounds. He couldn't look more regal or distinguished if he were wearing a crown. I extend my hand, but he throws his arms around me in fraternal embrace.

"How is it that I've turned into a fat old man," he says, "while you haven't changed a bit?"

"You've always been the lucky one," I say.

I take a moment to reacquaint myself with Louis' wife, Kayleigh, and their sons, the very embodiment of idyllic, middle-American charm. Kayleigh's hair is cut in a sensible bob, and the two freckle-faced boys are decked out in Broncos jerseys and caps. I set Blanche on a chair, but when one of the boys reaches to pet her, she bares her teeth. A server delivers a tray of dishes, revealing a patch of scabs up and down his arms.

Kayleigh places a tender hand on mine. "We hope you don't mind that we ordered without you."

"Am I late?"

"Only an hour, or so."

"Why don't we say grace?" Louis says.

The boys protest vehemently, spilling drinks and overturning bottles. It takes a lot to convince them, idle threats and so forth, but at last they dry their tears, and we join hands to thank Jesus for this bounty. It's unusual, but a feeling of deep belonging and contentment settles over me as we say "Amen."

I congratulate Louis on his promotion.

"After nineteen years of working at the hardware store," Kayleigh says, "he's finally been made the manager!"

Louis sighs. "Can you believe I started stocking shelves there when I was just a junior in high school?"

I nod contemptuously and cut up a piece of chicken parmesan for Blanche.

"Do you always let your dog eat at the table with you?" Kayleigh asks.

"Oh yes," I say, "always."

"You don't think that's a bit strange?"

"Do *you* think it's strange?"

The younger of the boys laughs so hard he nearly chokes on his breadstick.

"Mind your manners!" Kayleigh says, and slaps the boy's back. After an awkward silence, she says, "This afternoon we're going to the top of the Empire State Building. Have you ever been?"

"Oh no," I say, "not after what happened to Kong!"

"What about Broadway shows," she says, "do you enjoy them?"

"Actually," I say, my mouth full of ravioli, "I've never thought of going."

Louis and his family eat more per person than I imagine a village of peasants would in a week. Of course, our long-standing rivalry requires me to keep up. Never again will I be humiliated like I was on the roof of the cereal factory. After three plates of fettuccine Alfredo and two slices of tiramisu, I say, "Who wants to split an order of cheese-stuffed shells?"

"I couldn't eat another bite!" Louis says.

"Me either," Kayleigh says. "They're going to have to roll me out of here."

Neither the boys nor Blanche want more. She raises a paw to signal a waiter for the check while I finish the scraps on everyone's plates. When the bill comes, I tell Louis I'd love to contribute, but haven't got a cent.

CHAPTER 8

FINANCIAL SUCCESS and morals, I've come to see, go together like the moon and stars. There's no escaping this universal truth. Every man is a king, but he must pay his own admission. Today, my chance at salvation finally lays at hand: Today I deliver my sculpture to Susan at the gallery. Surely, once I'm wealthy, as I soon will be, I'll find peace in this world. If only someone had shared this secret back when I knew no better.

At the studio, prideful as a lion, I find Danny with a visitor. From behind, I'm certain she is another of the beautiful women Danny keeps in his sexual orbit—she's wearing a skirt and knee-high boots. But when she turns to greet me, I find myself shaking hands with Vincent and his abundant mustache and beard. I've done something wrong, I see. Vincent yanks his hand from mine and lifts it imperiously to my lips. Behind him, Danny is silently mouthing the word "please." For him alone, I bow my head and gently kiss the top of Vincent's hand. His skin is the softest I've ever touched.

"Vincent is from Inès."

"Ah, yes," I say, "I love fútbol!"

"Inès is a French luxury fashion brand," Danny says, his tone as serious as a coroner's.

"We're interested in doing a collaboration with Danny and his new bags."

"Looks like we're going to need way more cats," Danny says.

"One must always be as ambitious as one can," I say.

Danny's eyes bulge. "I've never heard you speak like that

before," he says, poking me in the chest. "You've always been so passive and blasé."

"Don't tell me you're so naïve that you believe a man should never contradict himself," I say. "Just because I've acted one way before doesn't mean that's how I'll always act."

Vincent takes Polaroids of Danny modeling the bags in his underwear, Blanche observing with cool interest. When Danny poses with a watering can, next to a potted tulip, Blanche teeters over to suggest he tilt his head to make better use of the diffuse light. The results are stunning. Never has the contrast between Danny's light eyes and dark complexion been so absolute.

It's garbage day, and someone's left their kid's red wagon on the curb. It's just what I need to haul my cellphone crucifixion sculpture to the gallery. I line the wagon with pillows and secure the sculpture with bungee cords. Wheeling the wagon through the studio, I knock a bottle of Danny's champagne to the floor.

"Would you mind taking that dreadful thing away?" Vincent says, looking at my sculpture with disgust. "It's making me deeply uncomfortable."

Out on the street, I walk with agonizing care. Every crack and bit of gravel causes the wagon to rattle and shake. Two kids kicking a soccer ball back and forth scamper down the street. When an errant pass sends their ball careening toward the wagon, I give it a swift boot and tell the kids to beat it.

I stop in front of a barber shop to readjust the bungees. Inside, a well-muscled barber takes a straight-blade razor to the lathered throat of his client. There's a baseball game on an old-style television box. A bald and wrinkled man whose pants are held up by red suspenders sits reading his paper. He sees my sculpture and rolls his eyes.

At the gallery at last, Susan shows little interest in my work. When I ask what she thinks, she glances at the wagon and says she's disappointed the sculpture isn't larger—collectors pay more for large pieces. The Best Buy recycling center I robbed, I say, was having a "slow week." She's concerned, as well, about the ambiguity of the baby's face. When I explain that I want the audience to make up their own minds about whether technology is offering salvation or doom, she tells me that's entirely wrongheaded, that, in fact, it's the artist's responsibility to beat people over the head with their ideas. It's paramount to make a statement, she says, whatever it may be, though, of course, the more polemical and provocative, the better.

"But do *you* like it?" I say.

"I'm the wrong person to ask."

"You're the gallerist!"

"To be perfectly frank, I've never been moved by a piece of art in my life. I inherited this place from my father."

If only that were the end of it. Susan's greatest regret, she goes on to say, is trafficking in the creations of "awful narcissists" who impose their "precious individualism" on the world. And yet she understands everyone needs to make a living. For herself, she's grown used to standards she'd miss if they were suddenly taken away.

Blanche's stomach is upset from the chicken parmesan, so she excuses herself to the restroom. Meantime, Susan assigns two workers to install my sculpture. They place it in the back corner of the gallery, tucked between a still-life painting of three bottles of wine atop a mid-century credenza, and a photograph of tumbleweed blowing across a desert. The creators of these two pieces are huddled together complaining how their work has been unfairly relegated to the nether regions of the gallery.

I overhear the still-life painter say his father's business partner has agreed to pay an exorbitant price for the painting to drive up its market value. The photographer is impressed with the scheme and plans to have her uncle do the same.

Blanche returns from the restroom flush in the face.

"How can anyone be expected to be sensitive to the collective emotion my sculpture invokes," I say, "when it's in proximity to such work?"

Blanche's antipathy for modern still-life paintings is unsurpassed. No work in this style can rise above a perversion of the masters. She rocks back on her hind wheels and scoots her butt across the floor, dragging anal gland secretions in her wake. The foul odor causes the painter and photographer to demand their work be moved, even after the floor had been mopped and polished, forcing Susan to relent. Now my work will appear beside two avant-garde performance artists showcasing a live sex act. On our way home, we swing by the nail salon, where I treat Blanche to a mani-pedi, in thanks for her quick thinking.

CHAPTER 9

I EMERGE from sleep to find my sheet wet, a welcome reprieve, honestly, from this wretched heat. My air conditioner has been useless since the power was shut off for failing to pay the bill. It's the sickly smell that finally rouses me. I'm lying in a yellow stain. Blanche has moved from her typical spot to a distant corner. When I scowl, she sighs.

I toss the sheets into a garbage bag with the rest of my laundry, then sit out on the fire escape with a glass of water and a cigarette from a pack that's been in my drawer since before Janie left.

It's art show day, and my stomach is upset. I spend ten minutes hunched over the toilet. A cold shower makes it difficult to catch my breath. I imagine riding a wave of critical acclaim after my sculpture is a tremendous success. Money pours in. I buy a Cadillac and find a new girlfriend. I've allowed myself to be devoured by my longings, I think as I brush my teeth. In the mirror, I note the tooth I chipped more than two years back, my crooked nose, my unbearably enormous ears.

I sift through my closet for an outfit. The last thing I want is to stand out as odd or unconventional. Self-expression via peculiar sartorial choices is in my opinion a cheap trick employed by the feeblest of artists. I seek only to appear respectable, composed. The blazer and shirt combination I bought a dozen years ago for an internship elicits from Blanche an unambiguous growl. Even my best button-down shirt looks cartoonishly big on me. The rest is splattered with paint or riddled with holes.

I comb the racks of the local discount store, aisle after aisle of castaway clothing priced to sell. The faces of the people here express a painful resignation. Their sole ambition, I see clearly, is to endure.

I buy a pretzel from a vendor. I have a mustard allergy, as well, but Blanche loves the stuff, so I dress the pretzel up for her, and we split the pretzel bite-for-bite. When the bus arrives, I try to board, but Blanche won't allow it, insisting instead we visit a store I've never noticed on our hundreds of walks up and down this street, Sal's Custom Suits. Blanche's judgment far exceeds my own, I know, so I do as she suggests.

Inside, an old man and woman are fighting. From all I can tell, he is refusing to take the nap she insists he have, going so far as to bombard her with terrible expletives. A collection of framed photos on the wall dates back what must be fifty years. The man in his prime had been quite strapping, but to see him now, it's not unfair to say time has not been kind. The woman, on the other hand, looks nearly as elegant and fetching as she had in her youth.

Frustrated with her man, the woman sits at her sewing machine. The man adjusts his tie and begins marking up a ledger. I clear my throat, to no avail.

"Salvador," the woman finally yells, "we have a customer!"

"Please, Alma," he says, "stop screaming. My nerves can't take anymore!"

Salvador greets me with the reverence and gusto customarily reserved only for foreign dignitaries and people of great purpose, then listens to my fear that I have nothing appropriate to wear for my opening with such attentiveness that I can't help but to continue from there about the details of my work and the hope that tonight will serve as a turning point in my career. Salvador pulls out his tape measure and sizes me up.

"To view the woman as prey adds greatly to love," he says, apropos of nothing, it seems. "The man who is chosen derives far less pleasure than the man who takes possession."

Alma smiles as she listens to the story of their courtship. "On your death bed," she says, "the only questions you will ask are, have I loved, and have I been loved?"

"If Alma were to die before me, I'd kill myself immediately," Salvador says, prompting Alma to step over and kiss his wrinkled hands. "When one's wife dies, she dies countless times—every time you crawl into the cold sheets of your bed, every time you eat spaghetti, every time you groom your mustache or lift the toilet seat to pee."

In response, I recount my own tale of lost love. After twenty minutes, I conclude: "She's a dermatologist in Soho, now."

Salvador is astounded. "If it's a loving relationship you want, you must seek out the marrying kind—an elementary school teacher, perhaps."

I push back against this logic, assuring him that a doctor can love a man just as well as a teacher. Both he and Alma laugh uproariously.

"It's a stupid man," Alma says, "who rejects happiness for intellectual principles."

Salvador shows me a dozen different fabrics. They're all magnificent, but there are two I can't imagine living without.

"Salvador, my friend," I say, "you're going to have to make me two suits."

"Are you sure about this?"

"I've never been so sure of anything."

I stay with the couple well into the afternoon. Alma and I play five chess matches, all of which she wins. For lunch, we have sandwiches and pickles. Blanche performs some tricks, and when at last she barks out the melody of "The Star-Spangled Banner," Salvador and Alma weep. At 3 p.m., Salvador announces his work complete, two splendidly bespoke suits he insists I model for him and Alma.

"Soft and thick in the shoulders and chest," Salvador says, as I pose, "but tapered at the waist."

Alma folds a white linen pocket square and tucks it into my pocket. My smile in the mirror is so foreign I hardly recognize myself.

Salvador then proceeds to punch away at his calculator and make notes in his ledger. Alma strains to smile as she bags the second suit.

"Two-thousand three-hundred and forty-seven dollars," Salvador says.

"Sounds fair to me!" I say after an inordinately pregnant moment. But when I fish out my wallet for a credit card, I recall that after maxing it out on cellphones for the sculpture, I cut it up. In my wallet are six wrinkly dollar bills. "Can I make a down payment now and pay the rest later?" I say, placing the bills and some change on the counter.

"Not to worry," Salvador says. "I understand that you are good for it."

Salvador shakes my hand and Alma hugs me warmly as they wish me luck at my opening. Out on the street, Blanche's tail is tucked far between her back wheels, and she refuses to look me in the eye.

"I promise I'll pay them!" I tell her.

The teeth she bares say everything I already know.

CHAPTER 10

BLANCHE AND I have been fighting. She's angry not only for my failure to pay Salvador and Alma, but also because Susan banned her from the gallery for her dragging her anal glands across the floor. Blanche insists I not attend the opening, in protest, then chews up the last of my fresh canvases when I won't be swayed.

"I'm sorry," I say, "but we must think of our career prospects!"

On the subway, I take a seat beside a Puerto Rican woman and her young daughter. The girl is sucking on a lollipop and waving a glittery wand. When her mother plays a game on her cellphone, the girl wanders off to bless her fellow passengers. Even the surliest of the passengers bow to let the girl tap the wand to their heads. But just as I'm about to genuflect to this princess, the train jolts, and her wand stabs me in the eye. The spanking she gets from her mother is rather vicious, I think, though my intervention only makes it worse, and soon the woman is violently berating me, as well, all in Spanish.

I'm an hour late to the gallery. My eye is swollen nearly shut, my pocket square is stained with blood, and I'm half-soaked from the light rain against which I forgot to bring an umbrella. Through the gallery's window, I can see Louis sipping beer in his plaid shirt and corduroy pants, a sartorial choice that to my mind makes him the most uniquely fashionable person in all of New York. Fate is malevolent, I think. The world teems with evil spirits.

Louis welcomes me with such warmth you'd think he was meeting God himself. "Man of the hour!" he shouts.

"I didn't expect to see you here," I say.

"I wouldn't miss it for the world," Louis says, an arm around my shoulder. "I'm so proud of you!"

I've never been much of a drinker, but guzzle two glasses of chardonnay to shield me from Louis' baleful company, and then I order a third.

"How people manage to make all this cool stuff seems like a miracle!" Louis says, beaming with contentment.

"We're all just trying to make good use of the time granted to us."

Louis' expression changes from a cheery grin to a pained grimace.

"This beer is going straight through me," he says. "I'm going to hit the head."

The first piece of art that catches my eye is the sculpture of a figure with a man's body and a sheep's head. I can't decide if this is an example of anthropomorphism or zoomorphism. A woman stands nearby, her eyes glistening and lips trembling. She appears genuinely taken by the work. I ask her opinion, but her phone rings. It's her daughter's nanny calling from São Paulo.

A bow-tied server passes with three crab rangoons left on his tray. I take them all, helpless to keep from thinking how banal art shows always are—eccentrically dressed misfits with lopsided haircuts making inane chitchat as they chug glass after glass of wine.

I'm drawn toward a painting of a cemetery in which a woman kneels with a bouquet before a headstone while the man with her drinks a beer. Its energy perfectly captures the bleakness of America's future, I think, as I clench my hands.

Years ago, I saw a therapist who after just two sessions

compiled a list of neurosis so long it filled three spiral notebooks. We argued bitterly over my compulsion to compare myself to other people. She assured me that my failure to address this habit would cause irreparable harm. I argued one can't possibly know where they stand in the world without measuring themselves against others. I never saw her again.

Louis returns to find me tying my shoe in front of the photograph of the tumbleweed in the desert.

"This is a nice image!" he says.

"I can't imagine the photographer is satisfied with it," I say.

"Oh, no?"

"No photographer is ever truly satisfied with their work. Secretly they all wish they had the skill to paint."

"That's one way to see it."

"It's like a dentist longing to be a brain surgeon."

Louis nods stupidly, as if I've unlocked the secrets of the universe. "Where is your sculpture?" he says. "I'm dying to see it!"

Every man, no matter how humiliated or broken, requires some degree of respect to maintain his dignity. Why would I empower the one person in the world who could rob me of this scarce resource?

"There's plenty of other work to see," I say. "You shouldn't waste your time with mine."

"I didn't come all the way to New York City not to see my brilliant cousin's art," Louis says. "You don't know what it means to me to see how well you're doing out here, so far from home."

Louis' power over me is absolute. Everyone eventually betrays everyone else, even themselves. How can I be expected to rise above this truth? Gloom settles into my bones. I lead Louis to the back of the gallery, and shut my eyes.

"Where is it?" he asks.

At first, I don't believe what I see. I wonder if I'm hallucinating. The doctor warned me I might experience such a thing when I stopped taking my pills. I rub my eyes. The sculpture has transformed into a pedestrian painting of a flower garden. Susan, the gallerist, materializes by my side.

"I'm sorry, Paul," she says, "but we had to remove your sculpture from the show."

"Pardon me?"

"As you can see, we had to make room for this Chagall."

"I'm afraid you've been had," I say, squinting my eyes to examine the painting's brushwork. "This is no Chagall."

"*Wendy* Chagall. Her mother is my chiropractor. I'm showing the work as a favor. Danny said you wouldn't mind."

Susan turns her back on me. A wealthy collector has a question about another piece. I stand by, listening. High class people frighten and intimidate me to no end, especially women from the highest echelons—they speak in pretentious half-baked phrases that are as well-polished as antique silverware. After a deal is struck, the conversation shifts to the collector's struggle with an ongoing kitchen renovation at her summer home in the Hamptons. She complains that she's already been through three different contractors and has spent upwards of a half-million dollars on the project. The construction has been so awful they've hardly even used the home this summer. Instead, they've been spending weekends at her in-laws' place in Martha's Vineyard.

"It's been a true nightmare," the collector says. "Richard's family absolutely refuses to hire a private chef."

Overhearing this tale, I realize it's far better to imagine

success than to experience it first-hand. The trappings of money breed countless new troubles. I'm immensely grateful for the headaches I've been spared.

We retreat to the bar.

"How dare they do this to you!" Louis says.

I drink two more chardonnays. My stiff buzz is a welcome relief. Danny struts through the door in his camouflage shorts and beaded headband, flanked on all sides by an entourage of sycophants and models. Susan nearly breaks into a sprint as she crosses the gallery to greet him. Danny blows the smoke from his vape stick into her face, throwing her into a fit of coughing, then joins me at the bar.

"Nice suit!" he says, and rubs the material of my lapel. "Makes you look like a banker."

"Yeah?"

"Totally. I like it."

"I got two of them."

"That's the spirit."

We clink glasses and drink.

"Why did you allow for Paul's sculpture to be removed from the show?" Louis says.

"One mustn't upset their chiropractor," Danny says, eyeing Louis up and down. "You must be Paul's cousin."

Louis beams mawkishly. "We're more than just cousins," he says. "We've been best friends since we were kids!"

"You want to do some coke?"

Danny beckons to Susan and demands her keys. She doesn't question why, but simply hands them over. Several members of Danny's entourage join us in her office. At least three of them are famous. My sculpture, I see, is jammed into a corner behind a pile of third-rate artifacts. Danny dumps a pile of coke on Susan's desk and with the precision of a surgeon begins to cut it. A woman so elegant and stunning she must be royalty stands nearby. How he remains so cool under pressure is a mystery.

An actress with a small part in the new Alex Ross Perry film asks Louis if she can sit on his lap. Her wild gesticulations tell me she's very bad at what she does, the type who speaks too loudly or quietly, frowns grossly when expressing displeasure, laughs too hard when amused. Louis stops chewing his nails and springs to his feet, but she smiles cheekily and says she prefers to cuddle. Louis points to his wedding band and apologizes for any confusion.

A rolled up hundred-dollar bill gets passed around. Everyone attacks the drugs like lions their antelope on the Serengeti. I'm not nearly so well-versed as the others in the consumption of drugs, and sneeze when it's my turn, sending a puff of cocaine into the air. There is a communal groan. Danny simply produces another vial and cuts up more. The rush when at last I manage to get the stuff into my nose is immediate. My palms feel sweaty, my face flushes. There's no music playing, but I can't resist the urge to dance. I sway to the rhythm in my head, only to find myself stopping with paranoia to chew my lip.

"What happened to your eye?" says a woman with a thick, Eastern European accent.

Till now, I'd only seen her from behind, an alluring mystery. From the front she's something else entirely, high cheekbones and gypsy eyes, a face one wants to hold for eternity.

"A little girl on the subway stuck me with her wand."

"I hate the subway," Danny says.

The air conditioning is blasting. The beautiful woman says

she's cold. Danny gestures to the coat rack, and I stare as she slips on a black satin wrap and studies herself in the mirror. Then, in the mirror's reflection, she sees something and spins round to the corner where Susan hid my sculpture.

"What is this masterpiece doing here?" she says.

"It's a striking image," Danny says, "but I can't gather whether the piece is for or against technology."

"I like it," the woman says condescendingly, "because it leans toward conservatism when the trend is for revolution."

"Well," Danny says, and points my way, "you should meet the artist."

I cower behind Susan's desk, unable to process the attention. The woman steps my way. Her voluminous black hair is all the grander atop such a lithe and delicate body. I want to throw myself at her feet and beg her to spit on me, a baptism of sorts. Nothing would give me greater joy.

"Your worldview contradicts every other artist," she says.

"I find it very strange people don't see things as I do," I say.

Susan barges in and slams the door. "How I hate these awful affairs!" she says. Danny cuts her a line and hands her the bill. "Oh, no," she says, "money is filthy!" She takes a metal straw from her desk and inhales the drugs. "The Hermés duster looks marvelous on you," she says to the beautiful woman, then lies on the couch and rubs her temples while complaining about a migraine.

Danny invites everyone to an after party. We ride in a limousine and do more coke. My beautiful new friend is named Orsi. She's from Budapest and is now a graduate student at Columbia University, studying applied mathematics. Next to her in the limo, I pretend we're a bride and groom, fresh from our nuptials. When I ask her if she'd like crumpets and tea, she pats me on the head. I have trouble following what she says, due to her accent. I laugh hard at the story she's telling only to realize too late it's about the sacking of her grandmother's village in Hungary by the Nazis. I try to hurl myself from the car, but Louis grabs me, sparing my life, another sin for which I'll never forgive him.

The party's location is high in a Midtown building. The elevator opens directly into an apartment so large it takes up the entire floor. I strain with appreciation at the architectural grandeur, and wonder to Orsi about the height of the ceilings. Down on 5th Avenue, there's an endless sea of red and yellow lights. I ask Danny how much an apartment like this might cost.

"In the ballpark of twenty *mill*," he says, and yawns.

"A pittance for such an extravagance!" I say.

The bartender mixes Orsi and me whiskey and sodas. In French, she asks some men if they can make room for us on the couch. I'm nervous and terribly drunk, unable, really, to speak with any clarity.

"Forgive me for saying so," Orsi says, "but you make me a little uneasy. Your ideas about everything seem topsy-turvy. Your sculpture, on the other hand, reflects a deep understanding of the human condition."

"I'm drunk, I know, but allow me to tell you a story to illustrate just how true that is. While standing in line to buy some bubble gum," I say, and hiccup, "I met a man with golden hair and shiny teeth. He remarked that he liked my jacket. Its color suited me very well, he said. I blushed and looked away, because there's nothing more difficult than receiving a compliment, especially from a stranger. When I got to the register," I say, and hiccup, "it was to find I'd left my wallet in a locker at the YMCA. I tried to reason with the cashier, promising I'd come back the next day to pay him. Without my bubble gum, I wouldn't be able to sleep that night. But no matter what I said, he refused. Outside," I say, and hiccup, "I sat on the corner with my head in my hands. The YMCA was closed. Then, just as I started home, the man who had complimented me in the store approached with the bubble gum I had wanted. I thanked him," I say, and hiccup, "but said I couldn't possibly accept. In the end, however, he prevailed through sheer tenacity of will. My head was aching from not chewing bubble gum all day, so I went to the park to chew some and invited the man. We had been sitting there for ten minutes or so—discussing nothing of importance, perhaps even sports—when he asked me to follow him back to his apartment. In light of his generosity, how could I refuse?"

Orsi leans in close while I speak, as if moved by a mysterious sympathy. It isn't long before I'm foaming at the mouth and yelling like a sailor.

"This is where the story gets interesting," I say, and hiccup. "When we arrived at his apartment, the man realized he'd lost his keys. He said he was cooking dinner for his girlfriend that evening and needed to defrost a chicken. His window was open, he thought. Would I climb inside and unlock the door? He'd do it himself, he said, but he'd recently injured his back. No doubt I was struck by this serendipitous moment. The very man who'd just done me a selfless favor was now in need himself. I was more than happy to oblige. Once the man was in, he asked me to wait outside and yell "Mogadishu!" if I spotted anyone coming. His roommate, he said, was due any minute, and he wanted to make sure the kitchen was clean. A few minutes later, he raced out of the apartment with a handful of jewelry. I tried to apprehend him, but he was too fast. On the street, an officer arrested me. A neighbor," I said, and hiccupped, "had videoed me climbing through the window."

"That's a wonderfully interesting story," Orsi says, and sips her drink. "But I have to wonder how much of it is really true."

"Even in my lies," I say, and collapse hiccupping into the sofa, "there's more truth than in all the facts of natural science."

Orsi's face is calm, her eyes unblinking. "That still doesn't explain the sensitivity of your sculpture."

"Perhaps what you think is my understanding of the human condition is actually something else?" I say, as we return to the bar. "I'm not a good judge of people, really. I just like observing a person's peculiarities. For instance, I once knew a woman who couldn't help but blink her eyes every time she said the word 'tangerine.' Poor woman, she was powerless against this quirk. In the four or five years I knew her, I observed this tic at least a dozen times. And yet no one else ever said a word about it. Maybe it's this you saw in my work?"

Our drinks refreshed, Orsi leads me by the hand through the crowd. We pass through a room that is pitch black but for a storm of white strobes. The DJ plays deep house music. Everywhere bodies are flopping like fish on the deck of a boat. Fearful the lights might induce a seizure, I close my eyes and let Orsi guide me. The apartment is endless, each new room a scene in unto itself. One door opens onto a planetarium filled with people on blankets and pillows, sharing weed pens as they gaze into the universe. Another reveals a cigar lounge in which a group of very tall men are playing pool. One of them, I see, is the point guard for the Brooklyn Nets.

I have to pee, and step into a bathroom. Louis is there beside the sink with a screwdriver.

"The pipe was leaking," he says, "so I thought I'd fix it."

"Can you please leave?" I say. "I require absolute privacy to do my business."

"All finished," Louis says, and hugs me warmly. "And anyway, I need to head back to Kayleigh and the boys!"

It's not a lie to say I can't pee in less than perfect conditions. Several factors, honestly, require strict attention. First, I turn off the lights. The sight of my flaccid penis has never failed to shock me. Even a glimpse of it has in the past kept me from peeing for up to three days. In the dark, I strip my shoes, socks, and pants. I once wet myself on a school field trip to the aquarium, so now even the thought of a single drip on my clothes is traumatizing. Finally, I eat a bit of soap. Its awful taste distracts me from the shame that I am a slave to my bodily functions.

Orsi is waiting for me in the hall when finally, I emerge. She's ready to leave and asks if I'd like to come. In the elevator, I think, "When we pass the twentieth floor, I'll kiss her!" Of course, instead, I make a disparaging remark about an author whose work is popular with a certain type of reader.

"That Ben Lerner's no thinker," I say. "He's just a two-bit preacher."

"I quite liked his last novel," Orsi says with narrowed eyes.

"A total waste of time," I say, feeling my cheeks turn red, knowing I've never actually read the man's work. "All he does is vulgarize ready-made ideas for the masses."

At the corner of 53rd and 6th, I prepare to part ways. It's better to initiate the separation myself than to suffer the humiliation of waiting for her to do it first.

"It's getting late," I say, "and my dog won't sleep unless I read to her from the day's financial page."

"In some respects, you're as brave as a matador" Orsi says, taking a cigarette from a case. "In others, you're a meek little lamb."

Orsi flags a taxi with a wave. She flicks her cigarette away and scoots to the far side of the backseat so I can join her. The driver's playing pop music on the radio. On the screen before us, a commercial for the Jimmy Fallon show repeats on a loop until I turn it off. Orsi rests her head on my shoulder, and we don't speak at all.

CHAPTER 11

ORSI LIVES on the third floor of a five-story walkup in Chelsea. On the ground floor is a luxury clothing boutique, and on the second, a tattoo shop. I count three wine bars on her block, as well. Several bikes are chained to the banister in the hall to her door. Inside, she flips the light switch and the room is suffused in a yellow glow. I've never seen so many books in all my life, in every European language, finely bound, many of them first editions. And such curious and eclectic art. I recognize a piece from a Japanese painter I once saw speak on a panel. He had, as I recall, quite a grip on the art market's demand for novelty.

"Did a German Shepard used to live here?" I say.

"How did you know?" Orsi asks, sniffing. "Does the apartment smell of it?"

"Nothing like that," I say, and note the High Line Park directly across the way. "It's just that sometimes my head gets filled with little bits of mysterious knowledge. It doesn't happen often."

Orsi leads me to her room, where we tumble onto the bed mid-kiss. She tastes like mint gum and whiskey. Our clothes come off piece by piece. This is the first time I've been with a woman since Janie left me. It feels so foreign that it seems almost impossible that other people have sex on a regular basis. Orsi positions me on top of her. She spreads her legs and reaches down and takes it, hard as the Empire State Building. I almost ask about a condom, but am afraid to sour the mood. Orsi is engulfed by passion and longing. I'm not so foolish to think

I'm the first man to ever stir her, but it's deeply satisfying to know I play at least some role in her enjoyment.

Now she's on top, twisting and squirming, sucking greedily on my fingers. She guides my hand down her backside, leans forward, and implores me to slip a finger in. In all my life, I've never had such erotic good fortune. Then she grabs a fistful of my hair, and I'm reminded that I have a few peculiarities of my own in this department. Any touching of my hair makes me deeply uncomfortable. Once Janie brushed a few loose strands back behind my ear while we were in the act. I was so upset I spent the rest of the night walking around the neighborhood telling anyone who'd listen I planned to become a park ranger in Wyoming. With Orsi, however, I'm determined not to let my compulsions get the best of me. I employ a relaxation technique I read in a biography of a seventeenth-century Tibetan monk, counting backwards from one hundred. By the time I reach forty-six, Orsi hollers she's about to come. I cease counting and commit my full attention to her orgasm. Just as she climaxes, she bites my lip, hard, and I fall off the bed and then finish into a sock. Afterwards, we lie together in silence for a few minutes.

"I'm going to make a sandwich," she says finally. "Would you like one?"

"I could eat."

She goes to work on an impressive assortment of Italian meats and cheeses. I inform her I'm a vegetarian, and she rolls her eyes. An open bottle of red wine sits on a table made of an old church door, from which I pour us glasses. Halfway through my sandwich, though, bits of tomato and provolone falling from my mouth, I see Orsi has barely taken a nibble, so I stop eating, too.

A spider crawls up the leg of the table as we light cigarettes. Orsi asks where I took my MFA.

"I have no formal education beyond a GED and a scuba diving certification," I say humbly.

"What did you intend to do when you were young?"

"A palm reader once told me I have a short life-line, so I never bothered to prepare for a future."

"Sometimes in life one is lucky, and the right thing finds you."

The room is too smoky, so I open the window. On the mantle stand a series of framed pictures, many of them showing Orsi as a young child with her family back in Budapest. In others, she's an adult, and almost always with the same man. There's something heroically dishonest about him that I'm immediately attracted to.

"Is this your ex?" I say, pointing to the man.

She takes a long drag. "That's my husband."

"Where is he now?"

"In India, I believe," she says. "Have you heard of the Pure Cosmos Club?"

"Never."

"My husband is developing quite a following."

"And it's okay if you sleep with other people?"

"One has to follow one's inclinations, doesn't one?"

Nausea surges through me. In the bathroom, I run the tap so Orsi can't hear me vomit. I splash water on my face and use Orsi's mouthwash. Looking in the mirror, I'm reminded that everything has an end—relationships, life, even the stars. Normally I feel no solidarity with myself. Since when does one have sympathy for his worst enemy?

Music is playing as I step into the bedroom to dress,

plaintive violins and cellos. My suit, I see, has a burn on the lapel. One of my shoes has disappeared. I find it under the bed, next to a jewelry box. Everything in it is lovely—an antique ruby necklace, a sapphire ring, a couple of golden bangles. I could sell these, I think, and pay off my debts to Salvador and Alma, and the landlord, too. There's also a bag of marbles. I pour a few into my hand, and am instantly transported to my childhood, where Louis and I spent countless hours playing ringers on the kitchen floor. Onionskins, corkscrews, peacocks, and lutzes are here, all with such wonderful colors and artistry. They might even be handmade, I think, and wonder whether kids play with marbles anymore. Parents, in all likelihood these days, consider marbles a choking hazard. The smooth green lutz with two orange bands feels so good in my hand. It's just a little memento, I tell myself, and put it in my pocket.

Orsi is still at the table smoking. The wine bottle is empty but for the butts we dropped into it. Orsi's eyes are red-rimmed, and her mascara is smeared. I didn't realize what a sensitive person she is, despite everything.

She shows me to the door. I go in for a kiss on the cheek, failing to remember that European custom calls for a kiss on each. Our lips lightly graze each other as I move to the other side. Sometimes the merest things are the most enchanting.

It's four in the morning and a long wait for the train back to Brooklyn. Even though it was but a single night, after sharing time with someone else, I feel I've fallen into nothingness.

CHAPTER 12

BLANCHE HAS untethered herself from her wheels and is pacing the apartment when I arrive. This is her coping mechanism whenever she's upset.

Her face is so droopy and sad she looks part hound dog. I strain to mask my emotions. Blanche has repeatedly insisted there's no romance in overt displays of passion. Nobility, she believes, is only found in the struggle against it. An appetite suppressed, I have often thought to myself, is the greatest victory in life. There is little evidence that Blanche will sympathize with my failure to live up to our shared ideals.

My body is filled with electric nerves. It's plain the only way I'll get any sleep is by chewing my bubble gum. I let Blanche off the leash as we walk to the bodega. Two squirrels cross our path, which, disturbingly, Blanche ignores. She has been demanding to know where I've been. Rather than let her think I've been disloyal, I slander Orsi.

"I met a terrible woman at the art show," I say. "A friend of Danny's, so you can imagine what kind of person she is. A monster, really. She comes from the Eastern bloc—if that tells you anything—and has the strangest accent. At first, I found it charming, I'll admit, like singing birds. But after a while, it fatigued me. In truth, I could really only listen to her speak for ten hours at a time, maybe twelve at most. After that, I'd need a rest, however brief."

Blanche looks at me with dead eyes. When she spits, as well—something I've never seen her or any other dog do—I'm made so alarmed that I begin talking even more erratically, making a fool of myself.

"Is she smart? I wouldn't say that, exactly. She's no Rimbaud, not by a far sight, nor has she the political savvy of a Nixon, or even of a Woodrow Wilson. I do suppose, though, in a traditional sort of way, yes, she's intelligent. She manages to get her shoes tied in the morning and make it out the door, and, if I remember correctly, which of course I may not, she's a mathematician at Columbia University, a PhD candidate, actually, with several top prizes for various formulas and proofs she's solved. But, you know me, I've never been impressed with anything to do with facts and figures. In fact, I hold ordinary genius in low esteem. What good is it?"

It goes on like this, which Blanche seems to accept, until we get our pack of bubble gum. After hours wandering the streets of Brooklyn, Blanche manages to get gum stuck in her fur. It takes an hour in a public fountain to remove it. By then, I have a tremendous craving for empanadas.

"Let's go into the city," I say. "I know just the place!"

Even at this early hour, the morning commute is fierce. I have to hold Blanche in my arms so she doesn't get trampled by commuters. Our destination is the West Village. Blanche grows suspicious of my motives. Surely, there's got to be a spot closer to home? What about La Isla or Arepera Guacuco? Both are quite well known for their empanadas. But I am adamant. Porteño's it must be. Have I even been there before? No, I tell Blanche, never, nor do I know anyone who has. I simply have a tremendous feeling about it, after reading a mediocre review in *The Times*. We sit at a table by the window, splitting an *espinaca y queso* empanada. Blanche keeps nodding off as we eat, while

I study the bustling street. When we're finished, to no avail, Blanche pleads to go home.

"Did you know there's a World War I memorial just across the street?" I say.

The Chelsea Doughboy is a statue of a soldier holding a rifle, with a flag draped over his shoulder. I salute the Doughboy, yet I'm not inspired to shed even a single tear, strange for a WWI buff like myself. Even as I explain to Blanche the origin of the term "doughboy" to describe an American soldier, I'm distracted, hyper-vigilant to everyone around us. We walk up and down the same row of restaurants and stores for the next six hours. So many different adventures and experiences to be had. A man could never leave this block and still lead a very full life.

Finally, after peering in the window of a candle shop, I see Orsi coming down the street, carrying two bags, and enter a building. What a coincidence, I think. I had totally forgotten that she lived on this block. It takes several minutes to recover from the shock of seeing her, then Blanche and I go home.

CHAPTER 13

THE BUBBLE gum we chewed has worked wonders on Blanche. On the train, she falls dead asleep. Now I must carry her. I'm tempted just to tuck her into bed, but first I have to brush her teeth. The veterinarian recommends I clean her teeth once a month, but she insists on twice a day, minimum. Ever since she learned of a greyhound who had to have two teeth pulled after a buildup caused infection, Blanche has had a dreadful fear of tarter. Obligingly, I provide daily inspections of her mouth.

At long last, I tuck her away and turn on the stereo. Blanche also requires background music to sleep. Lately, she's on a disco kick. Abba's "Dancing Queen" blasts from the speakers till our neighbor pounds on the wall. When I move to turn it down, Blanche growls. No sooner have I left to apologize to the neighbor than I see Louis and his family marching down the hall with a birthday cake with lighted candles.

I knock on my neighbor's door as they break into a horrible rendition of "Happy Birthday." A gruff old man with a grey beard and a silver tooth answers, leaning on his cane.

"I apologize for the loud music," I say. "My dog is trying to sleep."

The man slams the door in my face.

"Blow out the candles!" the older of Louis' sons says.

"What is all this about? Is it October already?"

"July, Paul," Louis says. "Your birthday is July eleventh."

I reluctantly grant them entry to my apartment. Louis' wife, Kayleigh, turns off the stereo, causing Blanche to wake with a jolt and fall off the bed. She rubs her eyes with her paws, utterly confused. The younger son presents me with a gift. He's covered in pink cotton candy stains, and the wrapping paper is sticky from his grimy hands.

"Why didn't you let me know you were coming?" I say.

"I must've called a dozen times," Louis says, "but you never picked up."

"Of course not," I say, "the FBI could have my phone tapped."

I unwrap the gift. It's a red tennis racket. I take a few practice swings, forehand and backhand, then lean the racket against the wall. This is a very cruel trick, even for Louis. My love affair with the game of tennis started in 1999, watching Andre Agassi on television come back from two sets to love to beat Andrei Medvedev in a five-set French Open final. To that point, Agassi's triumph was the most life-affirming thrill of my life. Fly swatter in hand, I played the entire match before my television, a marathon that pushed me to my limits. Between sets, I had to ice my knees and massage my elbow. Before the last grueling set, I even vomited under a couch cushion. When Medvedev's forehand sailed long on the match's final point, the victory was as much mine as Agassi's.

My great wish at the time, of course, was to become a pro. I begged my parents to let me play, but my father refused. The game, he said, was far too dangerous. After all, we had a family history of weak ligaments and joint pain. When on my birthday my parents gave me a six-pack of socks, I ran away. My first stop was the sporting goods store, where I waited in the fishing and hunting aisle for the manager to take his smoke break, so I could abscond with a tennis racket. I hid out at the local country club for a week, my days spent practicing my strokes. At night I slept behind the snack bar by the pool. My hard work caught the attention of the club's tennis pro, and he offered to give me lessons for free. Soon I entered a local tournament and finished in fourth place. It wasn't long before the local newspaper wrote a human-interest story on me, and my father turned me into the police for stealing the racket. I did community service after school for a year. By the time it was over, the window had closed on my competitive career.

"Do you love it?" Louis says.

"Is it your sole ambition in life to make me miserable, Louis?"

"I don't understand."

"That's it," I say, "you and me, on the roof, now!"

I shove Louis out the door and up the stairs. Blanche and the others follow. The sun beats down hard, reflecting off Louis' bald head. Kayleigh hurriedly applies sunscreen to her children's pasty faces. Blanche has heard me read aloud the passages from my high school journal. She looks worried. The roof is littered with obstacles, none of which I've committed to memory. I kneel down to Blanche and deliver a teary farewell.

"Don't worry, my darling, by this time next week, you'll have forgotten all about me. It'll be as if I never existed."

Louis taps me on the shoulder. "What are we doing up here?"

"Do you remember the cereal factory when we were kids?"

"Of course," he says. "On Wednesdays, they made Cinnamon Toast Crunch, and the town smelled wonderful."

"Yes," I say, raising a fist, "it did. But far more importantly, it's where you caused me to suffer my greatest humiliation!"

"I have no idea what you're talking about."

I recount my memory of the day we walked blindfolded to the roof's edge, risking certain death, adding fresh details to embellish the story, a tale so harrowing and tragic it causes Louis' children to sob hysterically.

"I'm sorry, Paul," Louis says, "but I have no recollection of anything of the sort."

My heart pounds with bewilderment. I see an unsettling sincerity in his eyes. His forgetful nature always has been his best defense. Our cruelest transgressions are at times the ones we disremember most.

"Nothing?" I say.

"Why don't we head back inside?"

As we eat cake in the apartment, Louis praises his wife's incredible baking skills. He's never tasted anything finer, he says. I'm more inclined to think his delicious feeling is that of having gotten away with a crime he too much enjoyed committing.

CHAPTER 14

As a child, I would steal things only to throw them away the moment I was free from being caught. Before I stole Orsi's marble, it had been years since I'd succumbed to my compulsion. Till now, I'd even believed myself free of it. My thrill, however, that today I alone possess such a treasure, is intoxicating. I can't say how often I hold the marble, reveling in its cool, round surface. It is, in fact, almost shameful I'm made so content by so little.

Sometimes, after I've been drinking, I vow to get rid of the marble, and dream up elaborate plans to purge it from my life. Yesterday, I rode a train forty minutes with the intention of throwing the marble into the ocean. Before that, I buried it in a park. But without the marble, I grieved. I ran back to dig it up only to find kids playing soccer on the field. I ended up interrupting their game so I could retrieve it.

Lately, I've been sleeping with the marble under my pillow, and my dreams have been filled with peculiarities. Last night I dreamt I was a rat that had fallen in love with a cat who wanted to eat me.

Susan calls to say I need to retrieve my sculpture immediately. She's preparing a show for a Norwegian artist who creates impressionistic renderings of the northern lights using the skin and blood of walruses. The artist has made nearly three hundred of these so-called paintings. It's been her life's work, actually, for the past twenty years. Susan is thrilled at the prospect of animal rights activists protesting the event. She's certain she's going to make a fortune.

"Collectors love to traffic in cruelty," she says.

"Twenty years of making essentially the same painting?"

"Her lack of imagination is, in fact, the key to her success."

I stop by the studio to get my wagon. Danny is hunched over a sewing table, hand-threading his cat-bags with sinew. With his aristocratic face, its large nose and shrewd eyes, he's the embodiment of erudition. My intrusion startles him, and his glasses fall to the floor and break. Half-blind, he lurches from one support to the next.

"My eyes must've been playing tricks on me," Danny says, and settles in a chair. "Did I see you leave the party with Orsi the other night?"

"She was quite taken with my sculpture."

"Don't tell me you slept with her!" Danny says, his mouth twitching. "She's way out of your league."

I do my best to resist smiling. "She's a married woman."

"Indeed, she is, to perhaps the most enigmatic man in the world."

My mind burns with questions, but it's important not to appear too eager, lest I court certain doom. "You know her husband?"

"In a way, I suppose, though I don't think anyone truly knows the multitudes that are James."

I seize Danny by the hand. "Not that it's of any interest, really, but perhaps you can tell me more."

"We haven't seen an individual so shrouded in mystery," Danny says, "since The Bible's Great Harlot of Babylon. If he's truly of no interest to you, however, I won't waste my time explaining."

My grip on Danny's hand tightens. "If I don't retrieve my

sculpture from the gallery, Susan's going chuck it out on the street. But I'm in no rush."

"I first met James in the dorms at Yale," Danny says, and lights a cigarette. "It was clear from the start he wasn't like the others. His father had been a Christian missionary, and James spent his youth in the most remote corners of India, teaching the natives the miracle of Christ and the intricacies of computer programming. He made his presence known on campus when he won a contentious election for student body president, unprecedented for a freshman. He captained the debate team to a national championship and starred in the school's intramural wrestling program. The summer after his sophomore year, he earned a prestigious internship in the Obama administration. It's not widely known, but it was James who penned Obama's acceptance speech for the Nobel Peace Prize."

"So he's a justice fanatic?" I say. "That's the type of maniac that irks me most!"

"Let me finish," Danny says, ashing his cigarette in a coffee mug. "James' junior year, he travelled to Tibet, where he never showed up for his classes. Rumors speculated he'd joined a Buddhist guerrilla fighting unit that had been captured by the Chinese and was being held in a prison in the Yunnan province. After that, nobody heard a peep about him for years. Then, two summers ago, we crossed paths again while I was attending a meditation retreat in Costa Rica. James was the retreat's surf instructor. He taught me how to 'hang ten.' Afterwards, we stayed in touch via postcards. From all I can gather, he's only just turned up in New York to start a new venture called the Pure Cosmos Club."

"The only thing worse than a revolutionary is an industrialist!"

I say, pounding my fist into the table. "What could Orsi possibly see in such a man?"

"You wouldn't believe how handsome and charming James is," Danny says. "His gravitational pull is like the Sun's."

"She doesn't seem like the type who'd go in for all that."

Danny returns to his sewing table, retrieves a new pair of glasses from a drawer, and renews his stitching-work. "Women respond to charisma and authority far more than they do even to money."

I collect my wagon and set off for the gallery. On the train, I study the faces of my fellow passengers. One day, I think, sadly, all these people will be dead. Worse, as time passes, each of them will be thought about less and less. The dead will become even deader.

The man and woman next to me are engaged in heated discussion. He has dark, smooth skin and is carrying a suitcase. She wears expensive clothing, and her face is heavily made up. Apparently, she's accompanying him to the airport for his trip back to Chicago and wants to know when he will return, to which he says, merely, "soon." The next couple months, the woman explains, will be very busy, so it's important she make the proper arrangements to ensure her availability. Then she recommends he check his luggage for the flight. The man leans his head against the window and closes his eyes. Although the bag between his feet is carry-on size, she assures him he'll be much more comfortable if he checks it.

"And anyway," she says, "the wait in line will give us a few extra minutes together."

But the man is adamant she must not follow him all the way to check-in, and rattles off the ways she can better spend her time.

"The airport here is very tricky," she says, "I wouldn't feel right just abandoning you."

The man reminds her he's flown out of this airport many times without any problems.

"Maybe," the woman says, "security will make an exception and allow me to escort you to the gate?"

As we approach my stop, the woman says she's never been to Chicago before. Perhaps she should take the next few days off to tour the city? The man wouldn't have to chaperone her entire visit, though she would appreciate his offer for a place to say. She could take him to a Chicago Cubs game, she says, and she's heard about some lovely bistros she'd love to try. I consider following them to the airport, but Susan has sent me a number of texts threatening to leave my sculpture in the alley. As the train speeds away, I see the man holding his head while the woman wags her finger.

It's raining when I hit the street. Most people are hoisting their umbrellas, confident they'll get where they're going dry as toasted almonds. I'm wearing the second of my two new suits—still pristine—and am wary of doing anything to sully it, so I stand beneath a hotel awning to consider my options. A garbage truck stops before me. A handsome man with a hint of stubble jumps off the back and makes his collection, then places an empty bag in the can. Aware of the six-block walk to the gallery, I make a beeline for the bag, to fashion myself a poncho. Several homeless men have done the same, I notice as I walk. We hold up our thumbs in recognition.

At the gallery, Susan is berating the team of Dominicans she's hired to install the new show. None of them are wearing the masks she insisted they don while transporting the art. Her concern, however, isn't that an errant sneeze will bring all of mankind to its knees by spreading the new virus from China, but that the art could be irrevocably harmed due to negligence. In short, she could be sued for damages.

Examining the paintings, she claims a fleck of saliva has tarnished one and threatens to garnish the worker's wages. But nobody appears overly concerned. Susan has a reputation for such behavior.

The paintings, I see, possess what is in my opinion the worst failure of any art: they've been labored over far too much. I approach one of the workers as he hangs one.

"These paintings just reek of effort," I say, while struggling to pull the wet bag over my head.

"I agree completely," he says, and helps me with the bag. "I'm only interested in art that falls like rain—a gift from God!"

The woman who took the picture of the tumbleweed in the desert stands with Susan, admiring the Norwegian's work. When at last they pause to rub their chins, I interject.

"The sky's the limit," I say, "when it comes to the commercial value of such, uh, *paintings.*"

My attempt at chitchat lacks conviction, and the two women ignore me. Susan asks about the photographer's process. As a matter of fact, the photographer says, she's only been taking photos for the last few months. The beauty of digital photography, she says, is that one can take an endless number of photos.

"Basically, I just point and click," the photographer says. "If I take enough shots, I'm bound to get at least a few good ones."

Susan congratulates the photographer on the sale of her picture and reminds her that she'll see a direct deposit of twelve thousand dollars in her account by the end of the week. The two women kiss each other's cheeks, and the photographer strolls merrily away.

"I'm sorry we weren't able to show your sculpture," Susan says. "It was actually quite inventive."

"Well," I say, nodding toward the photographer, "I'm glad the show worked out for someone."

"She's in the grip of happiness, now," Susan says. "It will pass."

"There are good moments," I say, impressed with how mature I seem, "and not-so good moments, right?"

"This goes against all my instincts," Susan says, "but do you need any money to tide you over?"

This strikes me as terribly offensive. My aversion to pity is profound. "Would I be wearing a suit like this," I say with all the dignity and prestige I can muster, "if I were out of sorts?"

"It is a very nice suit," Susan says, and runs her fingers along my sleeve.

"Thank you for your kindness, Susan, but I'm doing quite well."

I load the sculpture into the wagon and set off. A young woman with exquisite eyebrows and a Romanesque nose greets me at the crosswalk, and all at once we're talking about everything and nothing. The light turns green, but she's describing her beekeeping practice with such charm and verve I can't help but to stay. All around us the crowd is yammering and shoving, and some disgruntled individuals even go so far as to mutter at us nastily. An old lady in a motorized cart is upset enough to flip us off. The woman's name is Norah, she says with a sparkle in her eye, then suggests we might sometime soon share a cup of tea.

I've always been skeptical of anyone who takes an interest

in me, but there is something about Norah that gives me courage. I take out my phone to text her my number and hear a faint clatter at my feet. To my great dismay, Orsi's marble has bounced into the street and ricocheted off the tire of a blaring ambulance. I'm nearly struck by a motorcycle as I rush toward it. A police officer shouts at me through his squad car's speaker, yet I persist—I simply cannot lose this marble. Finally, after it has skipped off a delivery truck, and then a Japanese sedan, I dive at the marble just before it rolls through a sewer grate. Tears stream down my face as I sobbingly kiss the marble, whose meaning till now I hadn't fully grasped. A crowd has gathered. The officer from the squad car helps me to my feet. Not only have I destroyed my suit, I see, but I've badly torn the skin from my elbows, knees, and chin. The officer wants to know what on earth would compel me to act with such recklessness.

"I can't explain it, officer," I say. "I saw that I was going to lose my marble, and my body just sprang into action."

The police officer is hesitant. He lectures me for a moment, ending with something about my being a "danger" to myself.

"Unless you have legal recourse to hold me," I say, "I must insist you let me go my way."

My sculpture is still in the wagon on the corner. My phone is there, too. Norah, however, is gone.

CHAPTER 15

On the train, I pluck a section of my head clean of hair. It's impossible, I know, to be both happy and self-aware, so I decide then and there to forget myself entirely. I put my hand on my heart and tell myself a number of far-flung lies.

"You've done all the right things and made all the right choices," I whisper, drawing anxious stares from my fellow passengers. "You've made yourself indispensable in this life. The world would be lost without you!"

I remember the time I was forced to go hiking with Louis. Rocky Mountain Park is a destination I'd always found repellant. To this day, its rugged terrain and abundant conifers are for me the nadir of the quotidian. After a grueling day trudging up a jagged mountain, my muscles were exhausted, but when we happened across a particular cliff, Louis had an irresistible urge to scale it. He reached the summit easily and celebrated with a cheer. I had little choice but to take up the challenge myself. Louis shouted words of caution as I began, warning it was too dangerous.

"Please, Paul," he said, "don't do it! It was a mistake for me to climb this rock! I don't want to see you hurt!"

But, as anyone who knows Louis would understand, these were not words of concern so much as a direct affront to my humanity. To this day, I'm convinced he did something to the cliff to sabotage me. How else to explain my inability to climb more than a few feet? Surely, Louis had smeared the cliff with some undetectable concoction to ensure my failure. I struggled valiantly, but well past sunset, I'd made no headway at all, till, finally, empty, I collapsed and twisted my ankle.

At Louis' home that evening, his mother, my Aunt Abigail, asked why I was limping. Louis had tricked me, I said. Appalled by her son's cruelty, my aunt told me to decide Louis' punishment. The burden weighed heavily. After two lost nights of sleeplessness, I told my aunt that Louis should be kept from traveling with his baseball team to Fort Collins for the league championship. True to her word, my aunt restricted Louis to his bedroom, where he stoically awaited the fate of his team. As it happened, a freak snowstorm dropped eleven inches of snow that day, stranding the team on a mountain road twenty miles outside of Longmont. The team's leftfielder, catcher, and entire relief pitching staff were later hospitalized with frostbite and hypothermia.

As I wonder at the pile of plucked hair at my feet, it strikes me that my choice of punishment was doubly sound. Louis didn't merely learn a valuable lesson about treating others with kindness and dignity. My mercy spared him the fate of his teammates, what not even the cruelest of children deserves.

It's clear that I must throw myself at the mercy of those who I've wronged, and I force myself to Sal's Custom Suits. Salvador and Alma appear deeply concerned by my condition.

"What has happened to this wonderful suit?" Salvador says.

I stare at the floor, too ashamed to look this great man in his face.

"I'm so sorry," I say. "Things have gone horribly awry, and I don't have the money I owe you."

Salvador has left my side to examine the sculpture, which I must have dragged in with me. He walks around the wagon, pausing here and there to study the piece. Alma joins him, and the two whisper to each other.

"What you've created here," Alma says, "is a triumph of hope over experience."

"We'd like to make you a proposition," Salvador says. "In lieu of a cash payment, would you be interested in a trade? As compensation for the suits, of course."

"You want the sculpture for the suits?"

"Only if you think it's fair," Alma says. "It's a remarkable piece, and we would never want to take advantage of you."

To sweeten the deal, Salvador offers to make me a third suit to replace the ones I've ruined.

"I've got an incredible new houndstooth fabric," he says. "It will look marvelous on you."

I gratefully accept, and they invite me to stay for lunch. Alma has prepared her legendary *pozole*. The recipe has been handed down in her family for generations. In her grandmother's village, the soup is referred to as "*sopa de dios*." It's so good I eat three bowls, and when I leave they send leftovers for Blanche.

CHAPTER 16

THE LANDLORD has put a lock on my door, with a collection of eviction notices dating back two months. My eviction, it seems, has been done "by the book," as they say.

"Don't worry, Blanche," I shout, pounding on the door, "I'm here!" I can hear her barking plaintively, though not from my apartment, but the stairwell. My landlord is coming up with Blanche in his arms, his shirt stained with urine.

"What the hell have you done to Blanche?"

"You're lucky I don't call animal control on you," the landlord says as he sets Blanche down. He rolls up his sleeve to show me a fresh bite mark.

"I'm wondering if you would potentially take a painting in trade for the money I owe you?"

The landlord laughs. But what starts as mere sarcastic joy soon devolves into hysterics. He won't stop laughing. Then he begins to cough and choke, and his face turns crimson.

"You drive a hard bargain," I say. "Perhaps two paintings might be fairer?"

The landlord by now can only wheeze. A moment later, he's on the floor. I remember a CPR instructional poster from the kitchen of a Chinese restaurant where I once washed dishes, and run through the steps meticulously.

First, I check the area for safety hazards. I can't help anyone if I become a victim myself.

Second, I shake the landlord's shoulder. As I expected, this only exacerbates his condition.

Third, I yell for help, aware of its futility. Blanche is howling far too loudly.

Finally, I turn the landlord onto his back and press my ear over his heart. I trace a line from his armpit to the center of his chest, interlace my fingers, press my hands over his breastbone, and execute thirty compressions, which I count aloud. I tilt his head, pinch his nose, press my mouth to his, and blow into his lungs. I repeat this cycle until the landlord starts to breathe on his own. He lies there, covered with sweat, eyes glazed, aware only now, it seems, of what has happened.

"You saved my life," he says. "The only way I can think to repay is to let you live here rent-free till you get back on your feet."

Blanche nips at the landlord's ankles and growls, a surefire sign that we're in grave danger.

"That's very generous," I say, "but I'm afraid we can't stay here any longer."

"But where will you go?" the landlord says.

"It's difficult to say."

The landlord unlocks the door. I suck on a lollipop as I collect some things. I'm not the type who suffers delusions that time is meaningful. But with my thirty-seventh birthday having just passed, it's important I take a moment to reflect. Certainly, I don't want to be one of those vain men who considers their successes incomplete. It's no small feat to have come this far staving off the burdens that typically accompany adulthood. While the fountains of life have run dry for most men my age, I have no material possessions, or, for that matter, any allegiances, to constrain me. Anything but a full embrace of detachment rings false. It's time to carry the torch into the dark.

I've packed my worn paperback of Jane Bowles' *Two*

Serious Ladies, my Abba record, and a half-dozen paint brushes.
"Goodbye," I say to the apartment. "Goodbye, goodbye."

CHAPTER 17

AT THE studio, I build a makeshift bed out of broken picture frames and splattered tarps. The pitter-patter of rats darting across the floor has Blanche on high alert. We split a bottle of cheap white wine. Finally, at 3 a.m., Blanche drifts off to sleep.

Some time passes before I hear a cacophony of voices outside the door, and then the rattling of the lock. I reach for a paint brush from my can, but only knock it over, and scurry about on hands and knees until I find a brush, one, I'm relieved to see, whose handle in a fit of boredom I whittled to a point. When the door swings open to admit a throng of shadowy figures, I stab the nearest man in the leg. Howling, he assaults me.

"Get him, Winston!" someone says as we exchange blows.

Someone else flips the lights, and I can see my foe, a man in a threadbare military-issue coat and a matted beard. My brush is still lodged in his thigh, so I twist it, and he shrieks like all the devils.

"A cheap but effective move, Paul!" says the voice that had encouraged my enemy.

It's Danny, I see, squinting up. But just as I turn my vengeance to him, I'm sacked by a bevy of his followers.

"Enough!" Danny shouts. "That's my friend, Paul!"

A shirtless sunburnt man with fleshy cheeks and a bulbous nose pulls me to my feet and shakes my hand. Others follow, each fouler and more depraved than the last. One vomits on himself and makes no attempt to clean himself. Another is wearing sweatpants smeared with shit. A third offers me a toke from a crack pipe. Disliking to be rude, I accept. Blanche must be very drunk. She hasn't made a sound, or even moved.

Danny, I learn, met these miscreants several years ago while living on skid row. As I recall, he'd suffered a bout of amnesia after a head injury from a brawl sponsored by a conspiracy of underground streetfighters. They took Danny for dead, and simply dragged him to the street. The men here now found and nursed him back to health. He had been with them for several weeks when he was recognized by David Chang, owner of the Momofuku restaurant group. He had caught Danny digging through a dumpster behind his noodle bar. Chang made national news when he donated to the Sierra Club the two-million-dollar reward Danny's father had offered for information about his son.

Unbeknownst to me, Danny's been letting his skid row pals stay in our studio on nights when I'm not in here. No wonder the man I stabbed, Winston, knows the first aid kit is under the sink. He tends to his own wounds with an amused grin. Clearly, he has the spirit of a cannibal.

"Does it hurt very bad?" I say.

"Terribly," he says, and shakes my hand, his own cracked and hardened like that of a prison laborer, "and for that I must thank you."

"Do you find that physical pain helps fill the void?"

"Suffering is real, Paul. Pleasure is abstract and suspect."

"It's almost a pity, isn't it, that our wounds inevitably heal?"

"It's of no concern," he says, applying his bandage. "When this worry's gone, another will soon follow."

Blanche wakes from her drunken stupor and pees on my shoes, then staggers over to join us, where we are drinking bad wine and smoking cigarettes. As a child, Winston tells us, he went door-to-door selling cans of food at exorbitant prices, promising his neighbors that the proceeds would go to charity when, really, he spent it on candy and porn. For this, Winston says, and shows us the row of thick scars on his back and shoulders, his father beat him mercilessly.

"I wondered if old age would besiege me as naturally as all the other stages of life," he says, beaming. "The fact that it has is wonderfully comforting."

"Winston has been saved without the need for grace," Danny says, glaring at me with imperious eyes.

I find Danny's attitude and tastes to be precious to a fault, but say nothing. Instead, I squeeze my marble and take an extra-long pull from the bottle of pinot grigio being passed around.

It's nearly dawn by the time we fall asleep, piled up like cavemen.

CHAPTER 18

WHEN I wake in the morning Danny and his friends are gone, and, to my horror, Blanche with them. Did something happen during the night? Perhaps she went sleepwalking? Once she passed out at the dog groomer's after drinking too much champagne and woke up on the Staten Island ferry. Whatever the case, she's gone again. I search every inch of the studio, yet Blanche is nowhere to be found. I collapse to the floor and weep. Should anything have befallen her, I'd lose all reason to go on.

I whisper a prayer, asking God to lay all Blanche's suffering upon me, then lie on the floor and wait. It's not as if I've ever believed the injustices of this world will be righted. In many ways, I've been waiting for the next great event to crush the lot of us. After a time, I unscrew the lid from a bottle of bleach and promise to drink it all. Before I do, though, I pour a drop on my fingertip and lick it. The pain is immediate and excruciating. I simply don't have the strength required to end my troubles this way.

There's a bathtub in the studio I planned to use for a mixed-media sculpture called *Adam Drains Eden*. The tub is mounted on stilts to give it a greater sense of magnitude and requires a complex pulley system of counterweights and balances to lower. I do this, fill it with water, find the studio's sharpest razor, then strip and climb into the tub, only to realize I have no idea whether to cut my wrist lengthwise or crosswise.

I intended to find the answer with a Google search, but the bleach has left such an awful taste in my mouth that I pause for a glass of water. I drink another, and then another, and then so many I lose count. If I don't pee immediately, I fear, my bladder could suffer irreparably. By my estimation, it takes at least four minutes to empty out, some kind of record, I'm sure. The world record for longest urination, I find on the internet is five hundred and eight seconds—nearly eight and half minutes! This strains my belief to the utmost. A deeper search reveals there's no recorded video of the act. My pee, I'm certain, must be at least one of the ten longest in history.

Back in the tub, I cut my wrist but miss the artery by nearly an inch. Again, I climb back out to research "suicide by razor." There, stark naked in the middle of the studio, the miracle happens. Blanche bursts through the door ahead of Winston with a bagful of food.

"Did we interrupt your suicide?" Winston says.

"Life may be an interminable struggle, but it's cowardly not to fight!" I say as Blanche licks the blood from my wrist.

"I went for a walk and found her outside a French bakery," Winston says.

"She's quite fond of quiche," I say, and am somehow stricken with inspiration.

A mere canvas will not meet my needs. I pour through the mound of objects I've gathered over time—a ceramic plate, candle sticks, an air conditioner, a garbage can, a blender, an umbrella, shards from a broken window—until at the bottom I find the black multi-textured surface I require—a cast-iron skillet.

My mind clear of purpose or intention, I swab the brush I used to stab Winston into the blood dripping from my arm and begin to paint. There's nowhere near the amount of blood

I need, so I cut into my wound again, the room spinning like a carousel. I paint and paint, but run out of blood again. I'm ready to slice open my neck when Winston seizes the razor and cuts into the wound on his thigh. The outpouring of blood is far greater, I'm sure, than he'd have guessed.

"Hurry!" Winston says. "There's no time to lose!"

He's right, of course. I work frantically, until the painting is finished, and we collapse. I awaken to Blanche having wrapped my arm in a tourniquet (she truly is a marvelous creature!), which enables me to tend to Winston. Somehow, we see, I've painted myself standing under an advertisement for prescription painkillers, holding a tray of quiche, with Blanche's silhouette in the window of an apartment building. It's an archetype of the modern intellectual, racked with anxiety and disquiet. Not since Jesse's short story, "Two Bikes, One City," have I encountered such inspired work.

"Obviously," Winston says, exhausted and pale, "God was with us." His face hovers just inches from the work, his eyes squinting. "But who is this back here?"

I make a closer inspection of the painting and see he's right. There's a face in the background, like a shadow imploring the viewer to renounce their ego for something higher.

"I wish I could tell you," I say.

The studio's door swings open, and Danny rolls in on a vintage American motorcycle. He removes his sunglasses and surveys the area. None of the chores he's assigned Winston as a condition for staying in the studio have been completed. The floor is slick with blood. And Winston's leg requires immediate attention—already there are signs of an infection. Moreover, I'm completely naked and so delirious I'm unable, really, to speak in more than sign language and grunts. Blanche has a napkin tucked into her collar and is halfway through her second piece of quiche. Danny's eyes turn cold, and his mouth twitches.

"Did the three of you treat yourselves to my mescaline, or what?"

"Nothing like that," Winston says. "Paul was making a blood painting, but his veins ran dry, so I offered to help."

"Another painting riddled with religious symbolism?" Danny says.

Over the years, Danny has developed an authentic doctrine on art. And he's nothing if not principled about its values. By now he can scarcely understand a kind of painting whose point of departure lies beyond his own point of arrival.

I know I should be indifferent to the world's opinion of me—but, alas—I'm tortured with distress at how even a stranger on the street perceives me. Just the other day, I stopped a woman coming out of a yoga studio to ask her if she thought I might be a genius.

"How could I possibly know something like that?" she said. "We've never even met!"

Her words pushed me to despair, and I nearly threw myself off the Brooklyn Bridge. If it hadn't been for Blanche and a bicycle cop to coax me off the ledge, I'm certain I wouldn't be here.

After the police released me, Blanche insisted the woman was right. It would be impossible for someone to know whether a person they'd just met was a genius. She reminded me of the time I had a chance encounter with Quentin Tarantino at Washington Square Park. He'd been eating a sandwich by the fountain, while from my bench I studied him. The way he chewed with his mouth slightly open, how he swatted the flies from his food, seemed utterly commonplace.

I apologized for my behavior and promised to do better. But that night, as Blanche and I worked on a jigsaw puzzle, I remembered that when Tarantino was no longer hungry, he began to feed the pigeons with his crumbs. His casual elegance and sensitivity were unmistakably brilliant. Anyone who witnessed this could harbor no doubt that something startling and innovative was working in his mind. True genius oozes from one's pores, drips from one's fingertips, undeniable, impossible to miss.

Danny has always been suspect of my conviction that it's contradictory elements that most happily coexist. Once we quarreled viciously because I'd placed the Virgin Mary smack in the center of a painting of a three-ring circus. He said it was imperative I portray consistency in my imagery. "It's three in the morning," I said at the time, "and you want consistency?"

"I have to be honest," Danny says, evaluating my blood painting. "You're almost a really bad painter." He steps to the side a bit, assessing the work. "There's only one thing that keeps me from total insistence." Danny flips the skillet upside down, then again right-side up. "In all my life, I've only seen a handful of paintings that have successfully made blood stick. Normally, it just puts a hole in the painting. But you've managed to make it work. That's why I say you're only 'almost' a really bad painter." Danny takes a plum from his pocket and bites into it. With his eyes closed, he makes vaguely sexual groaning noises as he chews. "And one more thing," he says. "It was a very strange decision you made to put James in the painting."

"Who's James?" Winston asks.

"The husband of the woman Paul has a thing for."

Like a tightrope walker, I place one foot in front of the other as I seek out the pants to my suit, in whose pocket I left Orsi's marble. I feel torn between two beings, each as rare and unattainable as the other. I make a feeble and pathetic objection, knowing, right or wrong, one must always question the order of the world, or perish.

"Periods of intense closeness are always followed by feelings of abject indifference."

Finally, Danny tells us why he's here. He wants to invite me on a weekend getaway. He's only done this once before, two years ago. I was outside our studio, digging a pit, when Danny pulled up in a classic Jaguar roadster he'd won in a game of cards with the CFO of a Silicon Valley tech company. I mentioned that the 5.3L V12 engine was the finest Jaguar had ever manufactured.

"I didn't know you were a connoisseur of classic cars!" Danny said.

I neglected to tell him I had no interest whatsoever in cars, nor any idea where I'd gleaned this arcane bit. It's one of my "quirks," as Janie used to call them. Often, for example, with someone new, before they introduce themselves, I'll greet them with a random name and learn to both our surprises that in fact I was right. Danny was so impressed by my supposed knowledge that he invited me to join him for a weekend getaway at his family's apple farm in Vermont. I still had a lot of pit left to dig, but my hankering for apples was enormous, so I put down the shovel and climbed into his car. We spent three days picking apples, and in the evenings, the caretaker stuffed us full of lavish dinners and fresh apple pie. It was my finest weekend ever.

On the way home, Danny let me have the wheel, though he knew it had been years since I'd driven, after I stripped my moped for parts in a sculpture of a centaur. For two hours, I put the Jaguar through its paces, while Danny napped after his long night with the girl who tends the family's horses. When I pulled over to use the restroom—too many apples!—I left the engine running, failing to keep in mind what a tremendously sound sleeper Danny is. As luck would have it, two criminals lifted him from his seat and set him against a gas pump before making off with his car. Danny was more crestfallen we didn't make it back in time for his double date with Leonardo DiCaprio and a pair of Peruvian volleyball players than he was at the loss of his car.

"Meet me at the helipad on top of my father's building at four," Danny says. "We're going to the Hamptons!"

"Can I bring Blanche?"

Blanche is sitting up on her hind wheels staring at Danny like a sweet June bride.

"We've got a number of Dobermans on the property," Danny says. "I can't risk the liability."

He has a lot to do before we leave. At eleven he's meeting with Vincent from Inès to finalize the contract for their "cat bag" collaboration. It's been a difficult negotiation because Danny insists on a clause in the agreement that will ensure the performance of a Maloufian orchestra at the runway show in Paris. Years ago, while visiting Tunisia, Danny was kidnapped by a band of Sunni rebels. He spent four months in their capture, during which time he developed an appreciation for the local music. Even after his father paid the ransom, Danny insisted on staying for an extra month, to continue his study of the Tunisian oud, under the great master Anouar Brahem. Danny's insistence on curating the music has been the sole sticking point in finalizing the agreement, because Inès had already contracted Mark Ronson to DJ the event. But Danny says the only suitable musical accompaniment to the show is a special blend of violins, sitars, and flutes. Danny's lawyer has indicated to Inès' legal team that excluding the Maloufian performance is a deal-breaker.

Winston's assistance with my self-portrait has proven that he's more than deserving of my trust, so I ask him if he would do me the great favor of taking care of Blanche while I'm away. He insists that it would be the "honor of a lifetime" to be entrusted with such a "noble and esteemed lady." Even Blanche seems more than amenable to this. When I implore her to be a "good girl" for Winston, she wags her tail and licks my face.

CHAPTER 19

Security at Danny's father's building is state-of-the-art. It has to be, one of the guards informs me, because there have been multiple attempts to assassinate Danny's father in the past few months. At the start of the year, his hedge fund bought up eighty percent of the country's new utility interconnection permits, and is now selling them only to developers who agree to install natural gas power plants that buy gas from his fracking interests. This has made the man public enemy number one of the environmental community. Consequently, I'm subjected to three separate body scans, a strip search, and a polygraph test. The test's administrator is befuddled by the results. In his twenty years of doing this work, he says, he's never encountered anyone with such a puzzling perception of what is true.

As a further precautionary measure, they run an FBI background check. A painting I once made of a sad monkey scratching its head while standing next to a fallen coconut tree has warranted the concern of the officials.

"This painting of yours is a demonstration of an anti-capitalist sentiment, is it not?"

"It expresses a certain sympathy."

"Then you're a zealot, yes?"

"Of course not," I say. "Why does a man have to stick to an idea just because he thought it before?"

This bit of recondite logic is enough to allay their concerns, and a guard escorts me to the roof. Danny is running late but the helicopter pilot has a deck of cards, so we spend the next thirty minutes playing Go Fish. When Danny arrives, accompanied by six of the models he's personally selected for the runway show in Paris, all six of North African descent, he reports that things with Inès went very well. The pilot takes a headcount of all the prospective passengers and tells us we're one person too many.

"But they're models," Danny says. "They weigh half a normal person."

If we are caught with too many people aboard, the pilot says, he'll be stripped of his license.

"It's no problem," I say. "I'd be much happier taking the train."

"I'll simply charter another chopper," Danny says, searching his phone for the number. "Father won't be pleased, but it won't bother him so much, either."

In a world robbed of its manners and mores, I refuse to give way to conformity.

"I must insist," I say. "I wouldn't think of taking advantage of your generosity."

The train at Penn Station is pulling away just as I reach the platform. The next one doesn't come for another hour. Hunger stings my belly. It's been over twenty-fours since I last ate. I regret having allowed Blanche to eat my piece of quiche this morning. I check my pockets for money, knowing I spent most of it on my ticket. All that's left is four dollars and change. A young man and woman sit down next to me. The man wears expensive sneakers and sports a smart haircut. The woman's perfume smells of lilac and honey. She insists they have brunch on Saturday with her parents, but the man wants to go standup paddle-boarding with his old fraternity brothers.

"It's out of the question!" the woman says.

Willpower is a precious and scarce resource that should be rationed wisely, I think. This man is no dummy, as it turns out. He resigns himself to his fate without another word. The image of the triumphant woman and the defeated man inspires me. I take a notepad and pencil from my bag and start to sketch them.

"What the hell do you think you're doing?" the man says, when I reach out to adjust his collar.

"I've drawn a picture of you both," I say, and show them.

"Oh, my goodness," the woman says, "it's positively wonderful!"

"I look like a fool!" the man says.

"We'd like to buy it," the woman says. "How much?"

The sketch includes some of my finest line work. The thought of parting with this piece is unimaginable. "I'm sorry, but it's not for sale," I say.

"Nonsense," the woman says. "We'll give you twenty dollars for it."

"That's kind of you," I say, "but you're wasting your time."

The woman opens her pocketbook and takes out more money.

"Here's fifty bucks," the woman says. "Does this change your mind?"

I tuck the notebook into my bag and prepare to move, but the woman seizes me by the arm.

"What about a hundred dollars?" she says.

I yank my arm away and hurry up the stairs. The clerk at the convenience store across the concourse insists I leave my bag on the counter while I shop. I make several passes up and down the snack aisle figuring how best to stretch my money, and settle on a package of Gummy Bears. Back at the counter, I see my bag is gone.

"Excuse me, sir," I say to the clerk, "do you know what happened to my bag?"

"A man came in while you were shopping and took it."

"But you insisted I leave it here," I say. "That makes you responsible."

"Your bag is your problem," the clerk says without looking up.

"A failure to prevent a crime is as bad as committing it oneself!"

I fill my arms with snacks and make a run for it only to see my train about to pull away. Without a moment to spare, I throw myself headfirst through the train's doors, sliding across the ground on my chest.

Inside ten minutes, I've eaten all the Gummy Bears, two bags of Doritos, a box of Goldfish Crackers, and an ice cream sandwich. The man next to me falls asleep with his head against the window. Nothing repels me more than the sight of a grotesque sleeper—he's twitchy, and drool is running from his open mouth.

The train jolts to a stop. All the passengers have surrounded an old man collapsed in the aisle. A doctor kneeling at the man's side announces he's suffered a heart attack.

"I'm afraid nothing can be done," he says.

The authorities insist all passengers disembark. I still have my four dollars, but it's not nearly enough even for a bus ticket to Sagponack, thirty miles off. I decide to walk.

I take off my shirt and place it on my head to shield the blazing sun. The skin on my arms and chest transforms from ashy white to feverish red. A minivan drives by, filled with children. One throws a can of orange soda that strikes me in the neck. A few minutes later, a luxury German sedan pulls over. A man in an ill-fitting shirt and pleated khakis strides my way as I lie there, then helps me into his car, his face all the while the epitome of empathy and goodwill. Hall & Oates' timeless classic "Private Eyes" plays on the stereo.

The man, as I learn, lives in the same house where he was born forty-two years ago. When his younger brother and sister moved out after high school, his parents encouraged him to leave, as well, but he didn't see any reason to. He was perfectly happy in his childhood home, and his job at the pizza parlor was only a short bike-ride away. It took ten years to convince his parents to let him move into the basement. He believed his troubles over, then, yet found increasingly he was spending all his time obsessing about the plight of the world. A volcano in Sumatra had erupted, he recalled, and while no one had been killed, he couldn't escape the thought of what might happen next.

"I used to think it was a mistake for life to have been placed in my hands," he says, "because I had been such a terrible steward."

"It's best not to be so introspective," I say, removing a pebble from my shoe. "No one ever likes what they find."

"I used to dwell on the question of what would be left to show for myself when I die."

"A terrible question."

"If I were to die today, there would be a funeral, and people would say kind things about me. Then life would return to normal, and in a matter of weeks or months, I'd be completely forgotten."

"The heart beats," I say, "but to what purpose?"

The man looks like a wilted flower. "Can I show you something?" he says.

"Anything," I say. "Within reason, of course."

The man pulls onto the shoulder. The rolling grassy hills and farmland look like a painting by Alfred Thompson Bricher.

Sheep graze beyond an ancient split-rail fence. Beyond them, just over the knoll, stretches an expanse of dunes and wide-open beaches. We get out and walk into the meadow as the man explains how he's gone up and down this stretch of road since he was in diapers. There's not a house whose owners he doesn't know by name. Yet one day something unexpected happened, he said. As if under a spell, he felt taken with a particular tree, a white oak, quite stately, I agreed, that he'd passed a thousand times but had until then never noticed.

"Whenever I'm feeling low," the man says, "I come out here and sit under this tree."

I'm helpless to think of anything but the calamities that await this man. It's as if his fear has robbed him of all spirit. I wouldn't be the least surprised to learn he never made it out of his parents' basement.

An hour later, he delivers me to the gates of Danny's family home. Danny's father is a devout Francophile, and hired André Le Nôtre's direct descendent, Robert, to design the property's gardens, despite that Robert is by trade merely a dentist. "Landscaping is in the Le Nôtre blood!" Danny's father said. His instincts did not fail him. Robert created the most elaborately complex arrangement of gardens, groves, and parks on the eastern seaboard.

I stop to greet a gardener trimming a bush with geometric precision.

"The Sun King himself would be impressed," the gardener says, "wouldn't you agree?"

"I've never dreamed of such exquisite embroidery *parterre!*" I say.

Another of the manor's staff leads me to the pool, where

all of Danny's models have gathered under the gazebo. They are under strict orders to keep their skin pristinely waxen in preparation for the upcoming show. Danny is diving from his Olympic-scale boards. At Yale, he was the first alternate on the varsity diving team. Unlike riding a bike, Danny claims, one's diving technique escapes them the moment they let up. He has procured the services of Yale's diving coach for a private lesson today. The coach's attention to detail has clearly been effective. Danny's executes a flawless two-and-half-somersault dive off the five-meter platform, then swims over to insist I join him in the pool.

I'm without any trunks, so I strip down to my underwear. The unsightliness of my body must be more deplorable than I thought. A collective groan issues from the models across the way.

Danny's coach declares his formal opposition to my wish to dive from the ten-meter platform. Danny, on the other hand, says why not. I climb the ladder, regretting my failures and wondering at the magnitude of what I've managed under the wing of spontaneity. Halfway up, however, I make the critical error of looking down. My hands tremble, my knees shake, and a trickle of urine runs down my leg. Everyone is watching now as my ascent grows more and more listless. At the top, I cling to the rail and inch my way toward the edge. The pool below is a million miles off, the people around it mere ants. I once saw a shampoo commercial in which a man swan-dived from a waterfall in Acapulco. Everything about him exuded effortless cool, and ever since, I've washed my hair obsessively. I close my eyes and try to channel the spirit of that diver, then leap into the abyss, chest out, arms spread out eagle-wide.

I awaken by the side of the pool, Danny hovering over me. My body feels sore but nothing seems to be broken.

"You rescued me?" I say.

"Not me, him."

A member of the kitchen staff is kneeling in his white uniform, sopping wet, cleaning a mess of spilled shrimp cocktail. Danny helps me to my feet, and I stagger to my savior and kiss him on the forehead. His eyes radiate a virtuousness I'd thought long ago extinguished from this world.

"You've performed a godly deed," I say.

"It was nothing," he says. "I'll be back in a minute."

He leaves me there, the spell broken, and returns in a dry uniform just minutes later, with a fresh tray of shrimp. They are delicious.

CHAPTER 20

I PASS from room to room in this mansion, thinking. If I were to live forever, how bored would I be? Surely, I could evolve past the vicious creature I am today. It couldn't take more than a century or so to become more cultivated in the consumption of things like food and sex. Yet how long might it take to grow more attuned to eternal things, to become more godlike?

All around me I see things I never thought possible. A pregnant woman strolls past happily sipping a cocktail. A famous pop star sits in a corner, lonely and despondent. A politician—whom I helped vote into the Senate last election—lies passed out on the floor. I need to find a quiet place where I can call Winston and Blanche.

I stumble into a room and shut the door. Two women peer at me with grievous looks. One is Dana Torres, the lead actress of *Justice Served*, a long-running courtroom procedural. She's on the floor, banging her fists and wailing. The other woman sits huddled under a lamp scrutinizing what looks like a handwritten note.

"My apologies," I say, as I turn to make my exit, "I was just looking for a place to call my dog."

Dana latches onto my leg and drags me to a desk.

"Please, sir," Dana says, and takes the note from the other woman, "we need your opinion urgently."

It's from Dana's co-star, Bradley Sullivan.

My Sweet Dana, I'll always love and admire you. But I always have all sorts of mixed-up feelings. Please know that like your perfume on my pillow, my love for you will always be there even when I'm no longer present. Always, Bradley.

The other woman introduces herself as Veronica Popescu, Dana's graphologist. Veronica wears an inordinate amount of jewelry—her fingers, ears, and neck are wrapped in gold and semi-precious stones. If I had to guess her accent, I'd say Romanian. She's made her name analyzing characteristics and patterns of handwriting, by which, she claims, she can deduce the writer's psychological state, and even their innermost vulnerabilities.

"Every loop, cross, and dot says more about a person than I could learn in ten years of an intimate relationship," she says.

The tiny print of Bradley's note was written under heavy pressure, and the letters are erect, with no slant at all. Veronica insists this reveals he's prone to strong emotions and hasty reactions. Bradley, in short, wants to leave Dana, which stands to reason. His wife is pregnant.

"I don't believe a word she says," Dana cries. "Please tell me I'm right!"

"I'm by no means an expert in the dark art of graphology."

"But I can see in your eyes how wise you are."

I hold the note to the light. "This is obviously a man of weak character," I say. "Even if he wanted to leave you, he couldn't."

Dana slaps Veronica across the face, then executes a series of pirouettes as she recites a sonnet by Shakespeare.

"You've rescued me!" she says.

"I've been wrong about so many things, but of this I'm very sure."

Dana calls Veronica a "charlatan" and orders her away. It's a known fact, Dana says, that graphology is an exact science, but only when its practitioner is precise. Veronica's work, unfortunately, has been subpar now for some time. For my erudition, Dana lavishes me with praise. It's not long before I grow restless and leave.

That poor woman, I think. Another casualty of being loved too much as a child. Nothing causes more despair in adulthood. She's wasted a lifetime believing she's entitled to love, and, worse, that it's owed to her. Then I think about my own past troubles with love. There was a time, shortly before Janie and I split for good, when she spent her nights sleeping on the couch. Her excuse was that she liked to fall asleep in front of the television. The far-flung reality shows she watched helped her to unwind. I bought a third-rate television at a nearby pawnshop and installed it in our bedroom, yet Janie wouldn't leave the couch. A few weeks into this, I rearranged the living room furniture so I could see Janie's face in a mirror from our bed. Interestingly, she always appeared wide awake, and only fell asleep when I called to her. From then on, I spent all my nights alone watching *The Bachelor*, *The Bachelorette*, *The Bachelor in Paradise*, and even the foreign spinoff, *The Bachelor in New Zealand*.

Orsi's marble in my hand soothes me like a warm bath of serenity. When I trip over a footstool and tumble to the floor, a passerby snickers that I must be "roaring drunk," though I haven't had a drop. I'm too dazed from the fall to defend myself. Instead, I play with Orsi's marble.

"Look, darling," says a man. "This guy loves marbles at least as much as you."

Tall, but slightly stooped, the man is wearing a long white robe. His face is inordinately smooth and radiates tremendous sexual vitality. The intimacy I feel for him is overwhelming.

Orsi is just behind, with a smile to make a man on death row feel good. "This is my friend, Paul," she says.

"The two of you know each other. How wonderful!"

The man, of course, is Orsi's husband, James. I stand to greet him, and he kisses both my cheeks. His hair smells of patchouli. His touch is a shield from evil.

"May I see your marble?" Orsi says, looking hard into my eyes. "I used to have a green lutz with remarkably similar banding. I thought it was one-of-a-kind," she says, and returns the marble, "but apparently not."

"Last we spoke," I say to James, "Orsi said you were working in India."

James runs his fingers through his mane of silver curls. "I would hardly say what I do is 'work,'" he says. "It's more of a calling."

"James is in the guru-business," Orsi says.

"Sweetheart," he says. "You know I don't like to use that word." James places his hand on his heart and looks into my eyes. A tremor shoots through my body. "I'm an advocate for the maintenance of well-being. I help people refine their consciousness and expand their knowledge."

"James," Orsi says with an ironic smile on her lips, "is a master at helping people overcome self-deception and find their inner truth."

From the crowd, Danny joins us, a huge gold medallion hanging from his neck. "Ha!" he says and slaps James on the back. "No one I know has ever found happiness through too much truth!"

"Your soul," James says, "hasn't yet found peace, my friend. That's why you can't understand the power of truth."

James treats Danny like a son just home from war. His every

gesture cries out to Danny, as if he'd do anything to relieve the man's untold burdens. But Danny ignores James and moves to Orsi, his eyes aflame with rivalry. It's plain his humor is foul. A friend of his from childhood, he explains, Jeff, has just rejected his sexual advances. Orsi, no doubt, commands him to reveal the sordid details.

Danny has just returned from a jaunt on his fishing boat with Jeff and two of the Inès models. After an hour-long battle with a particularly ornery swordfish, he says, his invigoration was so irrepressible he couldn't keep from fornicating then and there with one of the models. This, however, to his great dismay, did little to assuage him, any more than did watching Jeff and the other model perform acrobatics he'd not seen in the most outlandish of darknet pornography. He needed something more, he says, and was on the verge of despair, when the notion came to him that he could perform oral sex on Jeff.

Orsi interrupts Danny to ask whether he has ever done such a thing, or even wanted to.

"You're missing the point," Danny says. "Let me finish."

Jeff, he says, was not at all inclined to this suggestion. But Danny, being Danny, wouldn't take no for an answer, and before he knew it, Jeff had thrown him overboard. In the end, it wasn't the nature of Danny's intention that upset Jeff—he was perfectly amenable to going both ways—but his strict opposition to incest. Danny is his second cousin.

"So now you can see why I'm so sick of all of my friends," Danny says. "All they do is reproach me for things they don't approve."

"They have no indulgence!" I say.

While Orsi is still laughing in sympathy with Danny, James suggests we go skinny-dipping in the sea.

Down on the beach, I realize I'd almost forgotten about the existence of stars. There they are, though, brightly shining. Everyone strips off their clothes, yet nobody seems in any rush to swim. Instead, the men perform feats of strength, and soon a wrestling match ensues. All the women strike poses, too, as they cheer the men on, a lurid and grotesque exhibition on all sides. James and Orsi mingle with the naked people like a bride and groom at a wedding reception.

It's not until everyone else has entered the water that I get naked. I fold my suit neatly and place it in the sand, then make a dash for the sea. As shockingly cold as the water is, I nevertheless swim beneath the surface as far as I can on a single breath. Never have I felt such solitude. I'm so free I forget my name and where I've come from. If only I could circle the globe like this, on a single breath. When at last I surface, it's far beyond the others playing among the breaking waves.

I'm reluctant to return, but my arms are tired. I fill my lungs with air and take twenty strokes toward the shore only to find when I look up I'm farther out than I had been. After thirty more strokes, the others are no longer in sight. I wish for money, a pill, a gun, all the tell-tale signs of panic. Pathetically, I cry out for Blanche. My muscles have begun to seize, so I decide to make one final push, recalling as I go as much Spanish as I can—*la mesa, el coche, la cuchara, el zapato, la tienda, el libro,* and on. When I run out of nouns, I conjugate verbs: *Yo duelo, tu dueles, el duele, nosotoros dolemos, ellos duelen.* It's not long before my body fails. I cease to fight and allow myself to sink. The humiliated happiness one experiences when making the decision not to pursue an overwhelming challenge—the hard work avoided, the dread of failure, the summoning of will—gives me instant peace.

I sit cross-legged before a surly crab flexing its giant pinchers. I'm a rootless drifting molecule. I wonder if I'll be able to take with me, like luggage, my memories of life into death? The anticipation is like fruit ripe for picking. Then, just as I've accepted my fate, I'm carried off by a powerful current. My resistance is no match for its force. I cartwheel along the ocean floor and everything grows dark.

Somehow, I've washed up on an empty stretch of beach. My nose, ears, eyes, and mouth are thick with sand. Half my life is spent struggling not to die—getting dressed, crossing the street, eating Brussels sprouts—and now a seagull is pecking at me. A warm breeze picks up, and I'm filled with a sense of victory. I am alive. I stride down the beach, naked. A couple on a late-night stroll turns away. Undaunted, I greet them enthusiastically.

"Have you ever imagined someone's last thoughts before death?"

But hardly have I finished before they sprint away. When the woman lags, the man drops her hand and abandons her.

The beach is littered with radiant shells. I pick one up, examine it, toss it to the sea, then do the same, again and again. The shells fill me with resentment. As a child, my parents refused to vacation at the beach. My father had visited the seaside once in his youth and swore never to go again.

"Sunburns and chaffing are the nadir of misery!" he said when I complained of having never seen the ocean.

Louis and his family, however, went to the seaside every summer, in San Diego. His days were spent building sandcastles, boogie boarding, and fishing off the pier. He developed a taste for fish tacos and ceviche. His skin browned like a vanilla latte. In the fall, back at school, he'd bring in his collection of shells

117

for show-and-tell, a waste of time, in my opinion. How could he not understand that in hunting shells, he'd failed to see the wealth of strangeness and wonder around him?

My suit is how I left it. I brush myself clear of sand and dress. The others have gathered around a bonfire. A member of Danny's staff—a handsome woman of Lebanese descent—hands me a skewer of vegetarian sausage. I approach the fire and listen as James expounds upon his mission.

"The Pure Cosmos Club's moral imperative is not guided by a political vision but a divine one. We have a duty to transcend the drudgery of our daily lives by tapping into the universal mind, the oneness of all things. Come and grow with us—emanate your energy and power!"

Everyone listens raptly. For many, I suspect, it's the first time they've glimpsed the possibility there's a means by which to label their existence. James pauses in his discourse to encourage us to take pictures. It's vital, he says, we share this moment on social media.

"Publicity is everything," James says. "Even Jesus would've been lost to the ages, had the twelve apostles not spread his message."

I finish eating my sausage as James turns his thoughts to reincarnation. He implores us not to feel guilty for the way we've conducted our lives. Everyone can become a higher being, though it may take a thousand years. It doesn't matter that James is preaching fantasy. He speaks with the conviction of Solomon himself.

Still very much hungry, I wave my arms to gain the attention of the handsome Lebanese woman, while at the same time the others stretch their arms to the sky. I call out to the woman, but it's no use, the group has begun to chant.

"Do you have a question, Paul?" James says.

"Are you really who you say you are?" I say, astounded at myself. I hadn't any such thought in mind.

James makes his way to me and fixes me with his eyes. "You already know I am," he says, "or you wouldn't be here."

I see Orsi alone on the beach as the group disbands, her arms folded and lips drawn tight. Every few moments she glares at James, surrounded by women. Not even I am immune to his charms. How wonderful it would be to find something to give myself over to, I think.

I plop down beside the fire. A fair-haired woman with a rosy complexion pours me a margarita from her pitcher. A man and a woman sit down next to me, talking to each other with British accents. The man is visiting from Berlin, where he's co-founded an architecture firm that, unfortunately, is facing powerful economic headwinds. The trouble started with a project to design a seaside resort for an Italian developer who after two years ran out of money, the project only half complete. To make matters worse, the man explains, he'd built himself a ski chalet in Austria, counting on profits from the resort. The last thing he wants to do is sell what he says has become "his special place."

His companion does everything she can to keep from laughing at the man's hard luck. According to her, making money is really very simple. The key, she explains, is to make "sound investments." The man's eyes swell as he scoots closer and asks her to explain.

"About a year ago," she says, "I received a tip on a line of beauty products. 'Martha,' my friend said, 'this company makes tremendous lipstick! It can't miss!' I had no reason to doubt her—we've known each other for years—so I invested a million dollars. When the company went public, it became fourteen million. Easy! All I had to do was go to brunch."

Until now, I'd always believed one had to be a genius to create great wealth, but clearly, I was mistaken. Really, all one needs to do is keep one's eyes and ears open to the opportunities lurking around every corner.

"Thank you so much for enlightening us!" I say.

"Where did you come from?" the woman says.

"I'm from Denver," I say.

The woman asks the man whether he knew I was there, but, like her, he had no idea. "He does," she says, "have a rather unremarkable face."

"I think he has a fine face," the man says.

"You really think so?" the woman says.

"It's appealing enough."

"There is a dash of bohemian charm," the woman says, "now that I really look. Nothing, however, I'd call beautiful."

"Now that is true," the man says, and empties his glass. "He's not beautiful the way that James is beautiful."

I dust myself off, and return to the mansion to sleep. There are at least fifteen bedrooms, all of which are accounted for with reservations on the doors. I pass through this hallway and that, but come up empty-handed at a dead end on the third floor. A man with a honey-brown face glistening with sweat—yet another servant—introduces himself as Manuel and asks if I need help.

"I've searched all the bedrooms," I say, "but for the life of me can't find mine."

"I'm sorry, sir," Manuel says, checking a list, "but it seems your name isn't here."

"Is there an attic somewhere about?"

"I'm afraid I don't understand."

"I've always felt at home in a cozy attic. As an infant, it's where my parents kept my crib. My father had incredibly sensitive hearing and couldn't stand my colicky wailing. I became so accustomed to my lodgings there, in fact, that I stayed until I was a teenager."

Manuel entertains me with a story as we make our way to the attic. He grew up in a fishing village in Honduras. His mother cooked *baleadas* for surfers and his father was a mason. At thirteen, after a year of studying English with a missionary from Salt Lake City, he snuck into the cabin of a racing yacht that drifted off course and docked for supplies. There he stayed, tucked away under a pile of life vests, for three full days and nights, listening to the sailors talk about the race. They were in last place at one point but had steadily gained, until fifty miles off the coast of Rhode Island, they were in third place. Hours later, with only a mile to the finish, they were a mere two boat lengths behind the first-place team. To lighten the load, the crew began to jettison cargo, but ran out of expendable provisions. Defeat was imminent. Unable to live with the burden of robbing these men of a great victory, Manuel threw himself into the sea. As the ship sailed away, the captain stood on the boat's stern and said: "There is a man who understands sacrifice for the greater good!" The tide carried Manuel to shore, where he was met with a hero's welcome. The ship's crew hoisted him to their shoulders while the captain began to chant, "*¡No sabemos de dónde vino, pero él es nuestro héroe!*" One sailor asked the captain to translate. "We don't know where he came from," the captain said, "but he is our hero!"

"The captain was Danny's grandfather," Manuel says.

"And you've been working for the family ever since?"

"Actually, I was soon deported, but years later I was granted a visa. I just got here two months ago."

Finally, we reach a hatch in the ceiling to the attic. Manuel squats down for me to climb onto his shoulders, then lifts me with ease. Once I'm in, Manuel tosses me a bottle of water and a flashlight.

"I'll be back at 7 a.m.," Manuel says.

A mischief of mice scurry away when I turn on the flashlight. Even on my hands and knees, my face gets caught in a spider's web. The attic stretches out in all directions. It must be as large as a football field. All around me are the forgotten treasures of past generations—a stuffed lion's head, two Renoir paintings, a signed first edition of Whitman's *Leaves of Grass*, and an eighty-year-old embroidered Nazi uniform. Then I find a box of unopened letters from the 1970s, addressed to a woman named Mary. I open one and begin to read.

Dear Mary,

I received your letter and was heartbroken to learn of the awful news regarding your health. For a woman of only twenty-three, cancer is certainly rotten luck. Also, I'm sorry that you're suffering financial troubles. Trust me when I say that no one better understands what a pitiless debt collector Uncle Sam is. Just last year I was forced to pay two million in capital gains tax because I'd had the good sense to dump my Chrysler stock when that numbskull John Riccardo took the helm. Did I ever tell you of the time when I devastated him in an arm-wrestling match at the club? That said, you're an adult now, so I'm going to have to decline your request to *pay the $3k you owe in taxes due to your failure to report the tips you earned last summer cocktailing at that nightclub in Chelsea.*

Love always,

Dad

P.S. Send along a photo? I've never seen you bald.

I'm opening another letter when I hear the faint but unmistakable sound of sexual relations. At first, I plug my ears and hum the theme song to "The Love Boat". I simply cannot bear to hear another's most private moments. And yet there's something familiar about these utterances. I crawl around with my ear to the floor, searching for the lovers' room. A faint light through a crack in the floorboard guides me. I peep into the crack and am astounded—Orsi is riding James, back arched as he kisses her breasts and shoves his fingers up her rear. My eyes fill with tears, and I begin to whimper. Then James flips Orsi over and takes her from behind. She's begging to be slapped and choked. James grabs a fistful of her hair and yanks back her head so forcefully I'm afraid he's snapped her neck. But she screams out, "Fuck me harder!" This is more than I can bear. I scurry away and pound on the door of the hatch, screaming to be freed from this torture. When no one comes, I tear a strip of insulation from the wall and wrap it around my head. I'm as baffled as could be to feel myself hardening, but I give it a stroke just the same. On one hand, I feel immense arousal, on the other, a deep sense of community. Soon I am in perfect rhythm with the couple. It's as if I'm the phantom third in this *ménage à trois*. As one, the three of us reach a fevered climax, screaming out in ecstasy. Then there's peace, and I fall into blissful slumber.

CHAPTER 21

MANUEL RETRIEVES me just as he said, at 7 a.m. sharp. A buffet is waiting on the veranda, where a broad-shouldered man in a tank-top reads from the morning headlines. "Thirteen Kurds Slain as Turkish Forces Go on the Offensive," he says. Everyone agrees that the loss of life is lamentable, but a leader's solemn duty is to quell any opposition to his power. The servants are offering us mimosas with Dom Perignon.

A tall man in a funny hat leans his golf bag against the table. A servant delivers him a cappuccino. A thin film of foam clings to the man's upper lip.

"Not a lot of wind today," I say when he smiles at me. "Much less than I expected."

James and Orsi appear in plush white bathrobes. They've just come from aromatherapy massages, looking peaceful as doves. Nothing, I think, is more stimulating than sincerity, rare as it is. James sits down next to me, and I begin to blabber. He listens intently, even as the others vie for his attention. I say I'm considering joining the military. Surely, there's no better place for a man so clumsy with the responsibilities of freedom.

After a time, James leads a group to the beach for morning prayer. Everyone bows their heads and closes their eyes, their faces serene. I wonder if it's possible to change human nature. Are we forever destined to eat too much, drink too much, sleep in beds, stumble through rain, eat salad with our forks?

James whispers affirmations. "Do not feel bad about your place in this world. Accepting our destiny is never a matter of cruelty or unkindness." His manner exudes dignity, astuteness, even arrogance, which I find appealing.

Orsi taps me on the shoulder. My smile is at once friendly and hostile.

"It's too early to listen to another one of his sermons," she says.

"Do you think James is right," I say, "that to know oneself is to know the world?"

"It's not that what he says isn't true, but that his words require a bit of interpretation."

The crashing waves distract me, and I turn to watch the surfers. A bikini-clad woman on the nose of her board glides across a wave. The feat reminds me how my defeatist attitude hurts no one but myself.

That things might be different than they are right now has never occurred to me. I've begun to sweat profusely.

Orsi presses the back of her hand to my brow. "You're burning up!" she says.

"Forgive me," I say, as I flee with my jacket over my eyes. "I'm not feeling very well."

I stagger into the house and bump into Manuel.

"Can you tell me where the restroom is?"

Manuel guides me to the facilities, where I lock the door and splash my face with water.

When I was eight, despising the idea that anyone but I might see the beauty of the flowers in our neighborhood community garden, I picked them all. A passerby, the founder of the garden, as it happened, stopped me as I was leaving.

"We planted this garden so that everyone in this community could enjoy it!" he said, waving his frighteningly hairy arms.

I told this man were it up to me I'd lock away all the flowers of the world for myself alone. The man laughed heartily at this and said someday I'd learn that the greatest gifts in life come from making others happy. He let me keep my bounty, but asked me not to pick the flowers again.

The next day after school I hid behind a tree across from the garden and waited for the man, then followed him to a little yellow house two blocks away. Only the year before, the house had been white. I had thought at the time that whoever had painted it yellow was an eccentric genius. I realized then, however, it wasn't genius that had inspired the man but a criminal sickness.

Finally, at midnight, I shimmed up a drainpipe, hoping when I got inside the house to find something truly wicked about the man, that he was a soccer fanatic or spent his free-time watching science fiction movies. Instead, through the balcony's sliding glass door, I laid eyes for the first time on a peacefully slumbering Madeline, my boyhood crush. My mind raced with options, yet in the end, I simply left, and never spoke of what I'd done.

As I dry my face, it strikes me, crushingly, that had I acted otherwise that night, my life would be very different today. Had I had the courage to sneak into Madeline's room, for instance, and introduced myself to her, she might have fallen in love with me, and spared my suffering when she chose Louis instead.

I leave the bathroom and I climb the stairs just down the hall. Servants of every sort are bustling about to a panglottal symphony—Spanish, Polish, Arabic, Yoruba, even Inuktitut. I greet them all in their native tongue, as best I can. Then a strange door appears, and I peek inside. It's a classroom filled with children at whose head stands Danny, writing on the chalkboard.

"Politics," he says, "is, above all, the art of the possible. What is not possible is absurd!"

"Someday," says a child with snot smeared all over his face, "the people will rise up and take to the streets. And when they do, a whole new way of being will be created where everyone is treated justly and fair!"

"It's the poor and oppressed who should be the most mistrustful of revolutions," Danny says, shaking his head. "It's almost always they who end up suffering most."

The students nod obsequiously, and Danny dismisses them. Before he leaves, the boy who spoke up leaves an apple on Danny's desk. I approach Danny, already marking up their assignments with a red pen.

"It's important always to tell the truth to children," he says, without looking up, "otherwise, they'll become accustomed to lies."

I pick up one of the reports and shiver as I read its title: "Modernity: How Everything Can Be Replaced by Something Else." "I had no idea you were so charitable with your free time, Danny."

"You mustn't tell anybody," he says. "Living with a secret is intoxicating."

"In a way," I say, "your contempt for vanity shows a deep strength of character."

"Now if you'll excuse me," Danny says, "I need to finish my work before my jiu jitsu master arrives."

Back on the veranda, the staff is cleaning up. Orsi is smoking on a chaise lounge and reading a book of philosophy. Two dolphins leap from the sea, side-by-side. Then a third dolphin leaps even higher, and swims off with his new mate. Absolute romantic security, I think, is impossible.

"What a wonderful experience we shared last night," I say to Orsi.

"Excuse me?"

"Surely you felt my presence?"

Before she can respond, James appears in just a pair of tiny running shorts and a crimson headband. He insists I join him for a jog along the beach.

"That's a wonderful idea!" Orsi says.

While James stretches, I hang my jacket on a chair, roll up my pants, and set off down the beach with the effortless stride of a cheetah. It's not long, though, before I'm sweating profusely, and no sooner have I unbuttoned my shirt than James is trotting alongside me, his breath calm and even. He's training for a marathon, he says, his third of the year.

"Are you familiar with the myth of Sisyphus?" he says.

"James," I say, "I'm far from uncivilized."

"Then you understand its core message?"

"You mean the persistent struggle against the absurdity of life?"

"That's one way to see it," James says. "Another is that man is nothing without his work. Zeus wasn't punishing Sisyphus. He was rewarding him." James can't be blind to my conviction that he's a swindler and a philistine, yet he persists. "May I ask you a personal question?" James says.

"Who is it that harmed you so terribly?"

"If this is about my father," I say, and will my pace to quicken, "I can assure you that we got along quite famously."

James runs alongside me with seeming effortlessness. My only means to silence him, I reason, is to bewilder him with a story to illustrate the filial bond between my father and me.

For instance, I tell James, my father and I invented a world of games. Often when he took me to run errands, he'd drive off without me, so that if I wanted to get home, I'd have to walk, sometimes tremendous distances. Then I got the idea to make him give me his keys anytime we left the car. Things went well until one day he pointed out a display of unusual wigs in the window of a beauty salon, and when I turned to look for him, he was gone. When I found our car wasn't where we'd parked it, I realized he'd made a spare key. There were many other such games. Over time I came to understand that it was through them that my father showed his affection.

"Paul," James says, and slows to a walk, "there is love inside you, yearning to be in the world. Let me help you to find a way to express it."

A seagull, we see, is flailing in the breaking surf. Again and again, it pops out of the water only to be swallowed by another wave. My instinct is to save it, but after last night's near-drowning, I'm afraid. I beg the seagull to forgive my cowardice. "I'm a selfish monster," I say, crying, "who's too afraid to die."

"Our worst impulses aren't inhuman," James says, "but merely secrets in the dark, insecurities, frailness. Overcoming these shortcomings is what makes us virtuous."

A renewed sense of power fills me, and I cast myself into the sea. But just as I reach the seagull, it disappears. I plunge beneath the surface, determined, and see the bird tumbling far below. With all my strength, I swim to it, secure its foot, and push hard off the ocean's floor, upward through a bed of churning kelp. On the beach, I am unable to diagnose the seagull's injury. It's only after it struggles to fly that I see its wing is broken.

"I don't know what to do," I say when James approaches.

"Listen to your heart, Paul."

I wrap the bird in my shirt and make my way to the boardwalk. I hop on a bike, and try to pedal away, but the bike is chained to a pole. Another bike leans against the side of a big house on the hill. I rush past the little girl tottering toward it and ride away at top speed.

At the animal hospital, a technician sweeps the seagull into an operating room. The veterinarian comes out after an hour to say the surgery was successful. In a matter of days, the seagull will be transferred to the local bird sanctuary, where she'll recuperate before being released back out into the wild.

"Can I see her?" I ask.

The veterinarian leads me to the recovery room. The bird is still woozy. I stroke her head and tell her how brave she was.

"It's best we let her rest," the veterinarian says.

I kiss the seagull and bid her adieu.

At the front desk, I complete a stack of paperwork. Unfortunately, I don't have medical insurance for seagulls and beg them to bill me at the studio.

I return the bike to the house. The little girl is thrilled to learn the seagull will survive, but her father threatens to call the police if I ever step foot on their property again.

Back at Danny's, the others have gathered by the tennis court. German tennis legend Boris Becker has just finished teaching a clinic on forehand topspin. Everyone, including Becker, is sitting around James, clapping.

"You may laugh at the absurdity of my story," James says, "but I assure you that I've invented nothing!" James spots me in the crowd. "And here he is, the hero!"

I'm met with pats on the back and words of praise from

these strangers. The wonderful sense of having adopted magical thinking courses through me. I corroborate James' story, and even add outrageous details to heighten my legend.

Orsi invites me to ride back to the city with her and James. For the duration of the four-hour trip, Orsi and I sit in the back of a black Range Rover while Hal, the driver, tells James up front that he's recently purchased a new speedboat. James shakes his head. He's worried that Hal is running at top speed toward damnation. Within thirty minutes, Hal is inconsolable. He's never felt more estranged from the love of God, he says, as James assures him we're all a mix of good and evil, right and wrong, endlessly tangled.

Cat Stevens' album *Tea for the Tillerman* plays on a loop. Orsi falls asleep with her head on my shoulder. Her hair smells of coconut and vanilla. Her gentle breath tickles my neck. I stare out the window and try to think pure thoughts. But it's no use. My desire is irrepressible.

James looks over his shoulder. "Orsi is tremendously fond of you," he says.

"I think she's just very tired." I adjust my pants to obscure my longing.

"She tells me that you'll surely come to be known as one of the defining artists of the generation."

At the studio, when Orsi stretches and yawns, her hand accidently brushes my erection.

"I hope I didn't make you *too* uncomfortable," she says.

I trot out the clichés required of a man in my position. "I'm only sorry I don't make for a more comfortable pillow."

I offer up my four dollars for gas money, but the gesture is refused.

"I know we've only just met," James says at the curb, "but I already feel that you're like a brother to me."

"Thanks for the lift," I say, taken by his vulnerability.

A rainbow forms on the horizon, peculiar, considering it hasn't rained. It's an omen, perhaps, I think, waving as their car speeds away.

CHAPTER 22

THE STUDIO is cozy and clean—Winston has even filled the place with bouquets of assorted flowers. He's sitting with Blanche on his lap, reading to her from Thomas Mann's *Doctor Faustus*. The two of them are so engrossed in this tale of a composer's pact with the Devil that they don't even notice me. I fix myself a cup of coffee and listen until Winston finishes.

"The book's major flaw," he says to Blanche with disgust, "is the conflict between Mann's symbolic intentions and his utterly absurd realistic ones."

Blanche barks her agreement.

"I have to disagree," I say, interrupting. "Never before has an author so successfully updated a classic work in contemporary trappings."

"You're home!" Winston says, as he and Blanche rise to greet me.

"Did the two of you have a nice time?" I say.

Blanche howls tunefully, and Winston insists that she was an absolute delight. They spent the evening, he says, rummaging through alleyways for discarded treasures. He can hardly believe their good luck.

"Can you imagine tossing out such a regal piece of furniture?" Winston says of the tattered recliner they were in.

The upholstery is stained with vomit and rusty springs are jutting from the cushion. "She's a jewel!" I say.

Winston has recuperated from his stab wound with little more to show for it than a slight limp. He yanks down his pants and shows me how he stitched the wound with fishing line, an old trick he learned as a boy working for a mountain guide in Montana. To demonstrate his restored powers, he taps a little dance with the grace of a swan.

"I must admit," I say, "I envy your elegance and style."

They were just about to head out for a late lunch, Winston says, at his favorite deli. As we walk, I share about my weekend at Danny's. Despite their obscene wealth, I say, he and his ilk don't seem entirely unhappy. Winston refuses this assessment. The wealthy, he insists, without exception, suffer from crushing loneliness and isolation. How could they not, after all, when they have no other reason to live?

"You don't believe material success is the path to salvation?" I say.

"What a slog chasing money is!" he says. "Think of all the loss of time one suffers trying to conquer financial battles. Simply admitting defeat removes all difficulties."

Nearly twenty-five years ago, Winston says, to illustrate his point, he worked as a beat reporter for a newspaper in a small Texas town. Unremarkable in almost every way, this town found itself in the national spotlight because of a controversial murder case. A black man had been accused of murdering a white woman. The details of the case were poorly understood. At first, the defendant swore he'd never met the victim. Later, before the evidence, he admitted he'd been having an affair with her. But the woman's husband, a local police officer, denied this story. His marriage had been happy from day one. The defendant was found guilty and sentenced to death. Later, however, the man's attorneys found new evidence. The murdered woman's neighbors had repeatedly witnessed the officer beating his wife. The prosecutor, moreover, had withheld evidence at the trial and sponsored false testimony. Despite all of this, and after many appeals, the day of execution arrived. The man, clearly innocent, was scheduled to die at midnight, and Winston was assigned to cover the event. But that evening, Winston's truck wouldn't start, and he had no way to reach the prison in time. He considered his options, concluding that, in the end, an execution was an execution, and sat down to write his eyewitness account, in fantastical detail, just in time to file before the 2 a.m. deadline.

"Hours later," he says, his face wistful with indignity, "my editor called to fire me. There had been a last-minute pardon, and the man was spared. But thousands of copies of the newspaper had been delivered, with my story on the front page. The city was suing for libel, and the paper's owner feared they go bankrupt."

"But it wouldn't have been fair to deny your readers a story as interesting as the one you wrote," I say. "How can you be blamed for a silly incident having to do with fickle executive clemency?"

The three of us parade through the neighborhood confident in the conviction that our shared view of the world isn't merely accurate but that everyone else is tragically wrong about everything that matters.

A breeze from the north carries the scent of freshly baked bread. Blanche strains against her leash, but Winston insists we not enter at the front of the deli. "We'll get much better service in the alley," he says.

To Winston's credit, everything he's told me contradicts popular wisdom. His non-conformity fills me with complete faith in his judgment. In the alley, three mustachioed Puerto Rican men with hairnets are smoking cigarettes.

"¡Hola, Winston! ¿Que pasa?"

"¡Vinimos a comer tu maravillosa comida, amigos!" Winston says as they fist bump.

One of the men asks Winston his opinion of the latest Alfonso Cuarón film. Though Winston hasn't seen it, he declares it an "absolute masterpiece." The men agree but wonder how Winston can be so certain.

"I can see exactly what Cuarón's doing two or even three pictures into the future."

The men finish their cigarettes and then head back to work.

"Are they going to bring us our lunch?" I say.

"No need for that," Winston says, and climbs into a dumpster. "Jackpot!" he says, and hands me a bag of day-old bread. "Eureka!" he shouts, tossing out a bag of produce. "Bingo!" he hollers, before a half-round of slightly molded cheese.

The weather couldn't be finer, so we take our bounty to the park. Winston lays his military-issue coat on the grass and sets to work preparing our meal. The man has real culinary flair—his avocado, hummus, carrot, and bell pepper sandwiches are unrivaled. After eating, we lie on our backs and take turns calling out what the clouds look like. Winston sees himself dressed as a witch doctor, captaining a Mardi Gras float. The same cloud looks to me like an ostrich with its head stuck in the sand while someone plucks feathers from its butt.

"They say that optimism is the most characteristic expression of a weak mind," Winston says. "But I've always found prudence to be the worst of follies."

The silhouettes of two figures, hand in hand, move toward

us. The details are blotted out by the sun. I rub my eyes, but all I see are exploding stars. I'm overcome by dread. My heart races, my mouth goes dry. I feel I'm going to vomit. Blanche strikes a defensive crouch, as if preparing for an attack. I throw my coat over my head.

"What's the matter?" Winston says.

"I'm having one of my spells."

"You're acting like you've seen Satan!"

"I'm afraid you have a front row seat to the suffering of the damned."

The rustle of footsteps grows closer and closer.

"Is that you, Paul?" a familiar voice says.

I press the coat to my face and squeeze my eyes. Even when someone taps my shoulder, I'm convinced that if I can only concentrate enough, all of this will vanish. I'm so fixed on manifesting nothingness I fail to realize I've bitten my tongue.

"I do not exist. I am invisible. Nothing can harm me," I repeat.

"I can't understand you," the voice says.

My silence incites this person to snatch away my coat. My instinct is to bare my teeth and hiss. Blood spews from my mouth and splatters across her blouse, and she shrieks.

"Paul," Janie says, "you're bleeding!"

This is the first time I've been face-to-face with her since that day in the park after we broke up, when I gave her the painting I made of Io. She's cut her hair short, with bangs. My God, I think, she's transformed—nothing like who she was with me. Even so, I find her lovely.

"I bit my tongue," I say. "It's nothing."

The man she's with is the same man who retrieved her things from our apartment and kissed her by the trailer. His chiseled good looks and muscular frame can't be anything but the product of supreme vanity coupled with dogged insecurity. Janie introduces him as Stephen, though she hadn't needed to. I already know everything about him from a series of dreams I had for weeks after our first encounter. I'm not surprised he's an orthopedic surgeon. As anyone who knows anything about doctors can tell you, orthopedic surgeons are the brutes of the medical profession. If this weren't enough to write him off as a lout, he's also a veteran who flew jets in the Air Force for seven years—a cheap ploy to get the American taxpayer to foot the bill for his medical school expenses. What's more, now that he's extorted all the free money available to him, he's set on capturing as much recognition for himself as he can, to validate his feeble existence. Just last week, he was honored by Doctors Without Borders for his volunteer work in West Africa. Never have I seen such a blatant display of narcissism. How Janie could fall for someone so trite is beyond reason.

"And who is this?" Janie says, kneeling to pet Blanche's head.

"This is Blanche," I say, as Blanche wags her tail and licks Janie's face. "Pet her at your own risk. She can be vicious."

Blanche rolls onto her back, courting belly rubs.

"You've always been so good with animals," Janie says.

"Just this morning, I rescued a seagull," I say, glaring at Stephen. "I don't suppose an orthopedic surgeon would know the first thing about treating a broken wing."

"You're right," Stephen says. "I'm a hip and knee specialist."

My tongue is really gushing now, making it difficult to speak. I ignore the pain and push on. "The intricacies of a bird's wing must be a thousand times more complex than a human hip or knee," I say.

"Are you sure you're okay?" Stephen says, and offers me his handkerchief. "You're really bleeding!"

I ignore this offering. This man is my sworn enemy. No matter what foolish romantics might espouse, love is a zero-sum game. Any positive connection between people is accompanied by loss—of self, for example, when engrossed in a tender kiss, or the terrible jealousy one suffers knowing their beloved has fallen for the charms of another. There's no increase or decrease in joy or sorrow, only a redistribution—the blessed and the cursed twisting and spinning like figure skaters.

Winston coughs into his hand, drawing our attention.

"Excuse me," I say, "I've failed to introduce my friend Winston."

Winston bows and kisses Janie's hand. When Stephen reaches for a shake, Winston takes his hand with the force of a strangler. The two men stay locked in a death-grip, battling for supremacy.

"Winston used to work as a journalist," I say, "but now he's a patron of the arts."

I encourage Winston to take off his pants to show them his leg.

"I was fortunate enough to contribute some of my blood for one of Paul's recent pieces," Winston says. "His new work is on the vanguard of experimental painting."

Janie musters a contrite smile, and I'm smitten with nostalgia. Any shortcoming I've ever attributed to this woman, however petty, has vanished.

"I'm so happy to hear your art is going well," she says.

"I'm long past the days when it seemed I was doomed to endlessly repeat the same mistakes."

Janie brushes a strand of hair from her face, and I'm struck by a glint of light from her hand. On her finger is the most garish engagement ring I've ever seen. It's a marvel her delicate bone structure can even support such an abomination.

"Is that what I think it is?" I say.

"I wasn't sure you'd heard."

"Well, congratulations!"

Stephen slings an arm around Janie and pulls her close. "We're getting married in Hawaii."

Blanche jingles her collar effusively at the mention of Hawaii. It's always been her dream to go on a tropical getaway.

"I don't know if it would be awkward for you," Stephen says. "But we're having an engagement party next weekend, and would love it for you to come."

Janie's face contorts with exasperation, inspiring me further to impose myself.

"I'd like nothing more than to attend my ex-girlfriend's engagement party. In fact, I wouldn't miss it for the world!"

Stephen and Janie are late to a wedding cake tasting, they say, and take their leave. Disappointment consumes me, yet I accept it. I feel like an old man welcoming his death.

CHAPTER 23

IT'S PRE-DAWN in the studio. Winston sleeps against the wall, an empty bottle of port between his legs. My back is sore from my lumpy bed. Blanche will awaken soon, and I'll have to do my dead-man's game. I check my horoscope in the pages of an old magazine. "True and false are merging into one." I sketch a drawing of three birds on a branch.

I've never found much to inspire me in the natural world. Even John Constable's most celebrated landscapes leave me cold as an ex-wife's heart. But there's something in this avian rendering that piques me on. By the time Blanche wakes up, I've painted two of the birds exquisitely. Not even Matisse ever demonstrated such a command of palette. I set down my brush and strike the most somber pose I can. Just as Blanche begins to yelp, Danny bursts through the door.

"This is no time to make a game of your mortality," he shouts. "Inès needs more cat bags!"

I jump up and straighten my jacket. Danny sees my work-in-progress and strokes the reddish goatee he's growing.

"I don't want you to get the wrong idea," he says. "While this still isn't very good, I will say it's interesting. Why you chose to paint two of the birds while leaving the third incomplete can only symbolize our sadly imperfect society. That was my first thought, at any rate. Then it struck me that the unpainted bird represents something far more tragic: a woman who's besmirched her own beauty to avoid the undesired attention of common men."

"That is interesting," I say.

"I'm not finished." Winston has risen from his port-induced stupor and begun to sweep. "The real problem lies in that—how should I say this?—for whatever reason, you are bereft of the emotional sophistication a man needs truly to understand the female plight. What you've created here is a graphic autobiography. The unpainted bird reminds us there will always be those who are made to suffer. In short," Danny concludes with a sniff, "this is nothing more than self-pitying dribble."

Winston pauses in his work to smile sympathetically.

"Have you nothing to say for yourself?" Danny says.

"This painting isn't a geometry proof in need of explanation. And anyway, you didn't come here so early to engage in futile dialectics. What do you want?"

"There's a man up in Poughkeepsie," Danny says, "one of the great cat hoarders of our time. Every year, Animal Control raids his place to put his cats in shelters, and every year he gathers a new clowder. My contact at Animal Control tells me their latest raid is scheduled for this week."

"You want me to buy this man's cats so you can slaughter them for your bags?"

"All of my bags will be cruelty-free, Paul. The busy stretch of highway around this man's lair is a road-kill mecca. On any given day, there are dozens of dead cats. Each year after their raid, Animal Control cleans the streets, as well. I've rented you a van so you can go up there to gather as many dead cats as you can before they get there."

"I'm pretty busy here, Danny, as you can see."

"I'll give you a hundred dollars for every cat."

"Obviously, that changes things."

The van is challenging. Not since I drove Danny's Jaguar have I been behind a wheel. I misjudge the turn-radius, hop a curb, clip a mailbox. Cars blare their horns from all directions. I straddle the lane divider, afraid to drive near the sidewalk. At a stoplight, a taxi driver spits at me.

Once I reach the city limits, however, the rhythms of the road return. I roll down the window and let the wind blow through my hair. The speed and power of this van is exhilarating. The speed limit is sixty-five, but I must be doing a hundred and ten. A glance at my speedometer quickly disabuses me, however, with a reading of forty-five. I remind myself that technology is nothing if not unreliable, and slow to a more comfortable pace. A peloton of cyclists in skintight suits nearly runs me off the road as they pass on my left. "Hands at ten and two!" I think.

Soon, my nose catches a whiff of something foul—the undeniable stench of rotting carcasses. I park alongside a shallow creek bed, throw two pillowcases over my shoulder, and set off. It doesn't take long before I find my first dead cat. This poor fellow, dragged off onto the road's shoulder by some thoughtful motorist, is easily identifiable by its smooth champagne-colored coat as an adolescent Burmese. Not more than twenty feet down the way, under a willow tree, I find a broad-headed Ragamuffin.

This really is heartbreaking work. While I have no love for pet cats, who do nothing more than idle on living room couches, I hold the highest regard for cats who spend their days hunting chipmunks and lizards.

After two hours, I've filled both pillowcases with fifteen bodies—enough to pay the vet bill for the seagull—and load them in the van. The second leg of my quest takes me miles in each direction. I fill the pillowcases again and am headed back to the van when I'm struck by the unmistakable cramping of impending diarrhea. It's a twenty-minute drive to the nearest gas station. But just as I'm beginning really to panic, as if gifted from the heavens, I spot a tiny cabin through the trees. A man with a face as heavy as lead answers the door.

"Are those dead cats in your bags?" he says in a thickly accented voice.

"Indeed, they are."

"So many cats in this area," he says.

I explain my dilemma, and the man is kind enough to offer his facilities. A leather-bound German children's book sits atop the toilet. Its introduction tells about a boy from a family of jewelers who spent his youth apprenticing with his father and uncle. Despite the boy's deep animus for the work, he carried on making necklaces, earrings, and bracelets until he died a wealthy but deeply unhappy man.

When at last I'm finished, I see this cabin's principal décor is militant. Along one wall are uniforms pinned with medals. Another wall is covered with weapons, and a third is lined with photographs and newspaper clippings. The man hands me a mug of tea as I study a picture of a young soldier being tried in a military courtroom.

"That's me," he says.

"What were you being charged with?"

"Crimes of war."

"You killed many people?"

The man's face turns grey, and he puts his hand to his heart. "Every night I see the dead marching through in my dreams."

Looking into the man's clear eyes, my conscience is at peace. He leads me to a door covered by a black velvet curtain. I have to squint to see the room he's showing me, mostly obscured in shadow. On the wall I make out a primitive wooden crucifix, and beneath it, a coffin. The man falls to his knees like Pascal and folds his hands into the prayer position. Though he babbles in a language I've never heard, I understand completely. The man when he's finished explains that after the war he travelled from town to town with this coffin in a wagon, preaching his newfound gospel, despite his rejection by everyone. The rejection, he says, only strengthened his resolve. He moved to the United States sixty years ago, and has been in this cabin for the last forty-six.

The man asks if I want to watch him polish his medals. I decline, explaining my obligation to deliver the dead cats. Outside, the chilly wind makes my eyes water, but I feel nothing.

CHAPTER 24

At the studio, Winston is serving lattes to Orsi and James. They've just come from an industrial space they're considering renting for a series of workshops hosted by the Pure Cosmos Club. Lucky for them, James says, Winston was nice enough to let them wait inside until I got home.

A large freezer has been delivered in which to store the dead cats. It takes me five round-trips to get them all in. As I work, I silently chant the Jesus Prayer—"Lord Jesus, son of God, have mercy on me"—inhaling Jesus, exhaling mercy.

Cat blood has leaked all over the floor. Winston says not to worry, he was just about to mop. Orsi, meantime, is reading from a nineteenth-century etiquette book. I sit on the floor to listen, eager to learn how better to comport myself. "Don't talk of 'the opera,'" Orsi intones, "in the presence of those who are not frequenters of it. Don't say 'gents' for 'gentlemen' or 'pants' for 'pantaloons.' These are inexcusable vulgarisms. Never say 'vest' for 'waistcoat.' Never speak aloud in a railway carriage, and thus obtrude upon the reading experience of your fellow passengers."

"Why all these dead cats?" James says when Orsi is finished.

"They're for Danny's collaboration with Inès."

"Speaking of whom," James says, "where is he? I want to speak with him about Pure Cosmos Club. He's surely going to want in on it."

"Danny never comes here when there's a full moon."

I pick up my brush to tinker with my bird painting, but

James knocks me over before I can touch the canvas. A lamp crashes to the floor, shattering its bulb.

"I'm sorry," James says, helping me up, "but I couldn't let you desecrate this amazing piece."

"You like it?"

"I've never seen a more accurate depiction of the crisis of modern man! Just look at how lonely and spiritually adrift this unpainted bird is. He lacks any semblance of tradition or faith—he has no bearings. All of that is gone. Like so many of us today, he's alone."

Orsi can't help herself, exploding with laughter. James' eyes cross. It's as if he were examining the tip of his nose.

"That is pure nonsense," Orsi says. "He simply hasn't gotten around to painting the last bird yet. Isn't that right, Paul?"

How could I not be in love with this woman? Were I to win her, I'd serve her tirelessly, and even in my failure to meet her expectations, however much she might demand, I'd strive on with an unwavering smile.

"James is most astute," I say, blushing. "Subconsciously, I may have had similar thoughts. Even so, I'm afraid you're right."

James tries to pet Blanche, but she scuttles away from him.

"If you truly like the painting," I say, "I want you to have it."

"That is far too generous of you. I simply cannot accept. Honestly, I'm much more concerned about your well-being. How expanded do you think your subconscious truly is?"

"I'm not sure?"

James turns to Orsi, who's helping Winston clean up the broken light bulb.

"How integrated with his authentic self do you think Paul is?"

"There's something blocking his vibrations," Orsi says. "I'm sure of it."

She's right, I know, unable to say why. I sit down, speechless.

"Paul has recently accepted an invitation to attend his ex-girlfriend's engagement party," Winston says.

"How strange," James says.

"A true test of one's character!" Winston says.

"Would you like me to go with you?" Orsi says, and takes my hand. "For moral support?"

James checks his watch, then says they must go. There's a pressing matter with his accountant that needs his attention.

"Please," I say, "take the painting. I want you to have it, more than anything!"

James takes the painting from the easel. "You're absolutely sure?"

"Nothing would please me more."

I scribble the address to Janie's party on a bubble gum wrapper and give it to Orsi. "Thank you," I say, and bow.

"And don't forget to tell Danny," James says, "we have exciting news!"

It takes me nearly the rest of the night to get the mud stains off my trousers. Winston's solution with vinegar and baking soda is a miracle tonic.

CHAPTER 25

YESTERDAY, I felt as good as a schoolboy on a snow day. But last night's dream ended all that. I was a man of sixty-five, with grey thinning hair, a wattle-face, and a belly, celebrating at my retirement party at the Owasco Lake Inn's banquet hall with more than fifty colleagues. For forty years I'd worked for the Rutherford Plastics Company, where I started as an Applications Technician and ended as a Senior Manufacturing Engineer. My daughter Teri even came, all the way from North Dakota. Of course, I had my wife by my side, wearing a blue dress she'd bought on-sale at the department store. There was salmon or chicken for dinner, and a cash bar. I had three scotch on the rocks and felt like the luckiest guy in the world.

Then I remembered I had to make a speech, which gave me frightful nerves. At Teri's wedding, I'd ended up rambling on about how she'd had an awful stutter as a child, and how we worried that she'd never find a nice young man like Ted to marry her. Teri didn't speak to me for two years.

During his introduction, my boss, Brian, made a joke about how he was only three years old when I started working at Rutherford. My wife didn't like Brian because he'd once given me a poor performance review that prevented my scheduled raise. Nevertheless, I held no ill-will for him. I'd always believed one must take accountability for their own misfortunes. "It's hard to summarize in a few words," I began, "the experience of forty years in the plastic-packaging industry." In the admiring faces of my family and colleagues, I saw my whole life had been building to this one grand moment.

I woke in a panic and have been in bed all day, inconsolable. It's abundantly clear I've ruined my life. The perfect path was laid out before me. All I had to do was take it.

CHAPTER 26

JANIE AND Stephen live in a neighborhood in Brooklyn called Cobble Hill, a magical wonderland of tree-lined streets, majestic brownstones, and storefronts so charming one is tempted to linger staring into their windows for hours. I stop to tie my shoe in front of a sidewalk café, and when I stand up, I'm penned on both sides by Filipino women pushing double-wide strollers. I step into the street, and am nearly struck by a man and woman out for a sunset ride on a tandem bike.

I wait for Orsi on the stoop in front of Janie and Stephen's. To the smart young couple strolling into the party, I say, "Excuse me, but do you believe life's only worth the trouble of living when one is in love?" Neither answers, but merely glare as they climb the steps. I'm convinced I can read their whispering lips as they wait at the door.

"Should we call the police and report this man for loitering?" the woman says.

"His presence can't be good for property values," the man says.

Finally, Orsi steps out of a taxi. She's wearing a sheer black top, and her hair is up to accentuate her collarbones and lovely neck. It wouldn't be an exaggeration to say her beauty rivals that of a Tolstoy novel. We ring the buzzer and are greeted by a man in a bow tie. The flat is filled with men in turtle-neck sweaters and women in modest, long-sleeved dresses. Caterers float about with trays of sushi and various Japanese delicacies.

A couple approaches. The man sports a neatly groomed

beard, and his wife is pregnant. She recognizes Orsi from school, where Orsi taught her graduate studies course in Number Theory and Cryptography. The woman is so awed by Orsi, you'd think she had invented mathematics itself.

The man's name is Amit. He and Stephen are racquetball buddies. The two met years ago when they competed against each other in the championship at their club. Now, in addition to playing racquetball together, Amit works as Stephen's architect. He did all the renovations to this apartment, in fact.

"It's a bohemian blend of traditional, modern, and industrial," he says, looking proudly about. "Stephen and Janie had a vision of clean and simple elegance."

"Nice work with the open vestibule in the parlor room," I say.

Amit is curious if I'm a mathematician, too.

"No such luck," I tell him.

"A physician, then?" he says. "Nearly all of Janie and Stephen's friends are physicians."

"Unemployed artist."

"Well," Amit says, and, to mask his discomfort, takes a piece of sashimi from a passing server, "to each his own."

The two quickly excuse themselves to chat with a couple from their Lamaze class. At the bar, Orsi and a woman make small talk for what feels like forever, allowing me to slip away. A painting I recognize hangs above the fireplace. It's the unmistakable creation of a molecular biologist-turned-artist whose work now fetches exceedingly high prices. He's created hundreds of hyper-detailed paintings of molecules and atoms. His subject and technique haven't changed since his work hit the market years ago. That his art sells so well is the best indication that he lacks any semblance of talent.

"I thought this piece might get your attention," Janie says. "Are you familiar with his work?"

"His paintings do very well with a certain type of buyer."

"Why don't you try making something similar? I bet you could do this just as well as him."

From across the room, Stephen taps a spoon on his glass, and Janie rushes over. Stephen thanks his friends for coming together in their beautiful new home to celebrate his and Janie's impending nuptials, and proceeds to eulogize Janie and his immense fortune in having been blessed to have her at his side for this amazing journey he calls life. Uproarious applause meets his remarks, and then Janie says a few words. She begins with platitudes nearly as stale as her fiancé's, but builds with tears in her eyes to a heartrending conclusion.

"I've tried so hard to give everything I have to other people. As a child, I dedicated my every waking hour to making my parents happy by earning straight-A's and be admitted to Princeton. Then I became a doctor because I wanted to heal those who are sick. My therapist tells me that even in my personal relationships I've always sought out broken people I thought I could fix. Always, I see, I was putting the needs of others before my own. But recently I experienced a deeply troubling period during which my resources utterly failed. Never before had I been the one in need. Enter Stephen, friends! With him, for the first time in my life, I didn't have to be the strong one. From the instant we met eight months ago, he has been my rock. And I'm profoundly humbled at the possibility that he will continue to be all that and more, so selfless and pure, for the rest of what I hope will be many, many more fruitful years. Everyone, please, raise your glasses in recognition of my wonderful soon-to-be-husband, Stephen!"

The room erupts with applause and cheers as Janie kisses Stephen long and slow. Bitterness courses through me like a disease. I dab at my tears with my pocket square, then take two flutes of champagne from a server and down them. Orsi when I find her is explaining to a trio of neurosurgeons a game theory problem whose solution requires nonlinear systems of differential equations. I feel sick and rush off to the facilities.

The rug beneath my knees is soft and plush, and somehow, I've managed to get vomit in my hair. I run a bath and strip off my clothes. The people knocking at the door will need to find other accommodations, I holler, as these facilities will be indeterminately occupied. A collection of hand towels hangs by the sink, each embroidered with verse from Rumi. I shove them into a cabinet and light a row of candles. There are three varieties of bubble bath, which I mix as one. Concerned voices continue to prattle out in the hall, but I ignore them and climb into the tub. Janie's collection of beauty products is unrivalled, I see. The scent of her shampoo transports me to the memory of her pillow on the bed we once shared. Sometimes, I recall, with a difficult day ahead, I'd pour a dollop of her shampoo onto a strip of cloth and carry it with me so that whenever I felt anxious, I could smell it. Then, all at once, having picked the lock on the door, Orsi is here.

"There you are," she says.

"I was feeling a little overwhelmed."

"What a brilliant idea to take a bath in the middle of a party!"

Orsi hands me a towel, and I dry and dress. Back at the party, everyone stares. Orsi shoves me against the wall and kisses me hard. Janie storms away, and Stephen gives chase. Orsi takes my hand, and like the Red Sea parting before Moses, a path clears before us. The bow-tied greeter wishes us a "good evening" as we leave the party.

Orsi lights a cigarette, and we walk slowly down the street. The leaves on the trees are beginning to turn gold. I try to hold Orsi's hand, but she draws away. The world ceases to make sense.

A jazz band plays near the window of a bar. Orsi asks if I'd like to get a drink. To my surprise and delight, she sits beside me in our booth.

"Do you always wear suits?"

"I always like to look my best."

Orsi points to the grass stains on my lapel and the hole on the knee of my trousers. "But this suit is in tatters!" she says.

My body stirs, and I wish for the death of my desire. There are times when neither solitude nor the company of someone we love can quell our torment. I am infected with a madness to understand this woman. The server brings us cocktails. Orsi spins her glass but doesn't drink.

"Are you fatherless?" I say.

"Why would you ask such a thing?"

"It's just something I presumed," I say, and take her arm. "You have very thin wrists. It's as if you're the product of neglect." Orsi turns away so that our knees no longer touch. "I didn't mean that in a bad way," I say. "It's just something I noticed."

"I have the finest father in all the world," she says, her eyes turned cold. "Have you heard of the Jeantet Prize? It's awarded annually for the most important achievement in medicine."

"Like the Nobel Prize?" I say.

"It's like the Nobel, but different. In fact, it's better in many ways, at least in the opinion of those who matter. Less political. Anyway, my father has developed many of the most important drugs of the twenty-first century. What do you know about targeted gene therapy?"

I feel terrible and say nothing.

"Just as I thought. I can't say I'm surprised."

"So, he's very successful?"

"He was," she says, fighting back tears. "But after the government fabricated political charges against him and had him arrested, he lost everything. They claimed at his trial that he was surrounded by 'suspicious elements,' presenting as evidence that one of his prized students was a relative of George Soros. If it wasn't for James, my father would be in prison to this day."

"James was your father's lawyer?"

"He has relationships with many high-ranking officials. Hungary is extremely corrupt."

"James bribed someone to get your father released?"

Orsi's eyes widen and become bright and expressive. "James says that when someone knows the truth, they bring great shame upon themselves if they don't speak it."

"Now I understand," I say, smiling as though I'd solved a complicated riddle. "You married James because you owed him."

"Of course not!" Orsi smacks the table so hard our drinks nearly spill. "I fell madly in love with him! How could I not have?"

Orsi finally lifts her drink, but before she can sip it, I snatch it away and slam it down with a gulp. Why I did this is beyond me. All I can do is grin as though I were trying to amuse her.

"What a strange thing to have done," Orsi says.

I say I need to get home to feed Blanche. When Orsi's taxi arrives, we hug.

"Could you love someone who does bad things?" she says.

Of course I could love someone who does bad things,

I think. People who act on principle alone are worse than dreadful. Principles alone are comic. Before I can say any of this, however, the taxi speeds away.

On my way home, I stop at a bodega to buy popsicles for me, Blanche, and Winston. The two of them are working with watercolors when I arrive. Winston has painted a seal sunning itself on a rock, with a speedboat in the distance. Blanche's painting is more abstract, a morass of browns and purples chaotically swirled about. They're both eager to hear about my night. We eat our popsicles as I recount the details. When the story's over, we retire to our corners, and fall asleep.

CHAPTER 27

It's been a week since the engagement party. Rain has fallen constantly, and I've started rewriting the history of my life. Tonight, Winston has taken Blanche to the cinema for a double-feature of *101 Dalmatians* and *Homeward Bound*. The studio is silent except for the whispering of mice. I lie in my bed reading my childhood journal. There was a time when I was full of ambition and guts, but today I'm terrified of everything. The only emotion my past inspires is mistrust. I'm developing a complete inability to rise above things. It takes three pieces of bubble gum to find even a hint of solace.

There's a knock at the door. To justify my existence, a sort of last campaign against a regression to total infantilism, I quickly dress and comb my hair, then open the door to find Janie dripping in the rain.

"I didn't get a chance to say goodbye the other night," she says, "so I thought I'd pop in for a visit."

Understandably, she excuses herself to the bathroom to gather herself. I boil water for tea and set out a plate of lemon macaroons. When Janie returns, she's wearing only my jacket.

"I hope this is okay?" she says.

I fiddle nervously with the nobs of a broken radio while Janie nibbles on a macaroon. There are two dozen cat-bags in various stages of completion lying about.

"You've moved in here full-time?"

"I know it doesn't much compare to your new home with Stephen."

"On the contrary, I quite like it," she says, and begins to pace about. "It suits you."

She stumbles over parts from a disassembled grandfather clock, then gets caught in the colony of furry bats I've made out of cellophane and carpet, all hanging from a beam.

"Do you know what the problem with happiness is?" she says.

"I wouldn't know the first thing on the subject."

"Even a chance at happiness requires us to give up all desire."

"Things not going well with Stephen?"

"When a man is as handsome as Stephen, it's easy to be good-natured. What he doesn't have is your vagabond spirit."

My thoughts go spinning like a thousand deranged ballerinas. My trouble with Janie has never been her per se, but with her effect on me. With her, always, I lose my sense of self. All my effort went toward anticipating her needs, which invariably I misjudged. Countless times my best intentions ended in tragedy. Once, I punched her uncle in the face over Thanksgiving dinner because of the things he did to her during childhood. Janie swore the ensuing rift between her and her family could never be repaired. The reason I couldn't see how I'd harmed her was that my powers of introspection were weak. In short, she said, I was prone to endless self-deception.

"That woman you brought to the party was very pretty," Janie says. "Is she your new girlfriend?"

I want to tell Janie of my love for Orsi—how I spend half my waking hours and three-quarters of my dream life thanking the heavens for her existence. Instead, I merely shrug.

Then, to my total amazement, Janie pounces on me like a leopard on a gazelle. She chews on my lips and thrusts her tongue in and out of my mouth. I try to push her off to catch my breath, but she pushes me onto my rickety bed and sets to ripping off my pants with her teeth. She yanks off my jacket and shirt, then slaps me hard, nicking my tooth in the process with her colossal diamond engagement ring. I spit blood all over her neck and breasts, which, against all reason, incites her. She takes me in her mouth, the whole thing, until she gags. Her eyes turn bloodshot and tears stream down her face, sooty with her makeup. She climbs on top of me and beats my chest with her fists, grinding so hard I'm afraid one wrong move will snap the whole thing off. Finally, she finishes and collapses.

"One thing I always appreciated about you," she says after a time, "is that I never had to feel bad about being brutal or savage."

"It's nice to have someone with whom to share familiar things."

She reaches for a macaroon and stands with it naked at the window. Her sweaty body shimmers in the moonlight. I get a bag of ice and press it to my cheek. She touches my swollen eye.

"My relationship with Orsi isn't serious," I say. "Truthfully, I hardly ever think about her. I can go seconds, even minutes, sometimes, without the image of her face forming in my mind."

"I hate to admit it," Janie says, as she puts on her bra, "but I became quite jealous when I saw her kiss you at our party."

"You don't think her teeth are too white?"

"Her teeth?"

"I think she bleaches them. How could she not?"

Janie lies down next to me, suddenly very wistful, and we don't speak until the whistle and pop of illegal fireworks interrupts our bliss.

"What is it?" Janie says, as I pound a fist against the wall.

"The other day I sketched a picture of three birds, but only painted two of them. Orsi's husband made a very keen insight about the work, only I didn't realize it at the time. But Orsi insisted I simply hadn't gotten around to finishing the painting. Her remark was so alarming that I just stupidly agreed."

Janie buries her face in a pillow and screams.

"Orsi's married?" she says. "So now you're making a hobby of breaking up relationships!"

I pick up the pillow and fire it across the room.

"What is wrong with you?" Janie says.

"Orsi was right. The crisis of modern man never crossed my mind when I left that bird unpainted."

Janie climbs out of bed and starts to dress, cursing at herself as she does. I've never known her to fall prey to petty envy. I place my hands on her shoulders and look into her cinnamon eyes.

"I know you said you like the studio," I say, "but we don't have to live here."

"I have to go home," she says. "Stephen gets back from his Doctors Without Borders trip in the morning."

"He seems like a good person," I say. "Please try to let him down gently."

"I'm afraid you have the wrong idea, Paul."

"If you want to keep us both," I say, "I'm not opposed."

"This was a terrible mistake. We can never see each other again."

Janie kisses me on the cheek and then is out the door. I stand there naked for several minutes before Winston and Blanche return from the movies.

CHAPTER 28

WINSTON POURS a bit of port into two coffee mugs and sits me down for a chat. His face—lumpy and pocked from teenage acne—radiates with tenderness and warmth. I take a knife from my pocket and start to whittle a broken table leg into the semblance of a totem. But Winston is well-versed in my tools of distraction, and chucks the knife into a bin of toys he's collected for donation to a local orphanage.

I'm falling victim to the cult of despair, Winston says. I should get comfortable with the idea that I'll never be able to satisfy anyone, nor will anyone ever satisfy me. As a member of destiny's elect, love will never be enough. I must be selfish with my talents.

"Don't you see?" he says. "The object of your affection will always pale in the light of your own brilliance!"

"My heart is with Orsi, but Janie would've made a fine substitute," I say.

"There are enough idiots in the world without you joining the parade!" Winston says, and laughs until he coughs. "Injuring oneself is a poor excuse for atonement."

I say nothing while Winston picks at the scab on his leg. Wanting badly to understand how Winston became so wise, I ask if there was ever a woman in his life. His face turns wonderfully animated, and he begins rhapsodizing about an ex-girlfriend of his from years before.

Her name was Darlene. They lived together in an apartment outside of Tucson, where she taught English as a Second

Language to Mexican children at the local elementary school. Darlene cooked the most incredible pirogues from scratch and loved to spend her Sunday afternoons ironing Winston's shirts. But as much as Darlene cared for Winston, he never truly loved her. There just wasn't that spark, he says. Their neighbor, however, a computer repairman named Samuel, thought the world of Darlene. The first time they met, he carried all Darlene's dry-cleaning up six flights of stairs after the elevator broke. Years passed, and Winston left Darlene for a woman named Sue, a recent divorcée who worked as a cashier at the corner grocery store, and Darlene soon moved into Samuel's apartment.

A few months on, when things with Winston and Sue began to fizzle, Winston got blind drunk and banged on Samuel and Darlene's door, begging Darlene to come back to him and threatening to kill himself if she didn't. Two days later, Winston and Darlene moved to Utah. For a month, Darlene worked hard to rehabilitate Winston. Yet as soon as he was better, he broke things off with her again. Unfortunately, Samuel was a man of personal honor, and refused to take Darlene back. It wasn't long, Winston says, until Darlene died of a rare condition called "Barlow's Syndrome," though Winston is convinced she'd died of a broken heart.

"You were able to remake yourself using your jealousy as a strength!" I say.

Winston bows his head and says a prayer for Darlene, then goes to the window for a breath of air.

Winston's right, all bonds are conditional. It's only work that frees us from boredom, need, and vice. I spend the day experimenting with lithography, making a series of seven prints of a man and woman holding rifles. The pictures depict the couple at various stages of abstraction, starting with a realistic portrayal and ending with nothing but a few lines.

CHAPTER 29

THE SUN has only risen, but Winston, typically a very late sleeper, is already up and hard at work installing workstations with sewing machines and framed photos of Charles de Gaulle and Victor Hugo. The French patisserie has delivered a basket of baguettes and croissants, and two cases of premium Bordeaux. Blanche, too, whom Winston has taken to calling his "L'assistant parfait," is humming with efficiency, arranging buttons and zippers. Serge Gainsbourg's "Je t'aime moi non plus" spins on the turntable.

Winston, moreover, I see, is wearing the uniform of the French guard's mounted *chasseurs*—a bicorne hat and an overcoat—quite dapper, I think, if a bit too Napoleonic. But it's the shoes that make an outfit, and Danny has given Winston a pair of leather boots to complete the look. Blanche has been snarling at him here and there, but it's only now I see why. "That's right," I say, "he does look like Puss in Boots!" Unable to bear further humiliation, Winston exchanges the boots for a pair of white sneakers.

Presently, a team of seamstresses fresh off a redeye from Paris come bustling in. Winston serves them espressos while they smoke and flit about, gossiping in delightful French voices. To my surprise, Winston speaks the language fluently. He delivers a rousing speech, voicing Danny's instructions for the cat-bags. The seamstresses' work takes on a steady rhythm, like a team of champion oarsmen. Blanche paces between the workstations, as chic in her red beret as a young Jane Birkin.

On their break, the seamstresses polish off several bottles of wine, then refuse to work anymore. Winston is on a tight production deadline and is afraid it won't be met. He pleads with the seamstresses, but they merely ridicule him.

"It's a mutiny!" he says.

"What can I do to help?" I say.

Winston doesn't believe I can be of any use. What have I become, he says, since losing the affection of both Orsi and Janie, but a diminished version of the man I was?

At this, Blanche raises her tail and growls. She sounds like a Rottweiler. The startled seamstresses rush back to their work. Winston is so grateful to Blanche that he begs her to stay on the job as his enforcer.

I sit in a corner with a box of pastels, watching Winston and Blanche run the place. Not once during the course of many hours of work does either of them so much as glance at me. I produce a series of morose sketches of the seamstresses toiling over their machines. Is each of us inextricably linked to those we love? My heart pounds at the hope that Orsi might think of me today, perhaps even miss me, if only for a moment. Yet it's likely that if she thinks of me at all, it will only be in boredom, reminded by a sneeze or a carton of leftover Chinese food that she throws in the trash. The past is only one of many possible futures.

CHAPTER 30

I SET off on a long walk, and determine to make two left turns for every right. Everything in life is a problem atop a problem, I think. Even the promise of a lifetime of love pales in comparison to James' accomplishment of sparing Orsi's father his doom in prison. The thrill of love fades quickly. The sting of it lost is forever.

Louis calls from Denver. I thought I'd heard the last of him when he and his family forced me to celebrate my birthday. And that he pretended not to remember our rooftop death match is simply a bridge too far. Nothing would please him more than to convince me I'd simply conjured the event from whole cloth. I must maintain an offensive position, not because I seek to cause harm or take revenge, but as a matter of self-preservation. He has, after all, defeated me at every turn thus far.

"Hi, Paul," he says. "Do you have a minute?"

His voice cracks, surely a ploy to make me think he's been crying and thereby suck even more from me than he already has.

"What is it, now, Louis?"

"I just wanted to share the good news. Kayleigh is pregnant. We're finally going to have the little girl we've always dreamt of."

"No wonder you're crying," I say.

"Tears of joy, Paul!"

"Three kids is a lot. Don't you think it's a bit irresponsible?"

Louis takes a breath so affected and loud I have to pull the phone from my ear.

"Every child is a tremendous responsibility," Louis says,

"and not one we take lightly. I must confess, it wasn't a planned pregnancy. To be honest, I was shocked at the news. Did I ever tell you about my vasectomy? I had to sit on a bag of frozen peas for a week. But my little baby girl's will-to-be-conceived overcame the best medical science has to offer. And yes, there's the financial considerations. Of course, you know that I recently received a promotion at the hardware store, but it's not as much money as you might think. We're going to have to do a lot of belt-tightening," Louis says, and chuckles. "I'm sorry to say there won't be any more vacations to New York City anytime soon. Not that we didn't have a great time. The boys had an absolute blast at Coney Island. I don't care who you are, nothing beats a Ferris wheel. And truthfully, I couldn't have been prouder seeing your art. Who cares that your sculpture didn't get included in the show?"

As Louis rambles on, my antipathy grows. My eyes blink rapidly, something they do whenever I'm bored. The fragrance of earth and trees fills my nose. A team of ants crosses my path carrying a morsel of discarded pretzel. An acorn falls to the ground with a thud. Everywhere I look I'm reminded of the goodness of nature's bounty. The sun is in the west, now, my shadow getting longer.

"And we'd be honored," Louis says, finally, "if you would be our little girl's godfather! What do you say?"

My hearing has always been as keen as a cat's. Somewhere nearby, one of God's creatures is meekly groaning. I cast about, looking for the source of this petition, and sure enough, in a patch of overgrown grass, I find a dying chipmunk.

"I'm sure everything will work out just fine, Louis," I say. "But I'm very busy right now. I have to go."

I take the chipmunk into my hands and consider the journey it has travelled. Looking into its face, I see we share a striking resemblance, not physically, but spiritually. It's clear that this poor creature suffers from crushing loneliness and no longer has any reason to go on. I stay with it until long past dark, soothing it as best I can as it passes from this world. When it's gone, I give it a proper burial. My only regret is that I lack the power to exorcise its sins.

CHAPTER 31

THIS MORNING, a bike messenger delivers an official invitation to an orientation for the Pure Cosmos Club. The invite is printed on gilded paper and decorated with hand-drawn pictures of distant planets and Christian saints. The note promises the opportunity to learn how to "transcend daily life by tapping into the universal mind." The event is today at noon, which is just as well, because I don't imagine I'll have any luck getting anything done at the studio, where Winston has the seamstresses working double-shifts.

James has converted an old prosthetic limbs factory into a modern-day ashram. The open floor plan has been renovated to form a lotus flower and is decorated in yellows and pinks. At the entrance, James has installed a koi pond in which three lily-white swans languidly drift. Silk tapestries embroidered with images of James holding hands with Lord Krishna hang from the walls. A woman with the face of an aristocrat rushes to chaperone me to the grand meeting hall, where James is standing on a podium that appears to float. Dozens of people are kneeling in orderly rows. The diversity of the audience is striking, men and women, young and old, across the spectrum of a rainbow. I take my position on a prayer rug behind a man and his granddaughter, their hands raised in praise.

"You have all come today," James says, his face like an ascetic's, "because you are children separated from your mothers. You long for the company of saints, but they remain hidden. You've met those who've promised to deliver truth, but have failed. Their path was not righteous. Theirs was a false God, apocryphal! But, here, together as one, we can overcome this evil. We are each endowed with the inner knowledge of the true God with which we can create the consciousness of our own salvation. Repeat after me: I won't be truly happy until I've been deprived of my illusory happiness!"

The audience intones James' mantra. "I won't be truly happy until I've been deprived of my illusory happiness!"

James possesses what must be a divinely conferred gift of persuasion. He sparkles like a diamond. Even so, my suffering is too great. How can mere high-minded speeches of celestial goodness cure me? Only a miracle, I think, can lift me from my sadness.

"Again!" James says. "Louder!"

"I won't be truly happy until I've been deprived of my illusory happiness!"

Again and again, the acolytes chant James' mantra. Their voices form a booming harmony that threatens to penetrate my steely heart. Reluctantly I chant, too, but my words are still my own, separate from the greater whole. Even when I join hands with my neighbors and sway with them, the spirit fails to move me.

Later, we're led into another room with tables attended by Senior Advisors of the Pure Cosmos Club. I'm weary of this mystical voodoo, and yet I have nowhere else to go.

Ahead of me, a man chewing on mints from a silver tin and buzzing with energy introduces himself as Amol. He made his fortune from a software program he wrote in his college dorm room, then sold to a behemoth tech company. After buying matching Lamborghinis for him and his boyfriend, and a second home in Aspen, he regrets to report that becoming fabulously wealthy by the age of twenty-three had left him spiritually adrift. He took a year off to work the land in Big Sur using sustainable farming practices. Growing his own carrots and kale was rewarding, he said, but came nowhere near curing him. It wasn't until he met James at a retreat in the Bahamas for Silicon Valley tech executives that he found what he'd been searching for.

"Did you know that James can calibrate his frequency to affect the weather?" Amol says.

A Senior Advisor has his paperwork ready for Amol. It's been determined, after a careful review of his financials, that advancing to the next level in his journey will require a donation of one hundred and sixty-two thousand dollars. Amol asks the Senior Advisor if there's a discount for paying for the next two levels upfront. The Senior Advisor makes some calculations, then consults with his colleague beside him. "Level-2 Attainment," the Senior Advisor says at last, "can be expedited for an additional forty thousand dollars." The transaction complete, the Advisor points Amol in the direction of the photo studio.

As for my own paperwork, things aren't so clear, the Senior Advisor says. "The financial statements we've procured indicate you don't have any assets."

"I own nothing in this world of material value."

"I'm afraid your presence here is a mistake. There are minimum financial baselines required to advance through our program of cosmic oneness."

"That's okay," I say. "Will you be serving lunch?"

The Senior Advisor waves over a member of the Pure Cosmos Club's legal team. A non-disclosure agreement is produced. By stepping onto this hallowed ground, it says, I've tacitly acknowledged that any disclosure of information about the Pure Cosmos Club will result in legal damages upwards of, but not limited to, three million dollars. Just as I'm about to sign, James appears. He snatches the agreement and tosses it away, then censures both of the Senior Advisors. They apologize like children and are led away by two men in black robes.

"I'm so sorry," James says. "My retainer mistook you for someone else. He'll spend the next three days in continuous penance."

"Just point me to the buffet, and I'll be on my way."

"We'll feed your body soon," James says, "but first we must feed your soul."

James links arms with me and escorts me to the photo studio. New members are instructed to take off their shoes and belts before stepping behind the curtain. When the shoot is over, the members return looking astonished and confused. I peek through a crack in the curtain to see a naked Amol striking a series of lewd poses while the photographer shoots. An assistant soon brings out a pygmy goat on a rope.

"What are they going to make Amol do with that goat?" I ask James.

"These photographs are just a way for new members to enhance their fidelity."

"But, James, I have a terrible fear of goats."

"When it's your turn, simply do whatever feels right."

The curtain opens and Amol walks out radiating incorporeal delight. The assistant calls me in.

"You promise that if I get my photo taken, there will be lunch after?" I say to James.

"My little *Voltairean* doubter," James says, holding my face, "once your picture is taken, you will feast like never before."

The photographer speaks to me in soothing tones, instructing me to undress. The theme of the shoot is "arctic expedition," the photographer says, and directs me to lie with a rifle as sensuously as possible on a polar-bearskin rug. After the shoot, I review the images. The sense of intimacy and vulnerability they convey evokes feelings stirred by a Modigliani portrait.

"Do you feel purified of your sins?" James says on my return.

"It turned out quite well," I say. "Let's eat!"

I join Amol in the packed dining hall for the most opulent smorgasbord I've ever seen. By the time I've finished, ideas that are obviously false seem somehow truer.

CHAPTER 32

THE OTHER Level-1 students and I have been paired off in groups of two and dropped deep in the woods of the Adirondacks to forage and hunt for ourselves while drawing for strength on the universal power to which James has given us access. Not since boyhood in Colorado have I witnessed life so pure. The mountain air is crisp, and golden leaves crunch delightfully underfoot. An eagle soars overhead with a fish in its talons. Deer drink from the babbling brook. I've been taken by senseless rapture.

Because of his zeal, Amol has been exposed to advanced teachings. His wisdom and guidance have helped to silence the little voices in my head. Last night, I got so cold that I questioned why James had sent us out here without sleeping bags or tents.

"You are a sheep, Paul, and must do everything you can to please the shepherd!"

Hours later, I'd lost all feeling in my arms and legs. The pain had simply disappeared.

This morning James has gathered us all on the banks of a roaring river. Each of us, he says, is to swim across, one by one. When a man asks whether we'll have lifejackets, James assures us that our faith itself will keep us safe. Amol volunteers to go first and steps gingerly to the edge. To our horror, no sooner has he entered the water than he's swept away with a pitiful scream, his arms and legs flailing. We call out to him, "Just believe harder!" though above the deafening roar it's certain he can't hear us. We stand by helplessly as Amol's head disappears in the raging current. There's nothing of him as he rounds a bend downstream but a weakly flapping hand.

Two kayakers appear expertly navigating this torrent. If there's anyone who can save Amol, it's them. James reminds us that now is the time to master our instincts, which in truth are merely social conventions turned against us. None of us tries to signal the kayakers, but, with James' approval, simply cheer as they pass. Once they're out of sight, our morale plummets. A young man with thick black glasses and narrow shoulders wants to call the police.

"What do you think happened here just now?" James says.

A pimply-faced teenager raises her hand. "Amol wasn't a true believer," she says.

"James is a charlatan and sent Amol off to die!" yells a bald man with a cane.

How it starts, I can't say, but soon the group is in open brawl, everyone punching, kicking, even biting. It goes on— men attacking women, women attacking children, parents against their own sons and daughters—until as quickly as it started, it ends.

James speaks to us in the hushed tones of a librarian as everyone lies about, tending to their wounds.

"I'm not disappointed in any of you," he says. "My love is too strong. You have yet to fully grasp my teachings. But you must know that until you abandon the false values you were raised on, and fully embrace my principles, you'll never be truly free. The river," he says, pointing across the river, at a smiling Amol, "saw the truth in Amol's heart and carried him safely to its other side."

As one, we bow our heads and begin to chant. "I won't be truly happy until I've been deprived of my illusory happiness!"

At sunset, James leads us to a mountaintop, where we gorge ourselves on a decadent meal prepared by the legendary Argentine chef Francis Mallmann, after which, beneath a sliver of yellow moon, commune around a fire. An owl hoots emphatically somewhere nearby, an auspicious omen, indeed, Amol says.

"Before everyone falls asleep," James says as he hands out very welcome blankets and pillows, as well as notebooks and pens, "I have one last thing to ask."

We are each to write a "commitment note" in which we promise to do anything James asks of us. He reminds us what happened earlier when we foundered.

"Practically speaking," I say, "are you suggesting we ought to give our lives, if that were your wish?"

Everyone stops to listen, even Mallmann, who until now has been cleaning up from dinner.

"In your note," James says, his gaze filling me with the comfort I feel in the presence of an airline pilot, "write what's in your heart."

I fill my notebook with words of profound dedication. Long after everyone else has fallen asleep, I scribble out page after page. I'm hardly interested in quibbling over the details that distinguish memory from fiction. I don't feel at all guilty for writing how I once trudged eleven miles through a Colorado blizzard to return a package delivered to me by mistake. A true story isn't meant to instruct, or to encourage virtue. What's important is I told my tale amusingly. By the time I'm finished, at sunrise, I feel the joy of a beggar.

James isn't by the fire, or in his tent, but at the river, stretching out after a sixteen-mile run. His training for the upcoming marathon is right on schedule, he says. I present him my notebook, over thirty pages of words. He's pleased I'm taking my spiritual journey seriously. He sees in me, he says, a man capable of a "gentle tyranny." I'm overjoyed that this most intriguing man hasn't merely recognized me, but considers me worthy of his time. I look over my shoulder as I make my way back to camp to see James reading my notebook as he does one-armed push-ups.

"The lengths you'll go to so as not to be alone are astounding!" he shouts. A single tear runs down my cheek.

CHAPTER 33

A COCKROACH as long as my thumb scurries across my pillow and wakes me. It's four in the morning, and the studio is still for the first time in weeks. The seamstresses finally completed their work on the cat-bags and are now halfway over the Atlantic. Blanche and Winston are exhausted. The executives at Inès are so impressed with them that they're considering how to keep them for future endeavors.

I set about gathering material for a new sculpture—a cat ear, a tail, a shopping cart, frayed manila rope, the shattered remains of dozens of champagne bottles, a box of silver buttons, two bowling balls, and Winston's discarded leather boots. My process feels guided by an almighty hand. Perhaps I'm feeling the touch of Jesse, my dead friend? Either way, it's not for me to question my inspiration.

Disinclined to wake my friends, I work by the light of a kerosene lamp. My good intentions become moot, however, once I ignite my welding torch. Blanche and Winston yawn and rub their eyes. Blanche unplugs my electric sander while Winston dumps my circular saw into the toilet.

By mid-morning I'm pleased with my work and full of pride. And yet I'm leery of foolish happiness, as well, the disease of our time. At the very least, the condition is compatible only with youth, and mine has long since vanished.

Danny kicks open the studio's door, then summersaults and flips across the room. The cat-bag collaboration, he announces, is an unqualified success. Clarisse Goncourt, the artistic director at Inès, just sent Danny a bouquet of daffodils with a note. "Not since Rembrandt's *Self-Portrait with Two Circles*," Goncourt wrote, "has an artist set himself so far apart from his contemporaries!"

Danny's rapture, however, ends as suddenly as it began when he lays eyes on my sculpture. "Having been brought up without religion," he says, "I've never known God. Yet here I am, somehow, a humble supplicant in the court of truth!"

Blanche and Winston are as stupefied as Danny at the sight of my sculpture of James piloting a spaceship. I, Danny says, have been transformed, and not merely artistically, but physically, as well. My posture is erect, my shoulders no longer hunched. I have found, at last, Danny explains, an "appropriate burden," without which, he insists we will be forever shackled.

Danny demands to know the source of my passion, as if I could explain. His base deficiency lies in his fixation on universal truths.

"I can't say what you want to know. What good can come from stripping life of its mysteries, Danny?"

He and I once argued bitterly over basic math after burgers at a diner. Danny had offered to pay the tab of thirty-seven dollars, and asked me to leave the tip. I was flush with cash that day, after a victory at the racetrack, and laid out sixty-four dollars.

"Twenty percent," Danny said with annoyance, "is standard. Seven or eight dollars will be plenty."

"You obviously failed to carry the one," I said. "Sixty-four dollars is right."

Danny scoffed and stuffed the bills into my pocket. But after he'd turned away, I tucked them under my plate. I simply could not accept his blindness to other universal possibilities.

With my hot-glue gun, I adhere two costume-jewelry rhinestones to the face of my sculpture—James' far-seeing eyes.

"I've long feared that the kingdom was lost," I say, "and that good was no longer possible. But the silly superstitions and hypocrisy of mundane law that have till now led me into dead ends are no more than apparitions, I see."

Danny's joy has vanished. He wishes he'd never borne witness to my success, he cries, which is his undoing. Certainly, his cat-bag collection is now tainted. The prestige he'd been so sure of garnering would only ever ring false to him. He commands Winston and Blanche to burn every bag. Winston disagrees, assuring Danny that the work is "brilliant" and "innovative," and Blanche howls dismayingly, but Winston retrieves a canister of gas from the supply closet anyway. Danny's sullenness has deafened him to reason. But as Danny steps to his display of bags, he trips over one of Blanche's wheels and drops the canister of gas, spraying the stuff all over my new sculpture. Only God knows how, but a spark somehow ignites, and before our gaping eyes my sculpture is engulfed in flames. In a matter of moments my sculpture is a pile of ash.

"What rotten luck!" Danny says, his spirits instantly lifted.

He takes out a stack of hundred dollar bills and counts out three thousand dollars on the table, enough to pay us to pack and ship his cat-bags to Inès' showroom in Paris. Anything extra is ours to keep, Danny says. Before Danny leaves, Winston asks him whether I should be compensated for my sculpture.

"The past is unimportant," Danny says, looking contentedly at the burnt remains. "What's the difference between *exists-no-longer* and *has-never-existed*?"

After staking out such a contrarian position against Danny's artistic judgment, it would be impossible to argue for reparations without making myself look like a hypocrite and an imbecile.

"It's better that the sculpture is gone," I say, reaching for a broom. "It was just something I threw together this morning. By tomorrow, I'll have made six pieces that are far better."

Winston and I spend the rest of the morning packing Danny's bags. Before we set off for the post office, Winston insists we eat. His blood-sugar is low, from his ill-treated diabetes. While he warms up a pot of last night's borscht, I sit with a book in the salvaged recliner. It's Andrew Roberts' Churchill biography, *Walking with Destiny*, nearly twelve hundred pages long. What an incredible life this man must've led to have had so many words written about him. My own puny accomplishments over thirty-seven years are scarcely enough to cover one side of a cocktail napkin. Churchill, I learn, defied John Maynard Keynes in returning Britain to the gold standard, and rashly supported Edward VIII during the abdication crisis. His combination of extreme courage and poor judgment must be unrivalled by anyone else in history. As Winston swirls a dollop of sour cream into our bowls, I recite a miscellany of attributes about history's finest Briton.

"And did you know," I conclude, "Churchill took sixty bottles of alcohol with him when he set out for the Boer War?"

Winston serves a side of corn muffins with the soup, then takes the book. He runs his fingers along its pages and begins to weep. "My parents' greatest gift was to name me after this preeminent statesman."

He wipes away his tears and apologizes for his mawkishness. As a child, Winston used to recite the transcripts of Churchill's wartime speeches. Even now, he admits, he gets goosebumps thinking about it. He shows me his arm, and indeed, it's covered in bumps.

Winston's too emotional to drive, but, worried I'll seek retribution against Danny for destroying my sculpture, he's reluctant to let me get behind the wheel. I assure him that nothing could be further from my mind. The driving force behind my creativity has nothing to do with competition. The universe has decided that today is Danny's, not mine. How can I fault him? Anything I can do to help Danny is reward enough. Winston turns away with a pained grimace.

"Don't flaunt your nobility at me!" he says.

The clouds have given way to a thin autumn sun. The van sputters as we crest the top of a rise. Winston and I marvel at the tremendous vista of New York City across the river. I catch my reflection in the rearview mirror. My eyes are wide and dreamy. The stoplight turns, and I step hard on the accelerator. The van hurtles away, and my stomach floats into my chest. The retail storefronts and bus stop benches whirl past. We zoom by car after car as the van's speedometer reaches eighty miles per hour. The stoplight ahead turns yellow, then red, but when I pump the brakes, there's nothing. A class of kindergarten children step into the crosswalk ahead, holding hands, their teacher leading them in song. Winston reaches for the door handle, but I engage the lock.

"Have you decided that it's time for us to die?" Winston says.

A voice not unlike James' enters my head to say there's no more empty feeling than the fulfillment of all life's desires. I close my eyes and take my hands from the wheel. The screeching of car horns and shrieking of children quiets my nerves. I am relaxed, even serene.

Winston reaches for my hand, and cries out, "I don't pretend to understand your motives, but I have complete faith in your judgment!"

I feel the van hop the curb, then a sudden impact, then stillness, and I open my eyes. The van, I see, had hopped a curb, and crashed through the plate-glass window of a mattress store. Against all odds, no one's been injured. The backdoor of the van swings open. Winston's face is white as Christmas snow.

"It's unbelievable," he says. "Not a single bag has been damaged."

The two of us break down in tears of joy. We've experienced a miracle.

CHAPTER 34

THAT AFTERNOON, I visit the Pure Cosmos Club. James is preparing for his sermon with an exercise routine. He does one hundred sit-ups without breaking a sweat, then launches into a set of lunges, all as I relate the story of our crash.

"Of course you were safe, my son," James says once I've finished. "I was there protecting you."

The gods have always been cruel and merciless, with not one stich of kindness in their lot. As one of fate's many pawns, I don't pretend what I do in this life matters. My fortune was written in the celestial ledgers. Nevertheless, I can't help but to wonder why I was spared this biblical terror. The sun's rays pour through the stain-glass windows above, bathing James in near-heavenly radiance.

"Do you believe I've been chosen for a special purpose?" I say.

"You have the power to become whatever you seek to be," James says, and takes his place in the pulpit.

The sanctuary is filled with followers preserved in their sins. A collective emotion imbues the air. The minds of one and all are determined to find peace, no matter the cost, and James' warm smile offers this—the promise of salvation.

"Who amongst you seeks deliverance?" James says. Like second graders, everyone throws up their hand. "This is wonderful!" James says benevolently. "Because I can help you achieve it. You must know, however, that it will require everything of you!"

James describes how from now on, to reflect our genderless,

non-dualistic self, we are all to dress in uniforms of loose-fitting, khaki pants and long, high-buttoned shirts. We are additionally required to become celibate. He himself, James says, has not had sex in over five years, a sacrifice, he now knows, that was prerequisite to his witnessing the inner truth of the Book of Revelation.

Orsi stands away from us, on the far side of the room, her jaw clenched, and her hands balled into fists. It's now that I remember my night in the attic of Danny's family villa, watching through a crack in the floorboard as James and Orsi made love. The thought brings me to the cusp of oblivion. Like a man in the clutches of his Tourette's syndrome, I begin helplessly to jerk and curse. When everyone turns to stare, I hum a gospel song I remember from childhood. I am, I realize, on the verge of a complete psychic breakdown. Why not embrace an all-or-nothing morality? If only I can accept James' assertion of celibacy, my suffering will end. It may even be the case that I hallucinated James and Orsi in the throes of ecstasy. Who, really, am I to say? I focus deeply, bearing down with all my strength on the ultimate primacy of the unseen over the seen, until my well-being is restored.

After the sermon, a Senior Advisor instructs me to surrender the suit that Sal tailored for me, and don my new uniform. My underwear, the Senior Advisor notes, leading me to the communal wardrobe, is riddled with holes. The Senior Advisor hands me my uniform and a pair of drawers, then tosses my beautiful suit into the incinerator.

"All is one," the Senior Advisor says, "one is all."

For an hour, I sit in grief before the incinerator. The commotion of Senior Advisors feeding more of the congregation's personal affects into the fire does nothing to break me. My life's efforts have been obliterated.

When after a long while I open my eyes, James is next to me. "Now repeat after me," he says. "'I want what you want.'"

His gaze is too much, and I turn away, but he takes my chin and lifts my face.

"I want what you want," I say.

"Say it again: 'I want what you want.'"

"I want what you want."

This goes on well into the evening, until I'm shouting at the top of my lungs, "I want what you want! I want what you want! I want what you want!" Another member brings me a glass of water, but James slaps it from my hand when I try to take a sip. Unbeknownst to me, the entire congregation has encircled us, holding hands as they sway to the rhythm of my declarations. Not once during the hours of my inculcation has James broken eye contact nor so much, it seems, as blinked. At last, at midnight, James dismisses the others. He wants to speak with me in private. I've coasted long enough without paying up, he says. My freeriding sets a bad example for the others. It's time I make an earnest financial benefaction to the Pure Cosmos Club.

"How much?" I say.

The number James quotes is disconcerting. For the benefits I've received thus far, James says, a contribution in the six-figure range is more than warranted. It's with no small amount of humiliation that I remind him of my financial woes.

"Perhaps I can offer you another painting?" I say.

"The sums I can fetch for your paintings aren't nearly enough, I'm afraid."

James, I learn, has already sold my bird painting for fifteen thousand dollars.

"That's more than I've made selling all my work combined," I say. "With that kind of money, I could afford to sleep in a real bed and buy my food from an actual store!"

James is disappointed in these selfish "material concerns" of mine. Real penance, he says, must entail my delivering to him an extreme sum of money.

"But how?" I say.

James' solution is so simple I'm ashamed I didn't think of it myself. All I have to do is convince Danny to join the Pure Cosmos Club. A donation from him would be more than enough to cover both of us.

CHAPTER 35

THE SKY is cloudless, but the sun is so weak I can barely feel its warmth. This morning Blanche and Winston left for a weekend getaway in the Catskills, a much-deserved vacation after their long hours lashing the seamstresses for Danny. For days, they made detailed preparations, mapping out trails to hike, creating shopping lists for gourmet meals, choosing board games to play during their cozy nights. It was kind of them to invite me along, but I didn't feel right about imposing. As they loaded the rental car, they expressed their concern for me. Blanche had found me in the alley scraping the skin from my thigh with a rusty razor. I reassured her and Winston saying this was an ancient homeopathic remedy for treating allergies.

Besides, I really do have work to accomplish. To start, I've volunteered my services to build a shed for the Pure Cosmos Club, whose design James and I created over the last week. The shed must be fortified with a concrete basement, James said.

"Like a bunker?" I said.

"Just a place with impenetrable walls where I can stay in case of an attack by the government."

Of course, I'm quite eager to demonstrate my value to James. My building skills I learned from my high school shop teacher, Mr. Beardsley. I can still picture his face—eyes bulging like a Boston Terrier, comb-over flapping, his frayed denim shirt tucked neatly into his frayed denim chinos—as he showed me how to work a belt sander with hands as manly as could be, despite the missing fingers on one, caused by a congenital birth defect.

I've asked Danny to deliver a ladder to the jobsite, a ruse to get him to join me. Once he sees how happy and well-adjusted I've become, he'll surely want to join the Pure Cosmos Club himself. Not to sound grim, but if it weren't for the Pure Cosmos Club, I'm not sure I'd have any reason to carry on. I've spent the last few days wading through a fog of emptiness, and my nights have been thick with anxiety and terror. To sleep, I've had to chew upwards of thirteen pieces of bubble gum.

By late afternoon, I've dug a large pit and am now ready to build the forms for the concrete. Despite the day's coolness, my face is badly sunburned, and several times already, mysteriously, I've broken down weeping. When Danny arrives in a brand-new pickup, I slap myself hard across the face, a reminder to smile for him. How else will he know how wonderful life is in the Pure Cosmos Club? Danny saunters to the pit, unzips his fly, and starts to pee.

"My father," he says, "forced me to take another drug test this morning."

"But you take drugs all the time!" I say, my spirits lifting. His getting caught using illicit substances could only send Danny spiraling, at which point he'd be vulnerable to the charms of salvation here at the Pure Cosmos Club.

"Not to worry," Danny says, shaking it out and putting it away. "I've got an inside guy at the lab."

I describe my project to Danny, who, surprisingly, thinks it's a fantastic idea. Like all children born to fabulously wealthy parents, he has a fierce libertarian streak in him, and is hell-bent on protecting his fortune from the government.

"James will be able to stockpile a massive arsenal of weapons down here!" Danny says.

We climb into the pit and set to work building the forms. I've rehearsed a speech about all the remarkable things one can see from the fringes of society—experiences and revelations not accessible to those still lulled by the false comforts of modernity—and deliver it to Danny as though my ideas are random musings.

"The mind," I say, "is never ready for seismic events. We must listen to our heart!"

I remind Danny of how impressed he was with my sculpture of James in his spaceship. He had been right all along, I say, about my having finally found my "appropriate burden," which has unshackled my potential and set free my imagination.

"Ah, yes," he says, "such a pity your sculpture was burned."

"Danny," I say, and drop my hammer. "My point is I no longer need the love of Blanche, or Orsi, or even Janie. I have the Pure Cosmos Club, now, a rock like no other!"

Danny climbs out of the pit to sit on the tailgate of his truck and smoke his hand-rolled cigarettes. "That's all well and fine for someone like you. But I drink champagne for breakfast. I sleep with models. I travel the world and go dancing every night."

Like most artists, Danny has a heart of stone, but is easily upset. When I remind him how shamefully indulgent it is to sleep with women he doesn't love, he flicks his cigarette in my face—a telltale sign he's still clinging to his primitive graces. How can I help my friend to realize he can't see the world as it is?

"Your resistance is reactive," I say. "I strongly suggest more forward thinking!"

Danny pulls his ladder from the pit and drives away. It strikes me that all too often success and failure are but mirror images, the difference being a matter of perspective.

CHAPTER 36

AFTER WEEKS of nonstop work, I complete the shed, and James conducts a ceremonial unveiling with a rousing speech to his followers.

"Holy spirits don't live in this world, my friends," he says, "they occupy it!"

He asks everyone to repeat another of his mantras. "I take refuge in my faith," we all say as one, "and thereby avoid the cruelties of this world!"

It's such a marvelous feeling to yield to one's impulses. My voice booms with conviction. James calls on me to join him at his podium. My work on the shed, he says, was an act of tremendous heart. His words fill me with joy and self-admiration. Not since the time I made Blanche a kite for her birthday, and she licked my face until her tongue went dry, have I felt so appreciated. James hands me a set of oversized shears, and I cut the ribbon around the white sheet over the shed. When the sheet falls, everyone cheers.

Eating cake after the ceremony, I'm seized by four Senior Advisors and led through a winding passage lit by candles, to a windowless dungeon filled with torture devices straight from the pages of medieval history books. The Senior Advisors ask why Danny wasn't at the ceremony. I invent a litany of excuses, all of them insufficient. A Senior Advisor forces me to the floor inside the circle they've formed, where I'm then interrogated. I make objection after feeble objection, but it's no use. My failure to deliver Danny to the fold, they say, has cast the Pure

Cosmos Club into dire jeopardy. Finally, the Senior Advisors leave me in the dark with a scroll of sins for which I must atone, foremost among them my financial dereliction.

CHAPTER 37

THE RAIN fell hard all night. A gray mist hangs outside the studio's window. Three days have passed since I was released from detention. I've filled a journal full of my treasonous thoughts. Something must be taking root because I am suffering terrible headaches. I'm comforted by the notion that my mind is transforming itself into something capable of manifesting its aims into existence.

Blanche no longer sleeps in the bed with me. She and Winston found a discarded futon mattress in a dumpster and have refurbished it. I lie down next to her on the futon, but she rolls away. I blow into her ear trying to wake her, then assume my best dead-man's pose. But Blanche never checks for a pulse or even to see if I'm still breathing. I eventually pass out from my efforts, and when I come to, Blanche is on her hind wheels by the stove, drinking French press coffee from a mug.

There's only one person I can go to for advice. I dress in my uniform and take a train into the city, only to get off at the wrong stop. A gust of cold wind chills my face. A street-sweeping truck blows past. Dust and debris cloud the air. Construction workers are lined up at a food cart for egg sandwiches and coffee. Steam pours from a manhole. The Hudson River plods slowly toward the Atlantic. Soon the streets become lined with lavish glass apartment buildings, luxury fitness centers, and gourmet coffee shops. At last, I reach my destination, a nineteenth century book-binding factory converted into extravagant condominiums. In the lobby there's a painting of a large-breasted, naked woman staring into oblivion. The concierge comes out from behind his desk and threatens to call the police. I tell him I'm here to see Amol.

"You're a friend of his, huh?" the concierge says with disdain.

"He and I once spent a night in the mountains and survived only by foraging for mushrooms and berries."

"Management will be thrilled to see the last of that guy," the concierge says. "After today, I don't ever want to see you here again."

The elevator door opens directly into Amol's penthouse apartment. The gallery foyer leads into a double-wide living room with floor-to-ceiling views of the river. Amol insists I remove my shoes. His white oak floors were just refurbished. The apartment exudes the woozy gray-gloom of New York City glamour. A stiletto-wearing woman—a cross between Cruella de Vil and Blake Lively—darts into the kitchen. In the sun through the skylight, she's like a ghost wearing skin. She barks instructions at a team of housekeepers about fluffing couch cushions and arranging the day's fresh bouquets. A private chef is already hard at work preparing hors d'oeuvres.

Amol's face has prematurely aged, but his eyes blaze like a wild animal's. He's the embodiment of mystical liberation.

"The open house doesn't start till noon," he says.

"You're selling this place?"

"I must free up funds for my celestial advancement, Paul."

With a bottle of champagne, we repair to the balcony, where Amol ignites a fireplace. His thoughts are myriad, from the chemical composition of the solar system to warnings of the war and destruction that will soon plague the Earth. He speaks of the promises of awakening, joy, unparalleled experiences for those who listen to and believe all that James has to offer.

"But so much of what James espouses," I say, "contradicts everything I know to be true."

A maid steps out to open a second bottle of champagne and refill our flutes.

"Don't you see?" Amol says. "It's precisely this conflicting evidence that increases the faith of the devout!"

"What happened that day at the river, when you escaped what we all believed was certain death?" I say.

"My near-drowning was no act. It was nothing short of a miracle. The river was deceptively shallow. No more than waist deep. Once I remembered James' teachings, I simply put my feet down, and walked to safety." -

The realtor appears to tell Amol the first potential buyer is here, the son of a Saudi oil baron. There's something menacing about the realtor, and I worry for Amol's welfare.

"Always be on the lookout for those who may not have your best interests at heart," I say, as Amol shows me to the elevator.

"I lived my whole life believing that fate rewarded those who work hard and are patient. But I've learned the mechanics of happiness need not be so complex. Do you understand?"

I nod, stupidly, as the elevator closes.

CHAPTER 38

WORD OF the sale of my bird painting has got out. A prominent film director saw the piece in his attorney's office and was so moved by it he rewrote the ending of his latest film, at enormous cost to the production company.

Now the director is in town and has requested a private showing of my work. Susan claims he's one of today's foremost collectors. "Not to mention," she said, "he's won two Academy Awards and his films have grossed over three billion dollars"

The night before the showing, Winston insisted we watch the director's debut film. He ordered pizza for us all and served three different flavors of popcorn. But while he and Blanche declared the film to be a "marvel of modern cinema," I was bored after ten minutes of watching a young boy stroll through the Russian countryside. For the rest of the film, I obsessed over a long-ago event involving my father and me.

His one real passion was the Crimean War. The Russians' defeat at the hands of the Ottomans and their French and British allies, he believed, was history's single greatest tragedy. For Christmas one year, he bought a rare copy of Tsar Nicholas I's diary, which foretold of the excruciating losses his forces would suffer to malnourishment and disease. The book meant more to my father than all the stars. Before dinner each night, he would read aloud passages describing the Ottoman's brutality, then force me to answer a series of arcane questions. When I failed to answer sufficiently, I was sent to bed hungry. On the night of my last day in fifth grade, my mother made me grilled cheese sandwiches, to celebrate. To prove my deficient education, however, my father demanded I explain why the terms of the Treaty of Paris had doomed Europe to a century of war. My impassioned defense of Ottoman rule enraged my father, and for it I received three smacks to the mouth and a night without my favorite meal.

I listened through the heating vents in my room as my father attacked my mother for "coddling" me. He threatened to withhold his taxes—why, he raged, should he waste his money when all it got his son was a third-rate education? I prayed to God that something awful should befall my father, and sure enough, later that night, drunk on cognac, he spilled his drink on the book and destroyed its first twenty pages.

Watching the director's paltry film, my only question was whether God had answered my prayer that night.

For the director's gallery visit, I've managed to produce but a minor sculpture, a gilded fishing rod made from toilet paper tubes, a plastic dolphin figurine, and pink dental floss. To limit my contact with outside forces, James has sent Orsi along to supervise. When she arrives in a black limo, I'm disconcerted to find her khaki uniform crumpled on the car's floor and her wearing a silk top with a severe décolleté.

"It seems you've developed a Stalinist view of art," Orsi says when she sees my sculpture.

"I've learned everything I could from the masters," I say, unwilling to meet her eyes, "and done exactly the opposite."

"The work does lend itself to the violent and depraved side of things," she says, and lights a cigarette.

The piece, I say, is meant to symbolize that in life we are all born with a hole in our beings that can't be filled with anything but the complete abandonment of our ambitions.

"It's bad enough that you're intent on displaying your personal tragedy," she says. "It's unforgivable you're so fixed on exhibiting it in cold blood."

I count the fire hydrants as we drive. Another cruel word from Orsi would break me irrevocably. When we arrive, Susan is waiting outside with a team of Dominicans to chaperone my sculpture. I browse the new art as we wait for the director to finish a call he's stepped away to take. There's a particularly bad painting of a woman on a bike, her bosoms and knees repulsive. A placard lists its sale price at two hundred and fifty thousand dollars.

"Practically a steal," Susan says. "The director just bought it a few minutes ago."

"He has interesting tastes."

"Decadence has its virtues," she says, turning to the director as he enters.

The director, appointed head to toe in shades of brown, refuses my hand. He's suffering a compromised immune system, he says, and can't expose himself to unnecessary risk. Susan recommends he visit her acupuncturist, a man known throughout the Xinjiang province for curing ailments that have baffled western medicine for decades. Appointments at his new Tribeca clinic are booked up for the remainder of the year, but the acupuncturist is a friend of Susan's, and she should be able to procure a slot. The director rejoices at Susan's offer. He's actually heard of this miracle worker and has been trying unsuccessfully to see him for months.

The director is anxious to hammer out a deal. He has a flight to New Brunswick, where he's scouting locations for a film about an eighteenth-century Maliseet Indian princess who developed a way to domesticate and breed beavers for the fur-trade. The whole time, he's got his eyes fixed on Orsi, who, for her part, is a willing interlocutor. She throws her hair back and laughs at the director's every word. At one point, when he suggests she visit the set, she even touches his knee.

"Why don't you take a closer look at the sculpture," I say, "to see if you'd like to make an offer?"

The director makes three laps around the piece, his face somehow malicious. After a tense moment, he shrugs his shoulders. "I'm not even sure what I'm looking at here."

"Isn't it obvious?" I say. "It's a golden fishing rod that's hooked a dolphin."

Orsi smiles and gives the director's hand a squeeze. "For me," she says, "this piece is saying that all God's creatures are obligated to live constrained by laws, subjugated to their determined natures. We, on the other hand, are unique. We have no limits. Moment by moment, we determine our own fate!"

"I see no need to look at it any further," the director says. "I have the utmost faith in this artist."

"For a piece of this caliber," Susan says, and suddenly I dread the idea of my name being attached to this work, "thirty-five is a more-than-fair price, I think."

"I'd rather throw it into the sea!" I say.

Orsi puts a finger to my lips. "What Paul is trying to say is that thirty-five thousand isn't nearly enough."

"What would you say is fairer?" the director says.

"We all know that in two years this sculpture will easily command a hundred thousand."

"Do we?" the director says, glancing at Susan.

"I'm disappointed in you," Orsi says. "I thought you were a man of judgment and foresight."

The director puffs up his chest. "I can offer sixty."

"You've got yourself a deal, pal!" I say, and slap the director hard on his back.

Susan draws up the paperwork, and we all sign it. The director nods in lieu of a handshake, and, for some reason—my profound joy, I suppose—I curtsy.

I'm ecstatic, as the limo returns to the studio, at the prospect of donating my newfound fortune to James' cause, but Orsi disagrees. In fact, she says, I ought to keep the bulk of the money, if not all of it. No one else is going to look after me, she says, and certainly not James. Sure that this is another loyalty test, I nevertheless insist on giving the entire sum to the Pure Cosmos Club.

CHAPTER 39

Now THAT I've made this first sizable contribution, I've been promoted from Level-1A to Level-1B, which automatically enrolls me in the Pure Cosmos Club's meal plan. From now on, I'm to take all my meals in the club's dining hall. A Senior Advisor lectures me that the average person wastes his energies in dozens of little ways, like shopping for and preparing food. These day-to-day expenditures distract a person from their life's mission. Meals at the club are a most ascetic affair. We follow the dietary rules of the Vinaya, a monastic code written by James himself. According to this code, we can only eat between the hours of dawn and noon.

For two weeks now I've had only turnips, lettuce, dark breads, cheese curds, and the occasional bowl of porridge. These new restrictions have been profound. Learning to tolerate hunger is the perfect training for suffering difficult emotions and physical pain.

Winston and Blanche are concerned about my weight loss. Two nights ago, when I undressed for bed, they gasped at my jutting ribs, stick-thin legs and arms, and concave chest. They were so alarmed that Winston pinned me to the floor while Blanche tried to force-feed me a pint of pistachio ice cream. Somehow, I managed to fend them off. Yes, I explained, it's hard to eat enough calories before midday, but the rewards of forgetting myself from then on far outweigh that disadvantage. I neglected to tell them about my mishap yesterday, of course, when I passed out on the street and knocked my head on the curb. The wound required several stiches, and, moreover, I suffered a mild concussion. The Senior Advisors are now allowing me a cup of tea with sugar and honey at sunset.

This morning, Winston prepares himself breakfast and politely asks if I'd like to join him.

"Hot lemon with a slice of tea would be wonderful!" I say.

The impact of this verbal slip is distressing. I break down like a hysterical child, kicking and scratching. I tear at my hair, and nearly swallow my tongue. Blanche has to lick my toes for twenty minutes to restore me.

I take a shower and brush my teeth, then stare into the mirror with my seething animal eyes. My hair has turned gray. Seeing that the devil lives in my deepest parts is the first step toward expelling him. I am so pleased by my spiritual progress that I decide to take a bike ride. Alas, I have no bike. Winston's never seen one at the studio, he says, to which I hiss about it having been stolen.

"What does it look like?" Winston says.

"I'll know it when I see it."

There were several bikes chained to the banister outside Orsi's apartment. Maybe that's where I left it?

On the train, no sooner have I sat beside two fast-food employees in their uniforms than they get up and move. They must be coming down with some illness they don't want to spread, I think. I drift off to sleep holding Orsi's marble and have a nightmare about my sixth-grade science fair. The first-place prize was a paid trip to space camp. At the time, I suspected I might be an alien with amnesia after crash-landing here on Earth. The answer to my return home, I was convinced, was at space camp. I spent months studying a physics textbook, hoping to learn the intricacies of lift. My aim was to build a paper airplane launcher. On a Wright Brothers calendar tacked up over my workbench in the garage, I marked off the days to the competition. But on the big day, I slept through my alarm clock and didn't wake up until dinnertime, and my coveted prize was awarded to Andrew Bolte, who had made an erupting volcano.

A nice woman wakes me up when the train reaches its final stop on the west side of town. Several dollar bills and a handful of change have mysteriously appeared in the pockets of my uniform.

Somehow Orsi knew I was coming. When I arrive, she's waiting at her window with a smile that fills me with nervous joy.

"James is away on club business," she says through the intercom.

"But I've only come to get my bike."

More than once, I need to catch my breath as I mount the stairs. Orsi is waiting in the hallway outside her door and looks appalled at the sight of me up close. It's hard to stand, I find, and in fact I'm so dizzy that I collapse into her arms.

"I can't find my bike," I say.

Orsi puts me in bed and takes my temperature, 103 degrees, then gets a bag of frozen carrots for my burning head. "I can't find my bike," I say, "I can't find my bike." Orsi disappears for a time and returns with a bowl of chicken noodle soup, which I spill across the bed when she tries to feed me.

"I know you're only a painter," Orsi says as she towels up the mess, "but you're smarter than all this."

I limply take her wrist, but she brushes me away.

"If you let me die with dignity," I say, "I'll sing your praises every day in heaven."

"You can't be so desperate as to believe all the lies you say."

"I'm a man of imagination," I say, and try to pull her onto the bed, "not of cold logic."

Orsi spends the day tending to me, forcing me to eat ice chips until my fever breaks. I tell her about the grand vision I once had, a life defined by some singular purpose and a final crowning achievement, that would make me a legend for all time.

"But the stars have led me astray!" I moan.

The mystical appeal of the accursed wanderer is now meaningless, I say. I just want to give myself over to someone else. Looking into Orsi's pretty eyes, notions of dignity and honor feel as distant as my childhood dreams.

I wake in the middle of the night to find Orsi asleep in a chair beside me. I rise and kiss her brow, and then I slip away.

CHAPTER 40

I'VE ALWAYS been a person who takes things lightly, never fearing the worst, even when it seems inevitable, but this morning I'm utterly shocked to find a stranger in my place at the table in the club's dining hall. His hands are clasped before him, and his eyes are closed as he silently mouths his morning prayers. The clean bald spot shaved from his crown imbues him with the peacefulness of a songbird.

"Pardon me, sir" I shout, and knock his porridge to the floor, "but that is my breakfast!"

He apologizes profusely, swearing he was only doing as he was told, yet I refuse these antics, reproving him that he can't possibly hope his ignorance of the law will excuse his guilt. A Senior Advisor arrives to investigate, and we explain. Apparently, just last week, the Senior Advisor says, the man deposited to the Pure Cosmos Club's coffers the entirety of his quarterly bonus from his job at Goldman Sachs—two hundred and twelve thousand dollars—a gesture of commitment and magnanimity I myself have come nowhere near. James, the Senior Advisor says finally, is waiting for me now in the butterfly conservatory. I would do well, the Senior Advisor says, not to test his patience.

I follow a songful stream, pass through a waterfall, and then a thicket of exotic foliage. James is sitting in the full lotus position amidst a flutter of monarchs, hundreds of them, like marigolds in the sky.

"You wanted to see me?" I say.

"The Creator felt sorry for the children of the world when

He realized their destiny was to grow old, wrinkled, fat, blind, and weak," James says. "This is why He gathered all the beautiful colors from the sunlight, flowers, and trees into a magical bag for His children. When the children opened the bag, butterflies flew out, and the children were enchanted."

"Life is tragic, and the world fragile," I say. "Existence is temporary. Happiness is a fleeting distraction."

"The only way one can avoid such an awful fate is to help others to avoid it, too."

"I am striving," I say.

"Danny is like a spoiled child basking in his false glory. He retreats from the world to hide his shame. We need to cure him of this hypocrisy."

My inability to bring Danny into the fold, I only now understand, is why I've been stripped of my rank. My place in the confederacy of the humbled has been confirmed. Can one ever recover from such a setback?

"Go with Danny to Paris for his fashion show," James says, and takes my hand. "Your task is to ensure it fails. His suffering a grand humiliation is the only way he'll abandon his materialist ways and set out on the path of renewal."

I've always believed that blind chance is responsible for everything in life. Now I see my future is written in the stars.

"If you fail," James says, "there will be no place for you here when you return."

A butterfly lands on the tip of my nose, then flies away. I scratch where it was and see on my finger a faint smudge of black.

CHAPTER 41

TODAY, I'M flying to Paris to sabotage Danny's runway show. It's so wonderful having purpose in one's life. I can't think of anything finer than helping a dear friend find cosmic oneness and true meaning.

Convincing Danny to hire me was no easy task. The man could murder God with his stubbornness. He made me give him a list of my most valuable skills—polishing rifles, holding my breath, guessing the number a person is thinking, and so forth. Throughout my pitch, Danny wore a pained expression that inspired me to press on. According to studies, the best way to persuade anyone is to appeal to their fear, so I reminded Danny of the "dark forces" at work in a country as socialistic as France. Blanche is the one who reminded me slyer men will always outwit slower men. If only she could've seen me there with Danny.

"You're as cunning as a lunatic!" he said finally and conceded.

I can't leave, however, until I've tended to my morning chores at the club. I arrive just after midnight, and by 7 a.m., I've scrubbed all the marble floors with a toothbrush, hand-washed twelve loads of communal underwear, peeled twenty pounds of parsnips, sorted eight new members' personal possessions for items to burn, and taught an introductory seminar on always directing one's curiosities inward. But just as I'm about to leave for the airport, a Senior Advisor summons me to their chambers. An inspection of my bag has revealed sacrilegious contraband—Andrew Roberts' Winston Churchill biography.

"Surely you're aware that such texts are not part of our program?"

"It's just a bit of light reading for the plane," I say.

"There can be no mixing of ideologies," the Senior Advisor says, and stamps the book, *Marked for Incineration*. "The lies in this book could easily undermine everything you've learned here."

"But how do you know what is true and what is a lie?"

"What is true is what serves the Pure Cosmos Club. Whatever harms it is a lie."

The Senior Advisor retrieves a stack of Pure Cosmos Club pamphlets. Every two weeks the pamphlets are amended to include James' newest epiphanies. Sometimes the revisions contradict the teachings of prior editions. In those cases, the outdated texts are deemed heresy—blasphemous propaganda planted by enemies of the club to subvert the teachings of the one true prophet, James.

The meeting keeps me so long that I miss my train to the airport and am forced to take a cab, a profligate expense I can't redress without confession in my Journal of Treasonous Thoughts. I haven't felt this guilty since the time I stole a winter coat from the Salvation Army after my father tossed mine out for taking up too much room in the closet. Even a boy on the verge of frost bite knows we can't get something for nothing.

At security, I tell the TSA agent that while I may look like the man in my passport photo, I am not him. The man in the picture is lost, whereas I am found. It's all in the eyes, I say, and pry open my lids so the agent can have a look. "Don't you see? The light in my eyes is completely gone!"

The agent turns red with frustration and calls in a colleague to sort me out. The rigmarole detains me further, and I am the last person on the plane before they close the gate. I pull back the curtain separating first-class from coach and see Danny, Winston, and Blanche drinking Dom Perignon from the bottle and stuffing their mouths with caviar. The flight attendant snaps the curtain shut and directs me to my seat at the rear, directly in front of the restrooms, as it happens.

A gigantic man wearing sweatpants stretched to their limit wants to use the facilities before takeoff. He's so large that despite my efforts I can't keep him from pressing into me. He emits a truly squishy fart that I'm sure everyone on the plane could hear, even over the rumbling of the engine. His face is one of sheer humiliation. A mother and young daughter exit the restroom and take their seats beside me. We all watch as the man tries to squeeze through the restroom door.

The young girl asks her mother if she can sit in the window seat, but the mother refuses. "Mommy likes to look at the clouds," she says. The girl rolls up the sleeves of her pink unicorn sweatshirt and begins to scratch uncontrollably. Already her arms were covered in blotchy marks. Now she's making new ones. Meantime, her mother really is transfixed by the puffy white tufts below us, so much so she seems impervious to her daughter's pain. When the flight attendant takes our orders, the mother orders two chardonnays, then downs them both while flipping through a magazine. She orders a third cup of wine, drinks it, and passes out against the window. The girl taps her mother on the shoulder, asking to go to the bathroom again, but the woman is out. I press the call button to alert the flight attendant. "I'd take her myself," I say, "but I'm afraid there could be legal ramifications." While the attendant escorts the girl, the woman wakes up, and complains about her empty cup.

"Your daughter had to pee," I say. "The flight attendant took her."

The woman pulls a bottle of Xanax from her purse and chews two of them, dry. When her daughter returns, she orders yet another glass of wine. The flight attendant is reluctant but can't summon the courage to say no. Now the mother is so chatty as to unburden herself to me. The purpose of their trip to Paris, she says, is to get her daughter as far away from the girl's father as possible.

"Is he abusive?" I say.

"Oh," the woman says, "he's far worse than that."

It soon grows clear that in fact the woman is kidnapping the child to extort money from her ex-husband. Apparently, she's pulled this same dastardly trick every couple of years, by way coercing from her ex ever higher alimony payments. The woman's therapist has convinced her that it was cruel and unusual punishment for her ex to have sold their "winter home" in West Palm Beach after the divorce.

"My ex claims he's on the brink of financial ruin," the woman says, "but he knows how much I hate New York winters!"

The more I learn about the woman's many misfortunes, the greater my sympathy for her. Halfway across the Atlantic, she's badly slurring her words and tapping my shoulder to emphasize her incomprehensible points. It's only a matter of time before she throws up violently. The flight attendant asks whether the woman needs help to the restroom, but the woman insists she's comfortable just where she is.

CHAPTER 42

A ROLLS-ROYCE delivers us to the Ritz Paris Hotel, where a bellhop in a blue uniform and cap escorts us through the lobby's corridor, past blue-and-gold draperies, gilded chairs, and furnishings in the style of Louis XVI. Danny has secured the famed Suite Impériale. At only twenty-seven thousand euros a night, he declares it to be the "best value" in town. Winston, Blanche, and I share a more modest room for a mere two thousand euros. Noticing the black smudges of ash caked onto my face from operating the incinerator this morning, Danny insists I freshen up before we meet for drinks. The bathroom's fixtures—golden swan faucet heads!— are absolutely first-rate, so I treat myself to a bubble bath. Luxuriating in the suds, I feel like the Duke of Windsor. Blanche barks outside the door. She needs help putting on her evening's attire, a bespoke cashmere sweater made by the team at Inès. Its specialty thread was hand-selected to compliment Blanche's brindle coat. Looking at her reflection in the mirror, she yelps with elation.

Winston wears a tuxedo borrowed from the concierge. He looks as cool as a young Jean Cocteau smoking on a balcony over a garden.

"You're not really going to wear that potato sack the whole time we're in Paris, are you?" he says, as I iron my uniform.

I don't dignify Winston's remark with a reply, but simply don my shirt. Blanche, for her part, pees on my leg.

We gather in front of the hotel's legendary Hemingway

Bar. As we wait for Danny, Winston tells the story of how the bar got its name.

"Hemingway was a war correspondent embedded with the US 4th Division troops when they landed on Normandy's beaches in 1944. For the next two months he stuck with the foot soldiers as they marched towards Paris. During that long slog across Europe, all Hemingway could think of was getting back to his favorite bar. In his diary at the time, he wrote, "When I dream of the afterlife in heaven, the action always takes place in the Paris Ritz!" Upon liberating the city, Hemingway and a band of Resistance fighters commandeered a jeep and stormed the Ritz with machine guns in hand. The hotel's manager informed Hemingway that the Germans had left long before and refused to allow them weapons in the hotel. Hemingway and his pals left their guns at the door, then proceeded to run up a tab of fifty-one martinis."

Danny arrives wearing his usual camouflage shorts and tie-dye tank-top, but with the flourish of an eagle feather in his headband.

"Monsieur Danny," the maître d' exclaims, "we didn't know you would be joining us this evening."

"Une table pour moi et mes amis!" Danny says.

"The bar is at capacity," the maître d' says, "but if you'll excuse me for just a moment, we will make accommodations."

The maître d' disappears, and we hear muffled shouting, followed by a woman's cries. In short order, an unfortunate-looking couple are scurried out of the bar by three members of the staff. Then the maître d' reappears to say our table will be ready soon. The man from the couple, newlyweds from Wisconsin on their honeymoon, is consoling his wife. From what I can make of it, the lovebirds had made their reservation sixteen months in advance and had only just begun to peruse the menu before the maître d' expelled them to make room for us.

I can see why the couple are so upset. This pocket-sized bar is still redolent with the gentlemen's club atmosphere of days when F. Scott Fitzgerald passed out here after too many gin rickeys. Hunting trophies line the walls, first edition novels, notes scribbled by Hemingway on coasters, a collection of American police badges. We sit in tufted leather armchairs. Colin Field—the guardian of the temple—sends over a round of his signature cocktail, the Serendipity.

"I'm sorry," I say, "but could I trouble you for a tea with honey?"

The waiter sneers as he turns, cursing under his breath. Winston empties a bowl of warm almonds into his pocket, then fills the bowl with my drink and gives it to Blanche.

"You have become a petty masochist, it seems," Danny says.

"Happiness is boring, Danny," I say. "Someday, maybe, you'll see."

"You know, I don't think I've ever met anyone whose every word is so disagreeable."

For the next thirty minutes I evangelize about James and the Pure Cosmos Club, taking extra care to use formal and esoteric language. There's no mystery in everyday speech. The plain manner with which postmen and grocers talk forces us to understand their every intention. Through James' benevolence and deep sagacity, I say, I've seen the secret wonders of the universe. Danny needn't inhabit a world in which the divine can't be found, I say. He can cultivate the conditions for his salvation here and now, if only he abandons the profane morals of our day. Most imperative of all, I stress, we must develop our capacity for illusion.

"Tell me," Danny says, "just how far does your loyalty to James extend?"

"If he were to order me to enter a gladiator's ring to battle with a tiger," I say, and sip my tea, "I would do so without a word."

Danny has drunk four cocktails and is waving his arms like a man lost at sea. He'd gladly shelter in the dark of ignorance, he says, were it to further his ambition.

"So, you are beginning to see," I say. "It's time to return God to his throne!"

A leggy blonde in a mini-skirt enters the bar on the arm of a man who is plainly a Russian oligarch. Danny turns positively gleeful.

"There are five pleasures everyone needs to be happy—sex, food, sport, relaxation, and accomplishment. The first four I have in spades. After tomorrow's show, I'll have the fifth, as well."

Danny tells us he's invited the provocateur of French letters, Michel Houellebecq, to dine with us. "He's the only man in Europe with a scrap of sense," Danny says. Initially, Houellebecq refused the invite, but changed his mind when Danny told him they'd be dining at La Tour d'Argent. I've never read Houellebecq, though I've heard about his scathing depictions of contemporary French anomie—just the sort of thinking James has cautioned me against. Citing extreme fatigue, I retire to our room to plan my sabotage of Danny's show.

I do all my best thinking while asleep, but I haven't any bubble gum to help me unwind. Having grown accustomed to sleeping on broken picture frames and dirty tarps, moreover, five minutes of repose on the hotel's premium Temper-Pedic mattress sends my back into excruciating spasm. I turn on the television to watch a political debate. I can't understand anything, but am quite taken with the modest, almost motherly image of the blonde politician holding forth. The man she's debating—quite young and handsome in his pinstripe suit, and reeking of health, vigor, and physical prowess—is definitively unappealing.

Perhaps a short walk might help my back, I think, and head out into the brisk night. A pack of French teenagers are flirting in the square outside the Louvre. A street vendor peddles berets. Every café teems with people guzzling wine. Peering in through the iron gate at the Jardin des Tuileries, I spy Rodin's sculpture "Le Baiser," and recall how the great master said, "The mind draws, the heart sculpts." I wander the banks of the Seine, past a band of guitarists on a blanket plucking out gypsy songs, through the coin-dropping tourists, and by a man behind his easel drawing caricatures for a mere thirty-five euros. A tour boat passes under a graffiti-covered bridge. I walk and walk, the means by which to humiliate Danny nowhere in sight.

A toothless, sickly man slouches in a chair before the gate to the Passy Cemetery, swearing to anyone who'll listen that he's the great-great grandson of Claude Debussy. "My great-great grandfather's dying wish," he tells me, after humming a few bars of "Clair de Lune," "was to be buried amongst the birds and trees." He now spends his evenings guarding the great composer's resting place from thieves. I beg him to give me a tour of the cemetery, and he's happy to oblige. "Here you'll find the tomb of Tristan Bernard," he says, pointing at a decrepit headstone, "and over there rests the famed statesman, Jean Giraudoux." Both the old man and I grow tired, and we sit on a bench. Within minutes, he's asleep, his head on my lap.

Before long, I myself lapse into slumber, as well. Lately I've been dreaming about my childhood, I've noticed, and in this one my family and I are eating dinner in a farmhouse in eastern Colorado, where my father took a job working for a municipal water company.

"Someday," I say, "I'm going to be President of the United State of America!"

My poor father looks like he might die on the spot of an aneurism.

"You could perhaps be a mayor," my mother says, "but never the president, or a governor, or even a senator or congressman." She then tells me it's in fact unlikely that I can ever be even the mayor of a big city. "It's best you limit your ambitions to a town like Lamar," she says.

When I wake, it's bitterly cold and the sky is the color of expired milk. The old man is gone, and wonderfully, so is my back pain. Sleeping on a cold park bench is a trick I won't forget next time I'm ailing. What an exciting time to be alive, I think, knowing what I do today will determine the fate of my very soul. Man must have faith, whether in God or Art. I feel fortunate to have both.

A hunched old woman with a red and yellow babushka is praying before the graves of her husband and two children, I learn. She visits the cemetery every day, she says, because she loves flowers so much. I sniff her bouquet of daffodils, and she points me toward my hotel.

CHAPTER 43

DANNY IS in bad spirits. Already he's fired fifteen members of the crew, and word is spreading that he slapped the face of the lead carpenter on the set. To avoid criminal charges, Inès' human resources department says, Danny will need to attend one hundred hours of anger-management counseling. Blanche lies on Danny's lap as he laments that one's character can be measured only by the tenacity with which he fulfills the world's expectations.

I'm an hour late reporting for duty and fear I won't escape unharmed from my impending confrontation with Danny. He didn't fly me to Paris for a vacation. To my surprise, he simply leads me backstage and then to a room filled with orchids, lilies, daisies, peonies, hyacinths, and tulips, a bounty rivaled only by the Jardin du Palais Royal. The flowers, Danny says, are for the show's climax, when Arab children toss them at the models in their triumph. My task is to drive a bus out to the *banlieue* near Charles de Gaulle airport to get the kids.

Traffic is horrendous. Protestors block every street. On the Rue de la Paix, transportation workers are on strike, and on Avenue de l'Opéra, there are teachers and nurses objecting to raising the national retirement age to sixty-four. I drive the bus onto the sidewalk to maneuver around the crowds. My fear of being jailed for reckless driving vanishes once I've turned on Place Jacques Rouché, however. The entire police force has taken the day off to join the picket line.

A plan begins to percolate as I drive. What would happen

should I fail to deliver the children? Undoubtedly it would set off a chain of events, none of which could redound to the grand success Danny believes is his destiny. The most poisonous of flowers often blooms from the smallest seed.

Danny has instructed me to meet a teacher named Ahmad at the El-Baraka Elementary School. Ahmad runs a program teaching Syrian refugee children how to speak French. For his efforts, he's won many awards, including a seat in the city council, representing the *Parti Socialiste,* and is now a rising star in French politics. Though I've determined not to collect the children, I'm curious to see with my own eyes one of the great men of our generation, so I drive past the school. There on the front lawn, under the French flag, is the man himself, surrounded by a veritable herd of children, beaming with anticipation. They all wave expectantly as I approach, thrilled at the prospect of visiting one of the world's finest hotels, and when I honk, the group breaks out in cheer. But, of course, I never stop. The children's disappointment, I reason, is a small price to pay for Danny's salvation.

A little way on, I park in a dirt lot next to an abandoned strip-mall and head inside a bar called Au Jocky Club. A group of bearded men sit at a rickety wooden table smoking a hukkah and playing cards, illuminated by blue and green neon lights. There's an old-style television box on a shelf above the bar. The horse races at Deuville are about to start. A man with puffy eyes and heavy jowls holds a betting ticket as he watches the screen. A horse named Pour le Salut prances to the gate with supreme confidence, and I know without doubt that she will win. When the race starts, sure enough, Pour le Salut takes an immediate three-length lead. The puffy-eyed man bangs his fists into the bar, screaming at the top of his lungs. By the time the field has entered the stretch, Pour le Salut has run away, and then across the finish line, a pay out of six-to-one for those with eyes to see. The puffy-eyed man tears his betting ticket into shreds and descends into a true fit, at which the bartender, in Arabic, eighty-sixes the man forever.

The man's defeat stirs my soul. Who am I to thwart Danny's hope and dreams? If I drive like hell, the children may still be waiting at the school. But of course, Ahmad and the kids are long gone. I park the bus and run through the school shouting for Ahmad, and am told by a kindly sanitary technician that the last class ended nearly an hour ago. Everyone, he says, has gone for the day.

Back in the bus, I see all the street signs are written in Arabic script. I holler out the window at a veiled woman carrying bags from the market, but she averts her eyes and turns away. I'm on the verge of surrendering to the certainty that Danny is destined for salvation regardless of my efforts, when up ahead, as if a gift from fate, a pack of men emerge from their afternoon prayer at the local mosque. With great difficulty, I explain that I'd like to pay them money to toss flowers at scantily clad models on a runway. The men grumble among themselves for a time, but finally decide that while they're happy to do me this service, they cannot accept my money.

If this doesn't make Danny happy, I can't imagine what would. The innocence of children is always a guaranteed spectacle, but these zealots will cause an uproar. As for my disloyalty to James, I expect no mercy. He will denounce and expel me from the Pure Cosmos Club, and I will return to my art. And of course, I'll have the consolation that though

I've sacrificed my and Danny's eternal peace and oneness, I'll have made a lasting contribution to the pantheon of fashion by ensuring Danny's triumph on the runway.

We arrive just minutes before the show begins. I whisk the men backstage and give them final instructions. The flowers, the set design, and the beauty of the women throw the men into a tizzy. They shout and bellow and cry. The eldest member leads them in a deeply solemn prayer. I'm positive these men have never witnessed such grandeur and are thanking God for their good fortune. After the prayer, the men look as grave as executioners. I wish them luck and take my place in the audience with Blanche and Winston.

The stage design features trashcan fires, crumbling shacks with red tile roofs, and graffiti. A foreboding concrete housing project in the brutalist style of Le Corbusier looms in the background. Over the catwalk hangs a giant banner that says, "No-Go Zone?" The tension in the room is palpable.

"Isn't Danny daring?" a woman with a self-inflicted, asymmetrical haircut says to her friend.

"That little man is nothing more than a third-rate provocateur!" the friend says.

An uneasy feeling takes me. Blanche is licking herself uncontrollably, and Winston, for some reason wearing a fur vest and cycling shorts, picks at the old wound on his thigh. The first melodious notes of violins peal through the room, and the whispering crowd goes silent. A procession of leggy North African girls march out in tweed playsuits, *garconne* coatdresses, tiny silk shorts and bell-shaped skirts, each sporting one of Danny's cat-bags, each more elegant than the last. The audience erupts as an ascending rhythm of hand-drums begins to pulse, followed by an orchestra of flutes, sitars, and ouds. Finally, just when the music climaxes, the men I brought from the mosque storm the stage like marauders, pelting the models with stones. The models are fearless, however, and trounce the men with haughty disdain. A struggle ensues, the house security wrestling with the miscreants, while meantime the models stream to and fro along the runway as if nothing could be finer. The audience responds with a mixed reaction, a violent cacophony of cheers and boos. Danny's face is that of a disgraced general surrendering the battlefield.

In the morning, room service wakens me delivering breakfast. Blanche is beside me, asleep in a cashmere robe. I take my bowl of lentils to the balcony and find a mob of left-wing protestors below with an actual guillotine, clamoring for Danny's head.

My left eye is swollen shut and my face is black and blue. After the show, I'd rushed backstage, where Danny's security team had escorted me to the private office in which he'd barricaded himself. A pack of snarling journalists were banging on the door, but Danny wouldn't see them. All his work, all his plans, had descended to chaos and devastation. Had I the chance, I'd have thrown myself at his feet and begged forgiveness. The first thing I saw stepping through the door, however, was Danny's fist driving toward my face.

The show's lasting effect was impossible to predict. It has provoked the largest public outcry in the history of fashion. The controversy is on the front page of every newspaper in Europe. Winston puffs on a cigarette as he translates the press. The *Libération* says, "Inès disgraces itself with a disgusting display of bigotry!" Winston guffaws. He is positively gleeful. For every detraction, there are at least two or three pieces that sing the show's praises. "Models prove that a liberal society must have no tolerance for intolerance!" says one report. Of course, the show is the talk of Paris, and the initial run of cat-bags sold out in minutes. The demand is so high that Inès plans to increase production tenfold. Overnight, Danny has become the most famous designer in the world.

"I don't understand," I say.

"The French aren't like Americans," Winston says. "They're not about to switch to a diet of hamburgers, my friend."

Danny shuffles into the room, red-faced and sulky. It looks as though he hasn't slept for days. I offer him a piece of bubble gum, but he's too depressed. He sits on the bed, waking Blanche, who growls lethargically, hung over from the after party. Danny can't stand the sight of the headlines and tosses all the papers off the balcony.

"Did you not read the reviews?"

"They're only trying to sell newspapers."

"Your cat-bags are the most sought-after luxury good in all of fashion!" I say.

"As you know, Paul, I'm already rich."

"So why are you upset?" Winston says.

"The show's success wasn't on my terms," Danny says, holding his face like a disappointed child. "The statement I wanted to make was artistic, not political. They love me for all the wrong reasons. I'm nothing but a two-bit fraud."

Danny's suffering, I see, was unavoidable, a curse from Mother Nature herself. His troubles have nothing to do with me. What's the difference between someone slowly losing their hearing to old age and Van Gogh cutting off his own ear? Both leave a person deaf.

CHAPTER 44

DANNY SPENDS the flight home writing detailed questions about the Pure Cosmos Club's doctrine. He completes a set, then summons the flight attendant, Wang Lei—a young Chinese man with the wiry frame of a featherweight boxing champion—to deliver them to me at the rear of the plane. Danny is convinced that ideas are fundamental to the collective consciousness, a view, I'm afraid, without poetry. We share a common language, Danny and I, yet there's a void of misunderstanding between us. The same words mean different things. When I say, "The Pure Cosmos Club has a love of truth!" Danny takes it literally, whereas for me it's simply rhetoric. Just before the plane touches down in New York, Danny concedes that the Pure Cosmos Club might offer the abiding philosophy he's been seeking. "The fashion show has left me directionless," his last note says. "I need someone to take the wheel and steer."

Delivering Danny to the Pure Cosmos Club has redounded to my swift ascension through the club's ranks. Now I must complete a week of solitary contemplation to prepare me for a rebirth. A team of Senior Advisors shackle and blindfold me, then drive me to a housing project in what I presume is Staten Island.

For five days, now, I've sat in this room with a cot, a bucket, and a single window facing a brick wall. If James hopes to draw me nearer by menacing me to the brink of insanity, he will get his wish. Civilized man, I've come to see, can't transform his environment without utmost will and all his faculties. I spent most of yesterday listening to my hair grow. That evening, a Senior Advisor delivered my cup of tea and asked whether I'd heard the gunshots earlier. Three people had been murdered in the room across the hall from mine, but I was blissfully unaware. The Senior Advisor was pleased. "This is terrific news, a clear sign of your increasing ascension."

This morning, I've committed myself to feeling the process of mitosis in my body. I direct my attention to the nail on my left big toe. It takes a bit, but soon the sensation of cells duplicating and splitting is as powerful as being cut with a blade.

I lie supine on the floor, at the threshold of deliverance, where once and for all I'll have purged the hellish repressions of modern life. I flap my arms through shimmering clouds and glide over peaks and lakes.

A Senior Advisor enters the room. "Your efforts to sully me with the common grief of man will be fruitless," I say.

James, the Senior Advisor tells me, has had an awakening, and we have been called to return to the fold.

James is in his pulpit when we arrive, with Danny at his side, head shaven, dressed like all of us in the club uniform. It's clear he's finally taken refuge in faith. His suffering has been unparalleled.

"Today, I deliver to you a message from another world," James says, "the Ultimate Level."

The congregation howls at this, as if infected with madness. James' voice drops another octave, into a fervent baritone.

"This world is wicked and cruel, refusing to slake our thirst, and yet we have persisted, and now, at last, the oasis of salvation is near. The Ultimate Level permits the saved but twice a millennium. Five hundred years have passed since last the gates have opened. Those who wish to enter now must be prepared. It is our humble honor not only to witness the end of this lamentable era but to be as well the agents of its destruction, just as it was written in the Bible's Revelations."

My body begins to tingle with these words, but James goes on.

"Do you feel that?" he says. "Do you feel the spirit coursing through your flesh? Yes! Yes! It is your spirit casting off its worldly garment, the shackles of your suffering, in preparation for its new and eternal life at the Ultimate Level."

All around me people are gasping, shaking, murmuring ecstatically.

"Yes!" James says, and wades into the crowd with Danny like a shadow at his side. "Yes! the Ultimate Level is a physical place, my friends, a quite literal heaven which, once entered, is unending and eternal. But you must be prepared. To attain this transcendence, we must give up all that's left of our worldly possessions, our friends, our family, even our very humanness."

Now, his voice is righteous with indignation. Sweat pours from his face. His body convulses with cosmic inspiration. The Pure Cosmos Club, James says, has great enemies bent upon its destruction, adversaries seduced by the Devil whose reach extends to the highest levels of government.

"There is but one way to attain the Ultimate Level, and thus eternal life," James shouts, "and it lies in our earthly demise!"

Beside James, Danny with his blank eyes presents a man transformed, a man whose instincts and ethics have been stripped away. He takes from a Senior Advisor a paper cup while others move among us dispensing the same, a reddish liquid and a small purple capsule. The congregation is now silent. We are, we realize only now, about to meet our destiny. The grizzled woman next to me is shaking so hard she drops her cup. The sound is like the crash of thunder. A Senior Advisor replaces her cup, and she bows. Orsi stands on the far side of the nave. It's been just two weeks since she saw me through my delirium, but that time has robbed her of much. Her hair is jagged and shorn, as if cut with a knife, and her face is red and sunken.

"There's no time to waste," James says boomingly. "Do it now, and we'll meet again soon on the Ultimate Level!"

Logic gives way to desire, and I pop the capsule, then chase it with my drink. With my luck, of course, the capsule lodges in my throat, and I begin mildly to choke. All around me the others are swallowing their capsules, their faces ecstatic. I wave my arms frantically, hoping for attention, but in this sea of flailing zealots, I'm ignored. The last thing I see before collapsing is Orsi skulking away like an aggrieved tigress. "He's ascending to the Ultimate Level!" I hear someone shout, and the congregation roars. In yet another stroke of kismet, however, when my body hits the floor, the capsule comes loose, and I cough it up. I know I should try again to swallow it, but can't summon the will to put it in my mouth. Confused and ashamed, I stick the capsule in my ear and watch as one by one the people around me succumb. No one struggles, no one cries for help. The congregation have surrendered as one.

A gravid moment passes before James addresses us once again from the pulpit. "My children," he shouts, "I've just received another message from Ultimate Level. We have more work yet to do here. Our time is not yet at hand. God is with us, and has rendered our capsules harmless. Praise be! Praise be, my friends! Let this moment be a testament to our commitment and faith. We shall be rewarded, all of us, beyond our wildest dreams!"

And with that, James leads Danny away by the hand through a curtained door. Slowly the congregation begins to rise and stumble about, babbling disappointedly until they conclude that they must work harder to prove themselves worthy of the Ultimate Level.

I search for Orsi, but she is gone. I go out to the street and stand in the shade of a tree. There, written in the dirt at my feet, I see a message—"I know what's in your ear."

CHAPTER 45

THE ONLY time I've seen a star in New York City was during a blackout caused by a heat wave. Janie and I sat on the roof of our building admiring the splendor of the universe. The next day I read in the news that fifteen people had died without air conditioning. The day after that I made a collage and called it, *God Didn't Build the City, He Built the Countryside.*

The other members of the club don't arrive until four a.m. to begin their work, but I've come early to get a head start. It's pitch black, still, so I light a candle to guide me through the temple. My first stop is the incinerator, where I destroy a cache of family photo albums seized from the homes of new members. In the penance chamber, I survey a collection of tools for self-flagellation, unable to decide which will be right to atone for the sin of hiding my suicide pill. There are so many—a lash, a rod, a switch, a cat o' nine tails, and on. At long length, I remove my uniform and strike my back repeatedly with a whip of knotted cords while chanting a mantra of redemption.

Afterwards, as I'm scrubbing the floor clean of my blood, I hear a sound in the hall, cooks preparing breakfast early, I think at first. When I don't hear the recordings of James' sermons the cooks always listen to, though, I put down my mop to investigate. Just as I feared, the kitchen is empty. The sound grows increasing louder as I pass the children's nursery, the nave, the greenhouse, and finally to James' private quarters, where I've never been.

"James," I say, and press my ear to the door, "is that you?"

I rap on the door, and when no one answers, I step in and flip on the lights. Orsi is there, of all people, a flashlight in hand and duffle bag at her feet half-full of paperwork, the space itself like a ransacked room in a detective film—lolling cabinet drawers, scattered files, gewgaws, and books strewn across the floor.

"I'm doing an internal audit," Orsi says after a mutual silence.

"You do all your accounting by flashlight?"

Before I can look into her bag, she zips it up and says, "Things have been so hectic, Paul. The only time I can do any real work is when everyone else is gone."

"What's in the bag?"

"Is this really necessary?"

Of course it's necessary, I tell her, and look inside. Not only has she taken all the club's financial statements, but also a file with my name, inside of which is a record of the money from my bird painting and fishing pole sculpture. The funds, I see, are now in an account on the island nation of Barbados.

"I saw what you did," Orsi says. "That nonsense about the Ultimate Level. You don't believe a word."

"James has shown me my destiny. It's spelled out clearly in the central plot of life!"

"Why didn't you swallow the capsule?"

"It got stuck."

"You can lie to yourself," Orsi says, laughing, "but please don't insult me with your transparent ruses."

A rage consumes me, and I shove Orsi to the ground. She isn't merely a genius mathematician, I quickly learn, but an adept fighter, too. I pin her momentarily with a half-nelson, but she claws my face with her nails, then hits me hard with a volley of rabbit punches to my kidney. I execute a kung fu leg sweep to trip her up, but hit the filing cabinet instead. Inexplicably, when it topples, it traps Orsi underneath it. She struggles valiantly, but once I've bound her hands and legs, she submits, and I gag her as well with my tunic. James cannot know what's happened here. I spend the next hour restoring the office, every document properly ordered and filed, then collapse to the floor next to Orsi.

Soon, we hear the sound of footsteps in the hall. In short order, I've freed Orsi and am sitting in a chair, just in time to greet James in his workout attire.

"What's going on, my friends?" he says.

"We're looking for the first aid kit," I say, and show James my mangled back. "I got a bit overzealous atoning for my sins this morning, and Orsi offered to stitch me up."

James assesses my wounds and hands a first aid kit to Orsi from his desk.

"Next time," he says, "try the infirmary first."

James applauds my commitment, but tells me I ought not be too harsh, then excuses himself and his tight schedule. He has much to do and needs to be available at any moment should the Ultimate Level attempt to contact him.

CHAPTER 46

I'M IN a terrible way as I walk back to the studio. My love for Orsi has blinded me to the value of my dignity. The memory of our night together looms larger in my heart and mind than the night itself. If I can't reinvent my perception of her soon, my damnation is certain. To do it, I must turn each of her many virtues into irredeemable flaws. Yet no matter how hard I will myself to see her as the paragon of immorality and wickedness, nothing changes, and after an hour I'm in tears. My feelings for her are my enemy, an impassable wall between me and the world as it truly is. I bite down hard on Orsi's marble, thinking if I can crush it, I'll be free, but get nothing for my effort but another chipped tooth.

I am, I see, a victim of Orsi's unassailable persuasion tactics. Only one other time has my mind betrayed me so completely. I was in the car with my mother and father, driving past a building downtown, and my mother had asked about it. My class had taken a field trip there just a few months prior, during which, in fact, a security guard had caught me stealing a book about T-Rex from the gift-shop, so I told her, "It's the Museum of Natural History."

To my complete surprise, my father snapped at both of us. "Don't you know anything about this city? That's the Law School at the University."

He said this with so much confidence that, from then on, I've second-guessed everything I think I know. It took years to recover from that moment, though clearly, I've lapsed. I berate myself for having allowed myself to fall under Orsi's influence, and vow not to let it go any further. Love is not an accomplishment. For a man to feel good, he must be proud of what he's done, and how he comports himself in the world. With the help of James and the Pure Cosmos Club, I have a chance to be a part of something larger than any one individual. I must at all costs eliminate anything that distracts me from this purpose.

CHAPTER 47

WINSTON AND Blanche are wearing matching berets and striped shirts, dancing like ecstatic children. An empty bottle of champagne leans against an easel. Depravity is afoot, I tell myself, beware.

"Inès has hired me to oversee another collaboration!" Winston says.

"The seamstresses are returning?"

"This time," Winston says, adjusting his beret, which keeps slipping over his eyes, "it's in Paris."

"You hear that, girl?" I say to Blanche, and scratch her belly. "It's going to be just you and me for a while."

Blanche looks at me mournfully and barks.

"Oh no," Winston says, "Inès has insisted on a team. They absolutely adore Blanche and have sent a contract for the two of us."

Blanche licks my face, her heart set. Who am I to stand in the way of an endless supply of good wine and quiche?

"I see," I say, with tears in my eyes. "What a wonderful opportunity."

"The production is imminent," Winston says. "Our flight departs later this evening."

I help them pack their bags. A cab arrives, and they promise to call as soon as they reach Paris. There's nothing more to say. They're gone.

I spend the night filling my Journal of Treasonous Thoughts with confessions about my struggles to detach myself from earthly relationships.

CHAPTER 48

THE THREE packs of bubble gum I've chewed since early evening yesterday haven't helped me even to have a nightmare, much less a wink or two. Now it's 5 a.m., I'm out of gum, and there's not a drop of any sort of alcohol. I've said my prayers, chanted my mantras, filed my feet, and read half of *Das Capital* in the original German. Truly desperate, I tie Blanche's extra leash to one of Winston's bottles and take it for a walk.

It's snowing for the first time this season. The bottle bumps and slides along the icy walk as we make our way, but I am sure to comfort it. "Be careful not to slip and fall," I say, soothingly, "you don't want to shatter." At the French bakery, we peer through the window as the workers knead their dough. When one of the lovely bakers sees me crying, she delivers me a piece of quiche straight from the oven.

"I'm sorry," I say, "but I haven't a franc to spare."

"It's on us," she says. "But, please, take this to the park or something? We can't have you out there mumbling to yourself when we open. You'll scare everyone away."

I've never considered myself the type of person who talks to themselves in public, but I believe the baker was in earnest and don't want to make her feel bad for having given me her wonderful quiche.

Time passes slower than I'd like as my bottle and I wander the streets, and I am bitter for no longer being young. My existence itself, I think, is an evasion. How many of us feel this, I wonder, and how many live as though their every moment is one of exile? I've never handled the company of others particularly well, and yet I do no better in solitude, either. I must hold faith in James' teachings. It pays no one anything to drag the past along wherever they go.

In the early light, I come across a pair of workers pouring concrete for a new stretch of sidewalk, and can't help but to envy their purpose. Finished, they cordon off the area with caution-tape and hang a sign that reads "Wet Cement" before they leave. People hustle by as though I don't exist. I snap a twig off a nearby tree and carve Blanche's name into the wet cement.

"Hurry now," I say to my bottle, as we slip away. "We don't want to be arrested for destruction of property!"

Back at the studio, I tuck the bottle into bed and sing it a lullaby, then realize that the pain in my stomach isn't illness, but hunger. I put the quiche in Blanche's bowl and eat.

CHAPTER 49

THREE YEARS ago, for Janie's birthday, I maxed out my credit card buying her a ticket to the New York Philharmonic. When I gave it to her, she was upset she'd have to go alone. I told her I could never attend such an event, suffering as I do from melophobia, an excuse that seemed for the time to satisfy her. She remarked simply that, ever since she'd learned of this condition in a first-year medical school lecture, she'd felt pity for those it afflicted. "What a tragedy to be robbed of the gift of music," she said.

On the night of the symphony, I waited for her at the Revson Fountain outside Lincoln Center. I wanted to be with her in spirit, I said. New York was suffering its worst blizzard of the season that night, and I'd recently pawned my coat at a secondhand store for money to buy paint. In less than an hour, I had all the tell-tale symptoms of hypothermia—weak pulse, shallow breathing, slurred speech. The warmth of a coffee shop across the street tempted me, but I didn't want to compound my lie about melophobia by breaking my promise to wait for Janie. A police officer saw me jumping up and down and offered to drive me to a shelter. When I refused, he subjected me to a host of sobriety tests, all of which I failed because of my hallucinations. I was nowhere to be found, of course, when the symphony concluded, so that, believing I'd been injured, or worse, Janie spent hours calling emergency rooms. I wasn't released from my cell until the morning, and got home to overhear Janie's mother on the phone telling her I must be having an affair. Cornered, I had no refuge but the truth, which I conveyed to Janie with utmost shame. She was both horrified and alarmed, far more so than I'd imagined. The next day she begged her uncle to give me a job selling software at one of the tech startups in which he'd invested, where I worked until I was fired six months later, for underperforming.

I've managed to relegate this sordid period to oblivion, right up to this afternoon, when James invited me to join him at the symphony. Now, here again before the fountain, it's hard not to feel a little sad.

"We have fantastic seats tonight," James says, beaming. "Nothing but the best for my favorite son!"

A dapper usher escorts us to our seats, and we watch attentively as the orchestra prepares. An oboe player with a mustache reminiscent of Clark Gable's blows an A for the lead violinist, who makes tiny adjustments to match the pitch, and, in turn, plays for others to get in tune. The lights dim, and a bald conductor with thick-rimmed glasses takes his place. A few errant coughs sound out as the musicians await their cue. Then the conductor flicks his baton, and the first two electrifying chords of Beethoven's Symphony No. 3 in E-flat major cut through the room. The symphony was inspired by the story of a great hero who strives, fails, dies, and then is miraculously reborn. This is music as triumphant as it is sublime.

"I brought you here tonight," James whispers, "to inform you that you're under consideration to join the board of Senior Advisors."

"It's not possible!" I say, unable to contain myself, and draw the baleful glare of an elderly tuxedoed man two rows in front of us.

"Life here on Earth," James whispers again after a time, and takes my hand, "is actually death. We must focus on the sky. Our lesson, our purpose, really," he says, "is to attain motivation that is selfless and pure, to serve the Creator in all we do, forever."

James' words remind me of Beethoven's disillusionment when he learned that Napoleon had crowned himself Emperor. Beethoven was at that very moment composing a symphony to honor Napoleon, but in his sadness, he destroyed it. Napoleon hadn't merely betrayed Beethoven, but all of mankind. I squeeze the arms of my chair tightly, feeling somewhat nauseated.

"You've suffered a terrible loss, Paul," James says, and strokes my cheek. "I can sense it."

Not too long ago, when a kitchen pot exploded, Blanche threw her tiny body in front of the shrapnel of vegetables and rice. Some would say Blanche was only hungry, but I know in my heart her impulse was that of a hero.

"I never miss anyone longer than forever," I whisper.

"Never forget, my friend," James says. "When God has been exiled, there's nothing that can take His place." The funeral march of the second movement begins. The somber violins and chthonic bass are almost too much to bear. "An attack on the Pure Cosmos Club," James says, "is a sin against life itself!"

I writhe in my chair like a wounded rabbit. A thousand manic voices squabble in my head. I'm saved only by the whisper of reason beneath them. James' utopian vision has always appealed to my own pragmatism. One can't distrust what one has never known.

After the symphony, James gives me an envelope he wants me to deliver to Amol. What's inside, he says, will help Amol to atone for his sins and rejoin the path of the righteous.

"Even though he's been lousy in this life," James says, "perhaps God will see something redeeming in him and give him another chance."

On the train ride home, I sit across from a young couple. The woman has a bruised eye and a badly battered lip. The man wraps his arm around her shoulder and holds her tightly to his body. He whispers sweetly in her ear about true love.

"I feel sorry for couples that don't fight like we do," she says, little tears forming in her eyes. "Their relationships lack passion."

Life consists of madness spiked with lies, but some people are guilty of only ever hearing what they want to hear.

At the studio, my bottle and I lie on our lumpy bed, staring at James' envelope on the overturned pickle bucket across the way. I want to open it, but know I can't.

CHAPTER 50

THERE'S A pile of chewed-up bubble gum on the floor by my bed, each wad wrapped in its own piece of tissue. Sleep never came. My bottle gives me no solace, either. I roll my eyes so only the whites show, and hold my breath, but my bottle doesn't want to play.

Amol's phone has been shut off. Luckily, I've received a tip from a fortune teller who's discerned his whereabouts by examining the palm of my hand. I take the train deep into Queens. At the station, a man is lying face-down on the platform, handcuffed. Blood drips from his nose and mouth. Two officers hover over him, talking into their radios. The perpetrator, they say, stole a bottle of water from a newspaper stand.

Fast food wrappers and plastic bags swirl about in the frigid wind. Decrepit brick buildings crumble along the main drag. Bedraggled townies huddle outside of the liquor store, scratching off numbers on lotto tickets. I make my way down the boardwalk, toward the housing projects and old folks' homes tucked away here for the better part of a century, passing countless lots riddled with weeds and rusting cars, and then a playground with no children. Finally, I reach the derelict building the fortune teller said would be here. All of its windows are shattered or boarded up. The walkway is thick with broken glass. I move into the dim caddywhompus hallways, and up a stairwell that reeks of urine.

Amol stands in the doorway of his hovel, seemingly waiting for me. He's grown a grizzly beard and his eyes are heavy with purple bags. He looks like a prisoner before his execution. Inside, black mold has crept up the flaking walls and steam spews from a broken pipe. There's a plastic card table with folding chairs, a futon, and, in the kitchen, a cast iron tub.

Amol has given up his fight against the travails of the world, I see. He natters on about the truth of things, how once you've seen it you can never return. Life in the Pure Cosmos Club, he says, has brought him to ruin. When at last he pauses, I remind him how foolish it is to blame his mistakes on others. In the end, it's only he who suffers.

"Let's get on with it," he says.

I hand Amol the envelope. He opens it slowly and lays the contents on the table—a series of black and white photos of him in sexually compromising positions with a goat, and a demand for further payments. Amol covers his face and weeps.

According to James, guilt and remorse are the effect of an earthly moral code. To suppress these emotions, I need only focus on the ethical framework James has taught me, whose precepts exclude all such ridiculous sentiment.

It's impossible for someone like me, whose childhood was a sanctuary of security and safekeeping, even to fathom clinging to the obvious lies of this world, and yet still I feel no contempt for this broken man.

"Nobody wants to hurt you," I say. "James just needs more money to help us all."

"Get out!" Amol shouts. "Get out!"

My ride home is filled with thoughts about how awful it must be to live behind a veil. Some people will forever be short on practical sense. Back at the studio, I cut my chin and forehead with a razor and sacrifice my blood to the flame of the candle at my little altar.

CHAPTER 51

WINSTON HAS complained bitterly about the lack of decent Mexican food in France, so this afternoon I went to our favorite taco shop for something I could send to him and Blanche. The restaurant's proprietor, Pedro, isn't actually Mexican, but Guatemalan. When no one would buy his *kak'ik* or *pupusas*, he changed the menu to traditional Mexican dishes. Now his *tacos al pastor* are considered the best in the tri-state area.

"What do you think will travel well?" I asked Pedro.

"No question about it," he said, "my mole enchiladas are indestructible."

Now, at the studio, as I seal up my package, four Senior Advisors burst through the door to blindfold me, bind my hands with zip ties, and drag me into a waiting van. They force a thick, bitter elixir into my mouth and soon my body begins to melt. Silver fur sprouts from my arms and legs, my nose becomes a snout, my hands and feet paws, and then a chain is slipped around my neck. The Senior Advisors are speaking to me in a foreign language I somehow understand. From now on, they say, I will live to serve my master.

Now we're climbing among steep jagged rocks. I complain of thirst, and an Advisor puts my face to a bowl of water, which I lap up greedily. Later, I'm shoved against a wall and my blindfold is removed. We're in a cave overlooking a forest-covered valley. The walls are decorated in hieroglyphics depicting scenes of spaceships and stars. The Senior Advisors, all in silver robes, shave my head and bathe me to the tune of ancient hymns on sacred flutes. James appears in white robes and kneels beside me.

"Everything you knew, I've taken from you," he says. "All you know now is what I tell you."

The Senior Advisors put me in a wooden chair and carry me to the edge of a cliff, where James leads us in a prayer. Then he cuts his wrist, dips his finger into the blood, and sticks it in my mouth. One of the Senior Advisors hands me a mirror and tells me to describe what I see when I look into it. At first, there's only a dark mist, but as I stare, a shape begins to form.

"It's James' face!" I say.

"He's no longer a man," the Senior Advisors chant, "but an Ultimate Level saint!"

"Ready him for the tattoo!" James says.

A Senior Advisor approaches with a needle and saucer full of ink. The others spread my legs, but just as the Advisor with the needle is about to start, the face in the mirror begins to shift. It's a mouse, then a snake, then a wriggling creature I've never seen. A haze sweeps over me, and when it passes, the image in the mirror is my own wretched face.

"Wait," I say. "James is gone."

"What is it?" the Advisors say. "What do you see?"

"It's me," I say, "it's only me."

"Hurl him off the cliff!" another of the Advisors shouts.

"No," James says. "There is still a chance for him to purify his heart. We shall see."

The kaleidoscope effect of the elixir eventually fades. I'm lying naked on a tree branch high up in a leafless maple in Prospect Park. My uniform sits in a crumpled pile at the tree's base. I'm shivering badly from the cold, but I manage to climb down. As I dress, a bird poops on my head. When I reach to wipe myself off, I realize I'm as bald as a coot.

CHAPTER 52

In times of great trouble, I head to Times Square, where, amidst the double-decker tour buses and endlessly blaring cabs, I have always found solace in the wisdom of the Naked Cowboy. This hulking man from Ohio, in nothing but his hat and boots and tactically slung guitar, is both a modern-day oracle and a genius who once had the good sense to run for President of the United States.

My first encounter with him was over a decade ago. I'd been applying for jobs at cafeterias and bodegas and sleeping in public parks. After my wallet was stolen by a pickpocket on the F-Train, my father had wired me eighty dollars for a bus ticket back to Colorado. I was, it goes without saying, a defeated man. Seeing me in so pitiable a state, the Naked Cowboy stopped mid-song to take me aside and share the story of his life.

He wasn't always the tremendous success he is today, he said with great humility. He, too, had once been down on his luck. It was only after he'd discovered a book filled with the sayings he now repeats to the Japanese tourists he lets photograph him for handsome sums that his life began to change. The book instructed him to write down his goals and assess them daily. To be remembered as the richest and most celebrated entertainer of all-time, he needed to exponentially grow his brand. Each morning before his first performance, he recited his goals and the means to achieve them. Miraculously, he said, this discipline carried him through his days. That very afternoon I began to make a series of drawings on the asphalt of Washington Square Park, in the style of Monet.

The next time I consulted the Naked Cowboy was the day after Janie left me. "Do you want to be the type of person who likes *foie grais*?" he said. When I told him I didn't understand, he instructed me to think it over. If I wanted to be the type of person who likes *foie gras*, I realized after weeks of scratching my head, I needed merely to recondition my preferences. This same mentality can be applied to anything in life.

Now I stand before this mighty sage in what is perhaps my worst state yet. I wait meekly while a woman squeezes his bicep and stuffs bills into the hole of his guitar. Then he strides over and takes me in a warm embrace.

"The lilies in the field neither toil nor spin!" he says after I've mumbled out my plight. "You must swim in the river of life!"

The Naked Cowboy is about to speak again, but before he can, we are both assaulted, he by a flock of divorcées from Poland and I by a sign-spinning solicitor with a badly scarred forehead, shilling coupons for Madame Tussauds' Wax Museum. Elated at the prospect of my long-awaited picture with Yoko Ono, I rush toward the museum only to be stopped dead by yet another vision: crossing 42nd Street is none other than James himself.

He doesn't hear me calling, so I race after him, banging into a vendor selling t-shirts and pins and then again, a mounted officer's horse. The officer scolds me as James slips through the heavy foot traffic. It's not for another eight blocks that I see him again, disappearing behind a mysterious red door.

I try to enter, but am stopped by a man just inside. Based on his enormous stature, I think while he pats me down and checks my pockets, looking for what I can't imagine, this man has missed his calling as an offensive lineman in professional football. The place must be highly sacred to require such strict security measures. Assured of my intentions, the behemoth directs me to a booth staffed by a woman in heavy makeup and a lace satin corset, who demands twenty dollars. Of course, I haven't a penny. The Senior Advisors took everything from me but my marble, which I jammed up my keister when they came for my belongings. In lieu of payment, I ask whether she'll accept a portrait of herself on the back of a cocktail napkin.

"The entrance fee is twenty dollars!" she says, laughing a lot more cruelly, in my opinion, than circumstances allow.

"Hold still," I say, grabbing a napkin and pen. "I really want to capture the sparkle in your eyes!"

The woman stares mesmerized at the picture I've made. "Why," she says, and hands me a heaping stack of dollar bills, "it's the most wonderful drawing I've ever seen! Go on in, and here's a little something to enjoy yourself with!"

I push through a heavy curtain into a dim chamber filled with men staring at half-naked women twisting and squirming around a pole on a stage. It's no secret that man's inability to conduct himself civilly renders him inferior to women, yet to my astonishment, the men in the place are rewarded for their bad behavior. Women who in other circumstances wouldn't pee on these men's flaming bodies are instead sitting on their laps, laughing with them as they gleefully cavort and slur.

None of this matters, though, I think. I'm here only to see James, whom I spot at last across the room in his white robe and beaded necklace. Two women, a blonde and a brunette whose physical gifts were ordained by no less than Ultimate Level, I'm sure, sit on James' lap cooing and giggling, fondling his arms and running their fingers through his hair. This, it occurs to me, must be a recruiting mission! Yes, James has seen in these women a heavenly quality beyond my poor eyes and has come to persuade them of their need for the sanctuary of the Pure Cosmos Club. I decide to join them, but no sooner have I left my bar stool than they slip behind a wall of velvet curtains. It's a rare occasion indeed to secure a private audience with James. These women must be exceedingly spiritually elevated.

I drink several hot teas while amusing the bartender with the story of how as a toddler my father made me take my meals in the backyard because he couldn't stand the sight of a messy child.

The rap song blaring from the speakers comes to its end. The woman onstage stops dancing and collects the loose money scattered around her, sweat pouring down her face. She puts her bra back on and catches my eye. She's worked so hard, I can't help but to flash her a thumbs-up.

"You look like a man who could use a private dance," she says, trying to pull me from my stool.

"I'm just waiting for my spiritual leader to come out from behind that door."

"He's in the Champagne Room?"

"Counseling two women in need of guidance."

"Do you mean James?"

"You know him?" I say, wondering if this woman, too, will be soon joining our fold.

"He's a regular here," the woman says. "Two or three times a week, I'd say."

"He should be out soon, then, I guess?"

"I don't think so. James likes to get the works."

The woman soon abandons her efforts and leaves me to my tea. Thirty minutes or so pass before I decide to go. My chores at the club are waiting. I pay the bartender, and when I turn back, the blonde woman who was with James hands me a manila envelope like the one I delivered to Amol. "This is your last chance to reach the Ultimate Level!" she says. The front of the envelope reads, "Confidential: for Orsi."

CHAPTER 53

MY FAILURE to achieve the status of Senior Advisor has called into question my commitment to the club, and no amount of penance will help. After three sleepless days and nights pouring through James' writings, I presented him with a list of nearly twelve hundred questions, to which he said, simply, "But, Paul, all of this is antithetical to faith." Despite my having delivered Danny to him, he told me my energies have been insufficient, and I need to make another contribution, if only with money from my paintings. He was so insistent, in fact, that he even pardoned me from my chores at the club. "While we're still here on Earth," he said, "there will always be the matter of money."

Back at the studio, I try hard to paint, but my hands are stiff and the only work I'm able to produce are crude renderings of milkmaids with heavy features and sagging breasts.

Orsi's envelope sits atop a stack of old weightlifting magazines. Even when we're apart, I suffer her burdens like they're my own. But the price of security is cowardice and ignorance, so I've refused myself permission to peek inside. I'm distressed at the prospect of losing anything else, and yet I'm horrified of things staying the same. Perhaps Venus and Apollo could make a happy couple in the end?

My God, I'm so disappointed in my faithlessness. James is like a father to me, and I've vowed to support him forever. But is faith a luxury I can still afford? After all, no matter how much I may wish it, the sun won't rise in the west. I don't expect mercy from the world, though a little sign of things to come would be nice.

I need to speak with Winston and Blanche. Where are they? My phone says I've called them forty-seven times today. What value does friendship possess unless it's actively demonstrated? When at last Winston calls, at 2 a.m., he apologizes for being so tough to get a hold of. Things at the atelier have been hectic. Inès is doing a collaboration with a tattoo-riddled, Swiss-born artist who, Winston says, is a true nightmare to work with. They're making rain jackets from condoms, but this pudgy sweaty artist insists they must be *used* condoms. The greater problem is that he wants to cum on each jacket himself. "That's what the people are paying for!" he says. After only a few days, however, they're way behind on production. The artist isn't so virile anymore and hasn't been able to muster more than a few loads each day. Winston proposed a compromise that they put just a tiny dollop of cum on each jacket, but the artist refuses to budge. "One load per jacket!" he says.

To make matters worse, Blanche has come down with a cold. She can't stop sneezing, and her eyes are watering so badly that people are mistaking her for a basset hound.

"The best thing for her is lizard soup," I say. "Go to the Chinese market and pick up some dried lizard, yams, and dates, and simmer them in filtered water for several hours."

Winston promises to send an intern to collect the ingredients and says he'll make himself more available.

At 6 a.m., I'm touched by a good but delicate inspiration—a strange phenomenon indeed, because this is the time of day I dislike most. My joy isn't vigorous, however, but somehow measured, also quite unusual. Every loneliness is a pinnacle. The only world I know is the one I myself perceive. When I die, it goes with me. Goethe was right—everything begins with the act.

For the next week, I work tirelessly on a series of paintings featuring Blanche. In each painting, she's on the deck of a boat. Every piece shares the same vantage, from a dock at a marina. The first painting shows the boat in the harbor, with Blanche sitting back on her wheels, near the boat's railing. She's so close it looks like you can reach out and pet her. The rest of the pieces show the boat a little farther out to sea. By the tenth and last work, the boat is a tiny dot in a great expanse of ocean.

My best childhood friend and true author of "Two Bikes, One City," Jesse, remains by my side as I work. There he is, in Winston's salvaged recliner, snacking on gummy bears, nodding with satisfaction. He hasn't done this until now, come to me while I work. He speaks to me of how one must sacrifice their past for the present. His very existence is a sacrament. Every brushstroke feels imbued with his wisdom. I enter a state close to prayer. The paintings are enormous, ten feet by eight feet. There's no question about it—this series represents an artist working at the pinnacle of his powers.

During my week-long torrent, Senior Advisors have appeared at the studio to monitor my progress. Art is a solitary endeavor, however. I've refused them all.

Finally, James himself calls. "Have you delivered on your promise to create a work of art that's heaven-sent?"

My body trembles, my teeth chatter. It's as if I've been filled with an impotent rage. I'm not normally given to such high-spirited behavior, but only a saint could resist this temptation. Instead of telling James about the new work, I conjure a thoughtless lie.

Tucked into a remote corner of the studio, behind a Cigar Store Indian and a rusted-out lawnmower, is a fishbowl I made years ago while taking a glassblowing class at the local YMCA. Inside the bowl are a dozen frayed and ripped origami monkeys that I picked up at a Panda Express fast-food restaurant back in 2016, in celebration of the Chinese New Year. This is what I tell James I've made.

"What do the monkeys represent?" James says.

Staring at my reflection in the fishbowl, I notice a mysterious vein running across my forehead. "According to the Chinese Zodiac," I say, "monkeys are calm and logical thinkers."

James is certain this can't be the only work I've managed to produce during my time away. I repeat my denials, sensing as I do that I'm shrinking more and more with every word. It's unusual for people to trust me. The feeling of disappointing someone is quite unpleasant. I'm on the verge of submitting to James, afraid I'll lose the gains I've worked so hard for, when a spirit of contradiction takes me. I simply cannot give James these paintings.

"I'll deliver the fishbowl to the Pure Cosmos Club," I say, "and the truth of things will be clear!"

No sooner have James and I concluded our talk than I set about hiding my paintings of Blanche behind a life-sized wooden model of Charles Lindbergh's plane—*The Spirit of St. Louis*—which Danny made at Yale. For the rest of the day, I reminisce about the days when Winston and Blanche ran the cat-bag atelier. Sometimes even the most painful memories can be pleasant.

CHAPTER 54

As I pull my wagon through the streets of Brooklyn, passersby ridicule the fishbowl with its origami monkeys. Mostly I'm paralyzed, but all at once, something breaks in me, and I burst into tears.

I have a recurring daydream in which I'm a prisoner wrongfully convicted of a crime and sentenced to spend my last years working on a farm. It's not a bad life. The food is plentiful and the weather agreeable. Once a month, I'm even permitted a conjugal visit from a lover. My job each day is to shepherd a flock of sheep across the valley. While they graze in lush fields, I skip stones on a lake and eat in the shade of an ancient tree. Not far from the lake a pickup truck is parked next to an abandoned barn. The keys are in it. The engine runs like new. No one would stop me from driving away, yet each evening, I return the sheep to their pens.

Every time the vision strikes, I'm overcome by intense claustrophobia. It's almost like I've lost my psychic bearing. A thousand outlandish thoughts race through my mind. Everything that truly matters is decided by the most ridiculous factors. And while I understand very well that life never turns out as one expects, I'm helpless to keep from speculating. My imagination always wins.

At the Pure Cosmos Club's entrance, the Level-1 worker tending the front desk refuses to greet me according to my status and even goes so far as to ignore my outstretched hand, which by rights they are bound to kiss. Every person I pass meets me with this disdain. I pretend nothing's wrong and greet them all with the club's preferred compliment.

"You look like you're transcending human existence quite nicely today."

I haven't changed underwear since the day of my failed Senior Advisor ceremony, and now I have an angry rash in my groin. I stop by the wardrobe for clean underwear, the room redolent with the scent of fresh laundry. But the attendant says they're out of medium-sized underwear, despite that the person behind them is stocking the dresser with fresh pairs. I wait until they turn away and steal a pair, then pass a room full of devotees genuflecting as they pledge. I no longer have anything to say to God.

I peek in the window of James' office, where he's speaking with a Senior Advisor. Watching someone with whom I share an intimate connection interact with someone else always stirs in me peculiar feelings. My friend's gestures and manners appear foreign, as though they're a stranger. People must have a thousand different natures. And anyway, what wisdom is James bestowing on this acolyte? The Senior Advisor's body is crouched, and their face is twisted. Perhaps they've reached that point in which joy comes to resemble suffering? It's not long before the Senior Advisor slinks out of the office.

I drag the wagon into James, present him with the fishbowl, and stand by while he makes his inspection. His deep-set eyes no longer appear crystal blue but black and small. He takes a handful of paper monkeys from the bowl and scrutinizes the shoddy craftsmanship.

"What desires drove you to create such a piece?" James says with unusual hostility.

"I work for pride," I say. The fishbowl was never intended as a piece of art, I well know, but for storing these origami monkeys. "I work for my humanity!"

The window of James' office looks onto an atrium, verdant with flowers and bees. Even as I marvel at this vision, I can't help but to ask myself whether James actually loves flowers and bees.

He holds the fishbowl to the light. His face looks severe yet elegant, like a judge. My pulse quickens. Every moment feels significant. Then, as if he'd grown bored, he drops the fishbowl, its glass shattering across the floor.

I shove James with all my might. He stumbles back, knocks his head on the wall, and falls into the broken glass. I stand over him trembling, admiring how handsome he looks with blood running down his cheek. Even in hell, a lord is still a lord. A beam of sun shines on me. I empty the filing cabinets of their financial documents and stuff them in a sack.

The wicked are doing just fine, I think, as I walk out of the Pure Cosmos Club. Nobody risks eye contact, much less a question.

I ride the subway gripping my marble, feeling tipsy, carefree, even young. Only a man who's fallen to his knees can truly rise. Life isn't calculus, I say to a young boy next to me. Not every equation makes sense. I close my eyes and picture my own death. I'm a soldier who's fallen in the heat of battle, under a dark and stormy sky, just before my side's final victory in a great war.

The subway comes to a grinding halt. Over the intercom, the conductor's muffled voice announces that an enormous sinkhole has opened up on the tracks, nearly a hundred feet deep, he says. It will be hours before a rescue team arrives. The stalwart woman next to me grips the crucifix around her neck.

"It's an act of God!" she says.

If the Old Testament has taught us anything, it's that God is a petty torturer. And it's with a serious heart that I vow to meet death with ceremony. But before I do, I must deliver these documents to Orsi. The passengers are in a panic. The women are weeping. The men are fighting. The children are the only beings handling the situation with any sort of grace. They have yet to learn the awful power of the Almighty, so they are immune to his cruelty. A toddler with splotchy red cheeks flashes a smile that fills me with courage. A force greater than Satan and more powerful than God blesses me with the strength of ten men, and I easily pry open the subway door, then race through the rat-infested tunnels. A line of prose from that heartless wretch, Rimbaud, comes to mind: "I am intact, and I don't give a damn!"

Yet back out on the street, I find myself afraid again. What if I fall and sprain my wrist? What if my teeth rot and fall out? I step into the street without looking and my leg is struck by a rushing cyclist. My shoe flies off. The cyclist and I crash to the ground. He picks himself up and checks his bike for damage.

"Watch where you're going, asshole!" he says.

In my confusion, I step on a rusty nail, then sit on a stoop to tend to my foot. A faint whistle sounds overhead, followed by a full can of beer smashing into the walk just a few feet away. Overhead, I see a man with a heavy belly and a wife-beater shirt lean over the fire escape's railing.

"Sorry, pal," he says, "I accidentally knocked it off the ledge when I went to light my cigarette."

Finally, at Orsi's apartment, she scurries me through the door asking whether I've been followed. The place has transformed since I last saw it. Heavy black curtains shroud the windows, and all the rare books and eccentric art have been piled across the kitchen floor. Flies buzz everywhere, feasting on the abundance of garbage.

Orsi's cheeks are gaunt, her face is slick with sweat, and, like a psych-ward patient's, her eyes are hard and narrow. Her marble in my pocket feels icy cold against my leg.

I empty my sack onto the table, file after file documenting the Pure Cosmos Club's complicated web of financial entanglements. Orsi parses through them, nodding with satisfaction when she finds a particularly revealing bit of information.

I take her face in my hands.

"Let's forget about all of this and run away together!" I say, conjuring a thousand different possibilities. "I don't have any money. You know that. Still, we can get a cottage in the woods. We can paint it pink or green or blue, whatever you want. We can decorate it, too, with flowers, and build our own furniture. Just think, we could really have a life, start our own traditions. Have you ever gone snorkeling on Thanksgiving? Of course not, nobody has. That could be something all our own. Maybe we could even have a child! A little girl named Alice, with a bad temper and freckles." Orsi presses her hand to her chest and starts to cry. I fear my heart will explode. "You don't like the name Alice? We can call her anything you like—Lucy, Ingrid, Ann? Whatever you want."

"Please don't do this!" she says.

"What's wrong?" I say. "Don't you love me?"

"Don't take this as an insult," she says, "because this isn't about you, but I don't want to love anyone anymore."

I drop to my knees and fold my hands. "I can carry the burden of love for the both of us!"

Orsi is resolute. She pushes away all the documents but one and with a red pen begins making notes. Still on my knees, I simply watch, afraid to interrupt. The tenderness of spirit she'd just revealed is gone, like a candle snuffed in the wind. She hands me the document. I have no knack for complicated figures, but with her notes it's plain that James was no savior to Orsi's father. In fact, it was James who'd caused Orsi's father all his troubles.

"Love is a dirty lie," she says, "perhaps the dirtiest of all!"

We sit on the couch for a long time. She weeps on my shoulder, and I stroke her cropped hair.

"The better you treat a man, the more love you show him," she says, reaching into my pocket for the envelope from James, "the more he deceives you."

The photos in the envelope are of Orsi and me making glorious love that long-ago single night.

"James knew about us?"

"There never was an us," Orsi says. "Only what James wanted of us."

The marble falls from my pocket, then rolls along a seam in the floor to a hole beneath the radiator, and disappears.

CHAPTER 55

A BEWILDERED man never makes a good philosopher. And when religion dies, superstition still remains. Yet here I am—a man of thirty-seven, in what is supposed to be the full bloom of my life—still uncertain how best to use what time I have left.

Rent is due at the studio. If I make a savvy wager on a horse race with the little money I have, I should be able to pay Danny. The snow falls hard and my body shakes as I shuffle to the pub where the bartender will take my bet.

"There's no excuse for my past bad judgment," I say to myself. "But from here on out, I vow to make every decision in life with the utmost care!"

Unfortunately, the racing season hasn't started. A Mexican soccer league match is about to begin, however, on the TV above the bar. Knowing nothing about either team, I flip a coin.

"Two hundred dollars on the team from Tijuana! "I say to the bartender.

Within minutes, the team from Chihuahua scores twice, and by halftime Tijuana's best player has been carted off the field with a knee injury. The second half is even worse for Tijuana. The fans are so dismayed that they begin throwing their concessions onto the field. We don't get to choose what happens in this world, but a terrible defeat like this suggests to me even grander adventures ahead.

I lay my cash on the counter, and the bartender pours me a whiskey, my first alcohol in months. The post-game highlights are nearly over when a news bulletin breaks through with grainy footage showing a team of men in full combat gear entering the Pure Cosmos Club.

"Heavily-armed FBI agents today stormed the compound of a doomsday cult called the Pure Cosmos Club," the newscaster says. "The FBI's intention was to arrest the cult's leader—known simply as "James"—for financial crimes including embezzlement, extortion, and tax fraud. Allegedly, documents obtained from the organization's accounting records show that James has appropriated over twenty-five million dollars from the club's members. Despite having been under constant surveillance for the past several weeks, however, the compound was empty when raided. Authorities have no leads as to the whereabouts of James or any of his affiliates..."

I walk home in a daze, heaving with cheerless laughter. The frequency with which I'm so wrong about people is deeply perplexing. Is it possible I've turned my back on eternal prosperity? I've always tried to make the right choices, do the things I believe will help me thrive, and though in countless ways I've succeeded beyond anyone's expectations, here I am, nevertheless, without a single provision.

I'm not vindictive by nature. It's never been my intention to bring the world to my feet. In most respects, my aims have always been far too modest—a loving woman, a loving dog, a working set of paintbrushes. When I compare myself to someone like James, of course I can't help but to laugh. Either we believe in something, or we wither. What we believe in makes little difference.

Danny has always been a pitiless landlord. Unable to pay him, I'm sure he'll promptly evict me. Even if he were to have some mercy, I'd refuse: a debt is simply intolerable. Tomorrow, then, I'll move out of the studio, even if just to a spot under a bridge. It's just as easy, on the other hand, to see myself becoming a hedge fund manager or a longshoreman, and I've always believed I'd make a fine dental assistant.

My belongings are so few it doesn't take long to pack, then I retire to the roof. It's simply too painful to sleep alone in my rickety bed. I miss my sweet Blanche dearly, but wish her only the best. Winston sent word earlier that they'd attended a jazz concert at the legendary Caveau De La Huchette, where the band's trumpet player had brought his French bulldog, Claude, who, as Winston tells it, adores Blanche. These are my thoughts as I doze off, only to be interrupted by my phone ringing with a request for a video call from an unlisted number. Typically, I ignore such invasions, but something compels me to accept this one. The connection is spotty, and at first, I don't recognize the face glaring from my screen, a man with flowing hair and a white goatee. Then, with a start, I see it's James, erect in the captain's seat of a rocket ship, the planet Saturn passing in the distance outside the window.

"You were blameless in your ways from the day you were created," James says, "till unrighteousness was found in you."

"I'm afraid I don't regret a thing," I say.

"Your heart grew proud because of your beauty, and you kept your greatest treasures from my grasp. Now I've cast you from our midst and exposed you before kings!"

"Sometimes, a bit of destruction is necessary."

"It's up to you now to create your own heaven on Earth," James says, just before the connection breaks, "as I can no longer protect you."

I lay down my phone and plummet into the most blissful sleep I can recall, and when I wake, it's with vigor and joy.

Whatever challenges life may bring, I vow to meet them with a quality of spirit unmatched since Caesar marched on Rome. I may go without food, clean clothes, or a roof over my head, but I will be free. "Yesterday I was a cat," I think, "but today I'm a rat!" I strip off my khaki uniform and toss it off the roof. It's wonderful to know that when I'm on my deathbed it will make little difference whether I'm depressed or content. Within a few days, I'm sure, I will be forgotten. My freedom is indescribable.

I stride down the stairs to bid farewell to the studio where I worked so well. To my surprise, Danny is already there, snooping through my things.

"Why aren't you on the rocket-ship with James?" I say.

"I have no interest in running off to wherever James is hiding," Danny says. "And besides, you know I've always been skeptical of zeal, whether political, religious, or mystical!"

"But you seemed so lost after your show in Paris."

"A temporary setback. A person like myself has no reason to upset the established order of things."

Danny's eyes are as furtive as a wolf's. Like all men of character, he harbors memories from life that make him blush in a contemplative hour. His madness is admirable. I'm confident he'll understand what I have to say.

"I'm flat broke, Danny. I can't pay my rent and have decided to leave."

Throughout our talk, Danny has been crawling about, peeking under this and that. At the tarp I used to cover my paintings of Blanche, he stops, then leaps to his feet and flings the tarp away. The paintings radiate an aura of grandiosity and magnificence that stun us both. For minutes, neither of us speak. Finally, I hand my keys to Danny.

"What's this about?" Danny says.

"I haven't the means to wallow in idleness," I say. "I'm thinking of pursuing a career as an insurance adjuster."

I pitch my Journal of Treasonous Thoughts into the sink, douse it with gasoline, and set it ablaze.

"But why," Danny says, his eyes half-innocent, half-worried, "would you renounce your genius just as you've begun to express it?"

"The Pure Cosmos Club has left for Ultimate Level. Blanche has fallen for a bulldog in Paris, and Orsi refuses to live with me in a cabin in the woods!"

"It's quite ironic, isn't it?" Danny says.

"Don't start with me," I say, turning away, "you know I have no appreciation for irony!"

"The greatest artist of a generation," Danny says, slapping his thighs with laughter, "lacks the imagination to see he need not be a slave!"

Danny asks whether I've shown my paintings to anyone and is thrilled to learn I haven't. He has decided, he says, to open his own gallery and wants his first exhibition to feature my work.

"Above all else," he says, "I pride myself on self-reliance."

Danny has his father's money, of course, but he takes it, he says, only because it's there, not because he needs it. He'd never invest in anything unless he stood to make a tidy profit. That afternoon we negotiate the terms of our business arrangement.

CHAPTER 56

DANNY SPARED no expense promoting the gallery's opening, and it made the front page of the Arts section of *The New York Times*. Anyone who's anyone in New York's high society attended. A woman named Scarlett—whom Danny said is quite a famous actor—became so smitten with me and my work that she left her husband on the spot and asked me to live with her. But just then a fist-fight broke out. One of my paintings had created such a furor that most of the room was bidding on it. In the end, the heir to a chocolate empire outbid a renowned venture capitalist, then sneeringly told the humiliated man a secret about his wife that only someone who'd seen her naked could know. Both men were arrested, to the rousing cheers of all. I simply couldn't believe my good fortune. I walked into the gallery a pauper and left if not a wealthy man then certainly an affluent one.

It's been two months since my success. There are no words to express the pleasure I get wearing a crisp, new suit, so the first thing I did with my money was commission Salvador to design me a new wardrobe.

Next, I bought a one-way ticket to Paris and rented a *pied-à-terre* in the 4th arrondissement, just two blocks from Winston and Blanche's atelier. My flat's ceiling leaks endlessly, and my neighbors are wonderfully noisy love-makers. On weekends, they host extravagant parties from which shouts of 'Ouuuiiiii!" can be heard until the early morning hours. Winston and Blanche have moved in, as well. The three of us aren't merely a family, but the best of friends. And, yes, I well know the old adage about artists being solitary creatures who can't create in the company of others, yet in my experience, this simply isn't true. I wake with the sun each morning and work until noon. Winston insists that it's my predilection for embracing fundamentalist orthodoxy that allows me to refute obvious truths about the world.

In Paris, nobody eats alone, so each day I meet Winston and Blanche at a café, where we share plates of *coquilles Saint Jacques* and ratatouille and sometimes even a bowl of French onion soup. It's not uncommon for us, like the French, to spend two hours eating and chatting. I'm proud to say, as well, that I've already put on a good twenty-five pounds, and am affectionately referred to by my new friends as *l'homme potelé*, which means, "chubby man." Every afternoon I take French lessons from a girl named Celeste, whom I met at a literary salon hosted by the sister of a famous French rock and roll singer. With tremendous effort, I've read two whole pages of Camus' *The Stranger*, in the original.

This evening, I'm meeting Danny at the Hemingway Bar. He's in town to view a new series of erotic paintings I've made inspired by Egyptian mythology. It's important I earn more money to help support my cousin Louis and his family. Swimming in the Seine recently, I suffered a vision in which Louis' hardware store is put out of business by a Home Depot that opens nearby. It won't be long now, I'm quite sure, before Louis calls to tell me of his life, his despairs, and his fears.

Since my arrival here, I've written daily impassioned letters to Orsi, none of which she's responded to until the other day, with a postcard featuring a photograph of the Taos Pueblo. Its text was a single line: "Please *stop* sending me letters—"

Quite obviously she'd scribbled this note in great haste. It's not like Orsi to speak so ambiguously. What, for instance, could she possibly have forgotten to include after that strange dash? I'll write one last time to inquire.

THE END

Matthew Binder is the author of the novels *Pure Cosmos Club*, *The Absolved*, and *High in the Streets*. He is also a primary member of the recording project Bang Bang Jet Away.